FLIGHT FROM OBLIVION

by

Kim Kacoroski

Cover art illustrations by Kim Kacoroski, Phillipe Velasquez, and Masha Tatarintsev

Visit the author website:
http://kimkacoroski.com

Library of Congress Control Number: 2013920852
ISBN: 978-1-947036-00-0 (Paperback)

Version 2017.05.03

Book Five of the Oblivion Series and the Beginning of Flight Series

Flight from Oblivion

Other Books in the Oblivion Series

Escape from Oblivion I

Beyond Oblivion II

Oblivion's Edge III

Oblivion's Deal IV

Other Books in Flight Series

Eagle's Flight in the American Revolution II

Flight of the Ascendants in the American Revolution III

Choices from the American Revolution IV

Bridges of Flight before the American Revolution V

Testimony VI

Books in the Camelon Series

The Promise of Camelon I

The Dragons of Camelon II

History of the World According to the Druids

New Beginnings IV

Kingdom of the Golden Tara V

Introduction

The tune references in *Fight from Oblivion* reflect the soul's journey toward individuation. Like a tether on the winged-Icarus, the songs offer safety in the pursuit of freedom, whereas in the myth they pursued flight for the sake of survival. This story embraces the same aesthetic qualities that lured Icarus to his demise. The music sets limits and boundaries through mindfulness. It is not enough to fly; one must do it safely without trepidation. The paradox of youth requires the individual to rise above dehumanizing entrapments, while realizing the extent of bonds making the flight a possibility. In escaping the prisons of the ancestors, an individual safeguards its freedom.

Chapter One

The questions of the 1976 US Bicentennial:

Where are we going?

And do we like it?

Tune Reference: *Theme From Mahogany (Do You Know Where You're Going*

To)

----Diana Ross

"THE VOTES HAVE been counted," the drama teacher announced. "You're president, Tobias Jones."

Those assembled in the portable building erupted into hearty applause. Humbled, Tobias looked around the room at the faces. Cheerleaders, drill team members, football players, and nerds were smiling at him. Never before in his life had he seen such hope and confidence in the future. His speech had struck chords in them, and now he wondered what exactly had resonated, so he could recapture their enthusiasm for the activities ahead. A passionless audience had suddenly taken flight---for what, he wasn't entirely sure. He questioned the dependence on his words, which had somehow stirred them from their oblivion.

Fortunately, the ringing of the bell interrupted Tobias's thoughts. It signaled that school would begin in five minutes. He didn't want to ponder the reaction, which sent an eerie chill up his spine. The shrill pitch encouraged Tobias to quit thinking and start doing. The drama club adjourned, and students left in a flurry to get to their first-period class on time. For the moment, the wandering dead had come to life. The white, placid faces of those passing through the outdoor corridors between portable classrooms contained a flicker of passion.

Tobias stayed behind to speak briefly with the club sponsor, who had counted the votes. He didn't need to hurry. His first-period class was speech, which was also taught by the club sponsor, Mrs. Denton.

Apparently impressed by his speech, she looked up at him and then at the outgoing chaos. She remained quiet as she rearranged the papers on her desk. Somehow, he had rallied the motley group and won the election hands down, a miraculous feat for a transfer student. It was his first year at the junior high, where the freshmen topped the hierarchy before they moved on to the high school with over two thousand students. She and Tobias had so many things to talk about for the new school year: the fall play, the debate team, and the talent show. After a hurried discussion, they set a date for the next club meeting, and Tobias walked back to his seat, nestling comfortably in the midst of his new classmates.

When class ended, he found his locker down the hall and pulled out a new binder for English class. Gazing quietly at the whirlwind of students swirling around him, he wasn't sure what to expect. He only had the class twice a week, and this was the first meeting of the semester. The English teacher doubled as an assistant football coach, which meant that football practice had priority in the schedule. Searching for social cues from those who were more familiar with the instructor, Tobias clutched his notebook and followed the throng piling into a portable classroom. Finding a desk near an open window, he sat down and waited for his second-period class to begin.

"We are going to listen to songs and write essays," the muscular instructor told his class as he sauntered into the room with a firm, businesslike air. Hinting that he might wander from stuffy, academic pursuits, he emanated confidence that the school district would support him on any lesson plan that he developed for the class. He lowered his voice abruptly while lapsing into small talk with some of the football players in the room, the ones that he had coached since the summer. Other students in the room strained to hear. After telling the football players a few jokes, he addressed the class, demanding full attention on educational issues, especially those that he lived. His voice became louder as he began relating stories about his close relationship with his twin sister and his new life as a married man. Tobias stretched and listened attentively. He noted that the stocky young teacher had hands the size of baseball gloves. He wondered whether he would learn any English this semester---not that it really concerned him.

This class was in contrast to the speech class, where the teen queens took over. In English class, the jocks ruled while the young women were quiet, retaining a posture of alert shyness. Some of them seemed almost scared, not knowing what to expect from the exuberant, seemingly worldly wise males in the room. In all their other classes, the football players stared dumbly into space, their eyes glazed over either from boredom or fear that they might be called on to answer.

The warm summer rolled into autumn. The English instructor's monologues became more informational, especially on what the local high school had been like ten years ago. The coach's eyes glistened as he reviewed the golden moments of his high-school years.

"So Plunckett and I pushed the car down the hill so that we could get it started," he softly rambled with a delighted twinkle in his eye. Using his thick hands for emphasis, the coach described how he'd managed to throw his crutches in the moving vehicle while he hobbled after it, somehow catching up with his buddy, the one who was steering.

The class remained quiet as they listened to his stories. Life at the big high school worried them, and the football stories soothed them. One day, the instructor assumed a more serious tone as he played a song for them on the phonograph. Most recognized the lyrics sung by a popular rock group. Intent on teaching more than English, he roamed past the desks of students until he stopped near one of the silent females. Like the instructor, she also had a twin, and this happenstance endeared her to him. She accepted his familiarity with a shy lack of commitment. He stood uncomfortably close to her. Almost touching her long, straight blonde hair, he questioned the class, "Who can tell me the meaning of this song?"

Looking around at the class, he left the side of the young woman with a deliberate lingering air. The needle from the arm of the phonograph circled over the spinning record. The words of the pop-rock song blared. Students shifted nervously in their chairs, hesitating to dive into this multidimensional conversation.

"I am looking for the solitary progeny of the devil ... as white as an angel..."

Nobody answered him for several minutes. Tobias noticed that even the football players squirmed uncomfortably in their seats, a few frozen solid. The students varied in their responses. Tobias watched and wondered where he fit in the scheme of things, knowing that the coach would not want an answer from him. He had a feeling that no matter what he conjectured, it would not satisfy the man. The instructor repeated his question several times, demanding a response. Although she was also an athlete, the young woman who had struck a chord with the instructor seemed relieved that he had returned the focus of attention to the rest of the class. She looked down at her desk without a word, placing one hand on the shoulder the coach had once touched. She seemed uncertain and a little anxious about his implications.

The star quarterback shot up his hand. He was also president of student council. Rather than respond as a student, he met the instructor's demands as a player. With a slight smile, the quarterback said, "Hey coach!"

The man brightened with a light blush, gently giving permission for the player to speak on his terms. He often let the class off easy after those from the football team had groaned, "Aw, coach." The football players knew his soft spot, and this considerably reduced the load of homework assignments. Whenever he heard his star players utter that phrase, he automatically dropped his academic guard.

"It is about the desire for a girl with experience, instead of purity," he asserted. "But you don't want them to seem like they've had experience."

Tobias glanced across the aisle at the quarterback's girlfriend. Her trophy boyfriend sat several rows ahead, closer to the teacher. Tobias knew that she threw frequent swim parties through the summer and identified with the same crowd that had elected him president of the drama club. Based on how they responded to his idealism in student leadership roles and musical entertainment, he fathomed the depths of their despair. For some reason, he never felt inclined to break into this girl's dispassionate circle, though he knew that he could if he tried. He wasn't sure that he wanted to take her away from the boy she entertained, which he knew would inevitably happen if he cultivated a social relationship. Tobias didn't want to win through his idealism, because it indicated how dead his classmates were inside. Like moths attracted to a flame, they frantically rushed into experiences that were beyond their capacity to integrate. Even if they possessed finesse, the premature spreading of wings would end in a swan song headed straight down to oblivion. The rite of passage did not guarantee enlightenment, not in the way they hungered for his leadership. Everyone wanted to score, and the drive to succeed sexually became paramount. Partnerships easily converted into sexual liaisons forged during summer pool parties. It was a scary thought, considering that he had won the presidency of a popular club with only a few well-timed, inspired words. To his horror, Tobias felt that he had been elected by spiritual vampires.

Refusing to deal with the answer to this question, he continued to eye the girlfriend's response to her hero's play. The bigger answer was the way that she managed the quarterback and brought him back into the fold. Tobias sensed that she was the silent hero, not her outspoken boyfriend who was attempting to involve the entire class in a man-to-man conversation with the instructor. Tobias decided that she knew more about games than the quarterback or the coach. This was something that he'd learned from the election sweep.

Looking down at her desk and pretending not to notice, she partially managed to conceal a proud, determined smile tugging at the corners of her mouth. She was head cheerleader, and she had chosen a seat near Tobias rather than the quarterback. She wore more makeup than the reserved female jock, though both young women had every hair in place. Tobias stretched out his legs under the desk in front of him. Leaning back in his chair slightly, he ran his fingers through his tousled hair. In his fantasies, he preferred angels that fought like devils. Rather than black and white, he desired angels with the colors of blue, purple, dark red, lime green---almost like the flowers and trees that grabbed at him during his walks to school. He resolved to become what he desired and achieve his dreams. Intending to turn their world upside down, Tobias determined to top the star football-playing student-council president by becoming emperor.

Knowing he could become more powerful by declining social engagements, he plotted his course of action as if by instinct. His heart belonged to the many associations cultivated in the Dallas-Fort Worth metroplex. The metroplex, or metropolitan area, consisted of a series of small cities, created by pioneers who had once driven their covered wagons off cattle trails in search of new lives. Now that a highway connected the perpetually mobile communities, the locals referred to the places between the two larger cities as one big *metroplex*. Tobias roved the area, making flirtations a way of life while practicing the lively art of noncommitment. His last official relationship with a girl had begun during the last two weeks of eighth grade, well-timed with end of school. Though she loved him dearly, he was ready to let the relationship fade into the scenery of wild fields and dusty winds as they pursued different paths. While at a spiritual retreat in the Catholic diocese of mixed ages and genders, he had discovered unconditional love and the need to cultivate that sense of joy in his relationships. The retreat had provided him the opportunity to leave a nonexistent family and given him a stepping-stone to a future where he could escape the past. His family of origin existed only as a group of people held together by economic necessity, relating to public image and traditional views. By definition, it was a dutiful mob rather than a family, and nobody really cared for each other. Tobias preferred to keep his life simple while he continued to move forward.

The people that he hung with on weekends managed to attract the notice of a nun from Calcutta, India. They invited her to come and speak publicly. When she accepted the invitation, Tobias served as an usher at the convention. As he surveyed the rows and rows of eager listeners, he imagined that he was helping usher in a new paradigm. The nun's lecture did not disappoint him.

Dressed in white, the worldly-wise woman from India walked briskly to the podium. She waved at the audience and there was a bounce in her step. "The poorest people on earth are in the United States. You people in America have your work cut out for you," Mother Theresa told the crowd. "All I have to do is hold the hand of the sick and dying. It is hard to get to get past the materialism here to make connection."

His group leaders had admired Mother Theresa for her ability to get past bureaucratic red tape and do what needed to be done in the worst circumstances. Recalling her perspective on life, Tobias watched the antics in class. The song about the sexual desire for an angel-demon seemed superficial.

The ancient Greeks referred to male gonads as orchids. Men were considered flowers in even the most patriarchal systems. He had learned biology from a mother of three handsome sons, an Italian goddess who dressed sharper than Sophia Loren, and had taught the class on the how tos of the plant and animal kingdoms. Tobias wasn't sure how to classify the singer's desire for the demonic, which seemed self-destructive. It was all about the birds and the bees; their secret lives could be fathomed by lengthy Latin terms. Life, when viewed through the ancestor of the romance languages, never stopped being sexual. There was no end, and if one thought about it too much, it would drive them crazy. Every bird and bee sensed that any self-absorbed flower never blossomed. By instinct, they avoided the diseased and contaminated flowers. When his Spanish instructor told him that objects which ended in *a* were female and those which ended in *o* were male, Tobias accepted this perception as a fact of life. Being well-adjusted or the ability to adapt to the terrain was a sign of a healthy plant or animal. Tobias enjoyed keeping life simple.

Meanwhile, the coach seemed happily animated at the quarterback's reply and he played the entire song for the class. For the moment, the rest of the class was off the hook. Tobias realized that he'd eluded the instructor's scrutiny because he was a competitive swimmer. This gave him the advantage over the social order. He was present, but he didn't belong to the parade of basketball, football, gymnastics, and volleyball stars around him. His destiny was elsewhere; these people, with their young, developed lives were growing old before their time. *Not me*, Tobias thought.

It appeared ironic that the answer had come from a student who had run away from home and dropped out of school for over a year. Tobias had heard his story from classmates, many of whom had known the young man since first grade. The former ward of the truant officer was now a school hero; he also played in a band at local sock hops.

Ditching the sexual mores of his spiritual associations in the proverbial closet, Tobias approached the man who served as the spiritual father for the jocks. He found him busy in a classroom filled with colorful posters and reading material. The instructor taught social studies and served the metroplex as a Protestant minister. The clean-cut, handsome teacher looked up from the organized stacks of books on his desk and greeted Tobias.

"Mr. Harwood, I'd like to sign up to lead one of the Friday meetings for Christian athletes," Tobias announced, looking at the reverend in the eye as a self-designated equal. Unspoken rules existed that steered cautious Catholics away from anything dubbed Christian, because of the de-emphasis on a single person. The Catholics armed themselves with collections of saints and stood with those who had died before the movement became suspiciously popular. Instead of taking issue with the reverend's work, Tobias offered, "I sing and play the guitar."

The pastor-teacher beamed at Tobias as if he were heaven sent. Discounting the fact that Tobias represented a Trojan horse regarding religious denominations, the professional preacher ignored the obvious question on spiritual affiliations and placed his bet on the horse that showed to do the run. Drawing Tobias aside in confidance, he slightly bowed his head and offered a book for Tobias to sign. He spoke no further words, but his manner assured Tobias that they were on the same side in their unique missions.

As a result of his public presentations, Tobias assumed patriarchal proportions to these people who were hardcore sport enthusiasts. Only once did the role create conflict, but it had been with a group that could easily be ignored. Before transferring to this school, Tobias had played in some baseball and basketball leagues during the off-season for the swim team. Earlier in the year, he had won a spot on the bench for the school basketball team. He took basketball more seriously than the clique members playing it did. When the coach finally let him loose, he turned a losing team around during one basketball game. Unfortunately, only the younger players appreciated his rising stardom and drive. The teammates whom he had edged out crowded him under the basket at the following practice. Tobias landed wrong on his ankle and sprained it. As several young men from the nearby gymnastics team carried him off the gym floor, he realized that his life with this peer group would be short-lived. Disappearing from the team as swiftly as he had entered, he developed a preference for making better use of his time. Rather than sit around and watch others play while his ankle healed, Tobias used the recovery time to hobble into the chemistry lab for extra-credit work. After finishing up a chemistry lab with an instructor that appreciated his inquisitiveness and overtime, she took him under her wing and gave him many pointers about life as a solo chemist. At this fortuitous moment, Tobias brightened with the realization that his peer group amounted to one. Although the teen queens feigned interest in order to get the grades required for their competitions, he watched how the science teacher gave them only token responses. The educator favored Tobias and took the time to spark his imagination. Having earned her valued attention, Tobias discovered that he had inadvertently found a way out of predetermined relationships and limited futures. In contrast to the other science instructors, her hair and makeup were usually undone by the end of the day. Something about the pursuit of inquiry unraveled her and brought out her cool, analytical inner scientist. She obviously was a chemist masquerading as a teacher, whereas the other teachers only possessed a passing interest in the subject, possibly in it only for the higher pay scale. Tobias found her rather fascinating, despite her aging skin, beaky nose, dark-rimmed glasses, and white-streaked, frizzy hair. As he probed beneath the surface of her polite manner, Tobias knew that he had found the anti-teen-queen. She would cut the artificial and leave no slack. He could learn many things from her, because he saw more to life than fashion sets, fingernail polish, and false eyelashes.

Toward the end of the semester, Tobias found that the bell rang too soon in science class. There never seemed to be enough time to pursue truth, and he felt lucky that his time in class passed swiftly, given the current facade. Young teens scurried outside of science class, while some of the female students caught up with the team-sport stars in the halls. Tobias left for another direction. He felt that he was just passing through. This junior-high scene would rapidly turn to dust once he moved on to the big high school.

He hurried to the locker rooms to change clothes for physical-education class. Today, for once, they were going to do something interesting rather than what was academically prescribed. Dark clouds were gathering overhead. This was tornado country, and education was not the priority this afternoon. The swirling winds of change in the distance made life the priority. A female instructor from the girls' class spontaneously organized a coed group to play a game of flag football. As they played on the green turf, Tobias kept an eye on the horizon. He noticed that the instructor also remained alert for a quickly descending tornado. Despite the graying skies, Tobias and his motley group of guys played with reckless abandon. Unlike the jocks in his classes, Tobias still played for fun. The stars up the street had quit playing neighborhood pickup games years ago. They had grown up too fast.

"Are you going to Dawn Roger's party this weekend?" a friend asked during the huddle.

Although, Dawn Rogers lived nearby, Tobias wasn't sure about the invite. If he showed up, would the parents think that he had crashed the party? Dawn Rogers cultivated alliances with the same troublemakers who frequently targeted his home with toilet paper and helped themselves to his family's swimming pool. Though he and the soft-mannered girl next door always crushed them during neighborhood baseball games, the needless, hostile animosity continued to loom just right under the surface.

"Her mother constantly reminds her to clip her toenails for the next teen competition," Tobias's soft-spoken friend, Clara, told him. "We can hear yelling several houses down." Being on the same swim team as Tobias, she told him, "These girls do these competitions like it is a sport, but without the sportsmanship. They are really hard-core, mean competitors---the worst."

On the night of the party, Tobias found himself hanging out with some high-school friends from the student council. Two of them decided to visit Dawn Rogers's party, and Tobias quietly tagged along. To his surprise, the parents seemed pleased to see him. Apparently they didn't know how intimidating their daughter could be.

Tobias and his friends didn't stay long.

"Let's go get some ice cream," Dana Miller entreated the high-school boys, who had cars. She seemed ready to cut the party and distance herself from Dawn Rogers. Occasionally Dawn Rogers's peers claimed that she was a snob.

Flattered by the teen queen's request, one of Tobias's friends volunteered his car. A few others joined them, and several vehicles made a trip to the local ice cream shop. Studying the appeal of the sophisticated young woman with the childlike demand, Tobias noticed that his high-school chums seemed quite happy to entertain her. They proudly shelled out coins for her ice cream and for the cones of the few young women who had dared accompany them. Then everyone drove back; there were no strings attached, just lighthearted chats in contrast to the serious tone of the party, where Dawn Rogers seemed intent on trying to prove that she was tops.

A few months later, Mr. Harwood greeted Tobias in the hall. Tobias occasionally did solo performances for the reverend's youth groups. All the young Christian athletes would cram into his social studies classroom for weekly rap sessions. Tobias enjoyed singing and playing his guitar for the attentive, packed audiences. It gave him the chance to teach his classmates a thing or too.

The reverend congratulated Tobias, saying, "Great job, my man." Extending a warm handshake with a pat on the back, the preacher told him, "I never thought you had it in you. You were quite the rascal in the school play."

"Well, there's nothing like a suit to make a man suave and debonair," Tobias retorted, waving his hand across his face to cover his perplexity at the reverend's new role. The success of his ruse surprised him. His last role on stage had been that of a drunken minister from an unpopular, lesser-known denomination. Though he didn't drink, Tobias had savored his freedom in the portrayal, almost having too much fun with the slapstick comedy. Perhaps this was the reason the drama instructor had reined him in and cast him in a more conventional bit piece. Though he secretly harbored some minor discomfort at the reverend's reaction to his previous performance, apparently his versatility had won the man over. The compliment had been personal, on the guy-to-guy level; it reminded him of the role shifts in his English class: teacher, coach, man, eternal student, lover, teammate, player. It never ended, and he sensed that he was growing up too fast, barely managing a shave of his fine whiskers once a year.

The instructor backed off and hurried to class with a warm wave. Of all the instructors in the school, the reverend provided the only advice for which Tobias willingly extended half an ear. Again, the theme of sexuality had surfaced in the academic environment from the top down.

Everyone's critic, Tobias thought, realizing suddenly how he matured in the eyes of those around him. Though he acknowledged the looming potency, he did not wish to be sexualized before his time. Instead, he resolved to dodge such innuendo in the future. It seemed empty, like a bottomless pit.

He wasn't sure why the drama teacher had placed him in the role, along with several other young men. She'd given the women roles as sexpots. What else was he supposed to do? Perhaps Mrs. Denton had entered them in a sophisticated bar scene in retaliation for Gerald's lewd, adolescent sense of humor. Gerald was one of their classmates. While the males merely laughed and rolled their eyes, Gerald's antics could make most of the women scream in a matter of a few obnoxious minutes and have them yelling, "Stop it. Stop it."

Like the instructor, Tobias eventually responded with his own counteraction. It occurred on the day that he brought his guitar to class. Because the instrument didn't fit in his locker, he had to haul it with him to class after morning practice with the choir. Even though he wasn't in the choir, he spent time with them before school started. The choir director had put out the word that she wanted a guitar accompanist, and Tobias had stepped in. It represented another clique that he enjoyed breaking into. He got around, and only a few adults seemed to catch on. To his surprise, teachers and students alike seemed to appreciate it, and he enjoyed being the mystery man, the unknown fellow from everywhere.

For various reasons, that day there were not enough students to do anything constructive in drama class, and so Tobias pulled out his guitar.

Playing and singing a tune, he melted the wild beasts of the class, including the instructor and Gerald. Though he didn't like the things that life was showing him, Tobias kept strumming along. He didn't like the sexual pressure, which seemed ungrounded and premature. He didn't care for the lack of meaning in the life around him. The shallowness haunted him. People strove for goals that appeared fruitless and self-destructive. It became a memorable fifteen minutes of mellow. He hadn't known they had any sense of the profound in them, or any notion of what made life worth living. All Tobias knew was that life did not amount to a fashion statement, particularly those alluding to sex as a panacea.

Tobias ruled, despite his initial set back due to the injured ankle. He could swim ten times further than he could run or walk. Having flown in his dreams with one foot anchored to the ground, he had transformed his fantasy into reality. By the end of the year, the English teacher offered his help in researching a future in the biological sciences, after having been convinced that there were holy assignments other than football goals. Though Tobias enjoyed success, angst tugged at his heart as he hobbled into high school. Keeping his sexual mores in the closet, he welcomed more wholesome friendships, which sometimes made him a target to those with other choices.

Chapter Two

Be your own best friend
Garden parties are for the tame

Tune Reference: *Garden Party*
----Ricky Nelson

TWO YEARS LATER, Tobias proudly held the legs of a swim teammate as he carried her on his shoulders for a pep rally. He could feel Clara's lithe, athletic body vibrate as she cheered and clapped over his head. Feeling as if he had arrived, he rejoiced that he had passed up the drill team and teen queens for this particular moment. It could not compare to the raw sensuality of the present. Clad in typical out-of-water attire of T-shirt and blue jeans, his teammates stood out in the crowd. None of his classmates could relate to this young woman as he could, after spending countless laps of swimming half-naked in skintight suits together through four seasons. He saw her more often out of clothes than in them. Nobody could fathom the joy he felt in balancing her above him as they cheered on another athletic team. The pressure was on the football team now, not them. They could scream and yell on the sidelines all they wanted without being the center of attention or needing to compete. Though they experienced a sense of relief at being out of the race for once, their spirited ways continued to rank them above the crowd. They were more flexible than the others, and their antics at the pep rally distinguished them from the fashion shows and frozen, apathetic faces. Having been district champions since Tobias's sophomore year, they saw themselves as winners.

When the rally ended, Tobias lifted Clara to the ground as his buddies off-loaded their friends. They all hit the wood floor of the gym with simultaneous exuberant bounces, happily gazing into each other's eyes for a few seconds of delight before looking away. Championship was something they could all share. Moreover, it was an understanding they held, knowing that it took hours of dedication and cooperation to make a winning team.

"Hey, Tobias!" shouted one of his teammates in passing. "Coming to the party on Saturday?"

"Where is it?" Tobias asked.

"It's at Barbara's home," his chum Brad answered. "Her parents said that she could throw one while they were out for the night."

"Yeah, I'll come after work," he responded. "I'll be a couple hours late. They have me closing the shoe department that night. It will take awhile to clean up after the sale. See ya there later."

Brad smiled, and they threw their palms up to meet in a congenial slap. Hard work, success, and good buddies made life meaningful. Unlike the teen-queen scene he'd avoided during his freshman year, Tobias reveled in the rewards that life had finally shown him. He was glad that he had never lingered in those times, merely passing through to get to this next stage.

After borrowing a family car, he drove the green Chevy to the Saturday-night party. He wondered what life would show him at this junction. Too busy working and studying, Tobias had missed most of the parties during the previous year. Now he parked the vehicle near the other automobiles on the street and sauntered to the door of the home.

Monica, the co-captain of the women's swim team, greeted him in the living room. Having given Tobias a book on Shakespeare for his last birthday, the young woman was one of Tobias's dear friends. Monica held a cola in her hand and explained some of the comings and goings of the party. She nodded in the direction of the bathroom down the hall. The best friend of the hostess was busy upchucking, along with a few other cohorts.

"Coffee!" the hostess hollered, hurrying to the bathroom. "Some of these people decided to start drinking early," she explained. "You missed it all."

Tobias eyed the flurry of activity around him that flowed through the living room, the bathroom, and outside to the swimming pool. He took a deep breath and tossed his head. Then his eyes fell to the glass in the co-captain's hands.

Covering her container, Monica admitted with a soft, serious grin, "Me? I don't drink."

Tobias glanced at the seriousness of her eyes and believed her. Looking up, he saw several of his teammates wave at him. He noticed that they were putting down their cups.

"Should have come sooner, Tobias," Monica chided. "Everyone might have stopped drinking."

"I seem to have that effect," he said with a shrug.

A shriek suddenly pierced the air from the next room, interrupting their conversation. They heard the sound of shattering glass, followed by cries of panic. Then the noise fell off, until there was just the eerie hum of hushed voices and shock.

Motioning Tobias to follow her, the co-captain directed him to the source of the commotion outside. At the doorway, Tobias left Monica behind him as he went in the yard, made his way around the still, blue swimming pool, and entered the playroom beyond. The other co-captain of the women's swim team knelt next to a broken sliding glass door. This time the hostess of the party was busy with a wet towel to mop the blood spilling off the wrists of the kneeling woman. Emergency attendants began spilling in the room as the hostess began to tell Tobias what had happened.

"She ran through the door," the hostess told Tobias. "She thought one of the sophomores was going to fall in the pool."

Tobias watched the young woman's tears fall on her bloody arms and dilute the red pools to a lighter, watery shade. He gently touched her elbow, and she responded with a faint smile underneath the stream of tears rolling down her face. Then he lightly sponged the excess blood on her arms to stop the bleeding without embedding any glass farther into her skin. Years ago, he had convinced his great-aunt to teach him first aid during a summer she'd spent with them. While his parents took a mini-vacation, Tobias and his younger sisters had stayed home and wrapped each other in triangular slings and Ace bandages. His aunt had been a field nurse at the WWII Battle of the Bulge. Tobias considered her the premier source on first aid. She was eager to share her knowledge and pass on lifesaving skills. Tonight his training comforted him as he tried to restore order to the chaos surrounding the injured woman and the broken glass.

The attendants already on the scene drew Tobias within their circle. Having taken a glimpse at the surroundings before approaching the badly injured woman, they let it be known by their discrete actions that they felt lucky for the invitation. The people karound them in the shadows were in much greater athletic condition than they could ever hope to be. Similar to other members of their generation, the teenagers were extremely devious and clever at eluding anyone trying to bring their lives back into balance without appreciating the journey to oblivion that had been handed to them by their surviving elders. The teenagers growing up deep in the heart of the military-industrial complex understood that the souls of their parents had been traded for the assassination of peaceful world leaders. Tobias knew that the captain was an orphan being raised by grandparents. He saw her clench her hand in a tight fist and let the EMTs know that she was restraining herself from a drama that would maul the established world. Other teenagers flexed their muscles and stepped forward to flank her. Standing together, they embodied a statement of their existence, conveying the sense that this was Texas, the lone-star state, where youngsters died in alcohol-related accidents like ants marching on a hill laced with insecticide. They were on the proud, fast track to oblivion.

"Had she been drinking?" one of the attendants asked, putting on metaphorical horse blinders to reassure the crowd that they had not been noticed, though he had read their minds, as would any good caregiver or cowboy who herded livestock. In such a culture, everyone knew how to look at someone between the eyes and read their intention. Focusing on the patient, the attendants made it clear that they were not there to break up the party. People calmed down. The inebriated hurriedly left the scene or hid in adjacent rooms until they found rides safely elsewhere.

"No, she was trying to save someone from falling in the pool outside," the hostess mentioned.

The young woman turned her attention to the attendants. Wishing to avoid interfering with their work, Tobias quietly left her side at a nod from one of the young men. He joined the hostess down the hall, who, with arms crossed, surveyed the scene from a detached distance.

"She is such a drama queen," the hostess murmured under her breath. "She would have to go through the window trying to rescue someone. I called my parents. They are on their way."

"The men's captain is taking the others home," Tobias agreed softly. "Time to go."

"The sober ones can help clean up," Monica interjected. "We'll clear the place out."

"Thanks for your help," the hostess answered. "See you at swim practice on Monday."

Tobias walked out the front door with the team captains and gently prodded the subdued partiers toward their vehicles. Satisfied with the joint efforts concerning risk management, he felt assured that there would be no further accidents involving his teammates tonight. Tobias entered his car and revved the 350 engine. Turning on the headlights, he slowly steered the Chevy onto the street underneath the tall oaks. Moonlight drifted between the tree leaves and soothed his thoughts. He had left the party as quickly as he'd arrived, almost as if he was simply passing through. He puzzled over this destiny.

The following Monday, the coach of the swim team gathered all the teammates around the starting blocks. He had them all sit down on the familiar damp concrete floor. Finding dry surfaces between small puddles, everyone quieted as he began a somewhat-familiar lecture.

"No less than six people called to tell me about the party," he began. "I have eyes and ears all over the metropolitan area. Even people who don't have kids phoned to let me know what my swim team was doing."

Those who had arrived early at the party hung their heads and stared at the paved deck around the pool. Despite the fact that they knew the coach enjoyed an occasional beer at the summer meets, they listened to him. His team gave him the respect of a leader, possibly because he was the only one addressing these issues with them.

"Athletes and alcohol don't mix," he told them. "If you want to be a champion, don't drink."

Then his eyes rested on the bandaged arm of the injured co-captain. He poked her in the ribs, and she squirmed uncomfortably. Then their eyes met, and they grinned firmly at each other.

"Now, what would have happened if you or one of your drinking buddies had decided to go out for a spin? You might have lost more than one teammate."

Those gazing at the light-gray pavement in front of them shuddered at the thought. By this time in their young lives, everyone had witnessed the numerous wrecks of classmates at the traffic light a block off campus. People took driver's education together and discussed the films depicting the carnage. The bleeding arm of the co-captain symbolized a rite of passage. Fragmented glass and bloody limbs would always be forever etched in their minds. The image of metallic violence contrasted with the steely, calm, blue water of the pool. Many looked at the stilled water as if they had found an edge.

The group dispersed, and Tobias came toward one teammate who could safely toss off the coach's lecture. She looked animated as she sat on the spectator bleachers near the coach's office. The co-ed swimmer sorted through her pile of books as if examining them for the first time that year.

"What were you doing on Saturday night?" he questioned her.

"I stayed at my boyfriend's apartment," she answered him with a warm smile.

Tobias acknowledged her admission with an understanding nod. Then he walked back to the locker room and considered her response, which said a lot about the comfort in her life. Being a star swimmer, she had admitted the simple secret of her success. It related to the contented life she shared with her older boyfriend, who had the tacit approval of her parents. Not the academic type, she proved a formidable rival in the water. Unlike Tobias, a collection of people on the team sported steady partners, almost as if they were already married. While others accepted the arrangements with a certain cultivation of naïveté, Tobias realized that he hungered for more in life. Questions that he could not articulate fueled the passions inside him. He could admire those who found peace in what seemed to be premature sexual companionships. It kept them out of trouble to some extent and provided some sense of security in an insecure, restless world.

****

Tobias didn't have time for another casual gathering until his senior year. The next one amounted to a replay of the first. The captain of the men's team decided to throw a party while his parents were gone. Usually Tobias arrived late, as he was always busy catching up on homework or working.

"There's beer in the fridge," Mike, the co-captain, offered as he displayed the open contents.

Tobias nodded at the assortment of hard and soft liquor, but he declined. Instead, he grabbed a glass of water and went to visit with the crowd in the den. His head was still swimming from the events of the day. For various reasons, he had never developed a taste for alcohol, which seem pungent to him. He was too pragmatic to force a bad thing or play games with his young life, too busy to indulge such rites of passage. Tobias minded his time and level of experience, while others apparently did not.

"Have you seen Laura Ann and Jessica?" Brad asked Tobias.

Tobias drove in the carpool that brought Jessica and their siblings to their various schools. A sophomore, Jessica had transferred from a private school, where she had been head cheerleader. Although, she had made the dive team, along with Laura Ann, the anonymous enormity of the public school continued to overwhelm her.

"Her mom asked me to give Jessica a ride home after the party," Tobias quipped. "Jessica and I agreed to meet up here."

"They stopped by earlier this afternoon," Brad, a responsible junior on the men's team, added. He studied Tobias closely as he looked at him in the eye. "They've been drinking all day."

Tobias met Brad's directness with a grateful nod and then stared into the far away distance. Apparently the younger members of the dive team had decided to drown their sorrows. Both Tobias and Brad knew that driving around the small, twisty country roads while under the influence of alcohol would only exacerbate their chosen feelings of isolation. The girls were truly lost. To make matters worse, a thick, heavy fog had descended on the wooded area, and visibility was only good for two feet ahead. Rolling their eyes at the ceiling, the young men expressed the notion that the choices of these wandering females were unimpressive.

After forty minutes had elapsed, Laura Ann and Jessica came strolling into the kitchen. With a slight, uninhibited swagger, Laura Ann placed a bottle of hard liquor on the counter and offered it as a trophy for the group. The older teammates maintained their position and observed the two wise fools. Completely oblivious of the effect of her words on the crowd,

Laura Ann complained about trivial details of their bitter joy ride. Mike, the captain and host of the party, stood back against the counter and slowly sipped his beer. Brad glanced at Mike and then eyed Tobias for his reaction.

Tobias didn't say a word. Instead he just watched, almost in disbelief at the stupidity of the two rebels. He wondered how he was going to get Jessica peacefully home. Having grown up with her, he knew to sidestep her mood, which he could tell would be impossible tonight. He wasn't looking forward to the confrontation. These young women knew better. Their actions dared the upperclassmen to bring them back in line and assert the pecking order.

Nudging her compatriot in the arm, Jessica motioned to Laura Ann that she was ready to leave. Teetering forward as if suddenly hit by a bowling ball, Laura Ann caught the heavy disapproval emanating toward them. It hit her like a silent wave in her presently inebriated state, where any repressed psychic sensitivities surfaced. Regaining her composure as a sure-footed diver, she announced her agreement with Jessica.

"All right, we're moving on," she stated, looking at the group with a harsh expression of dissatisfaction on her face. Though her footsteps failed to reflect her demeanor, she continued, "C'mon Jessica, let's go."

"Where are you going?" Brad politely asked without a hint of reprimand.

"I don't know," she said loudly, folding her arms across her chest. "Anywhere but here."

Jessica defiantly stretched out her hand to Laura Ann to pull her away from the gathered crowd.

"The fog is too thick to see the fingers on the hand in front of you," Tobias mentioned. He calmly extended his hand as if to reason with her. "It's not safe to go driving around, especially if you've been drinking all day."

Mike offered his palm to Laura Ann and gently asked for the car keys. Towering over the young women, he offered, "We'll drive you home."

"I don't want to go home," Laura Ann stated flatly, spurning Mike's offer. Instead she followed Jessica's steps as she marched out the front door. The women hopped into the car and spent a few minutes in the driveway, as Jessica took time to search for the knobs on the low beams and other controls.

Meanwhile, Tobias retrieved his car keys from his pocket and went directly to the Chevy. "I'm going after these guys. If I can get in front, they will have to slow down. I can light the way, so that they won't wind up in a ditch."

The rest of the group in the kitchen responded as if it were an emergency operation. Leaving their beverages on the counter, they enthusiastically grabbed their car keys and letter jackets with determined grins of fierce competitors. Taking several others with them, Brad and Mike headed out the door behind Tobias and started their engines. Tobias moved swiftly and managed to overtake the Laura Ann's vehicle when it slowed in the gray haze of a single street lamp. The lamp marked a nearby intersection, and Tobias passed the two women carefully under the light. Glancing at them sideways, he could tell that any indignation at his appearance was rapidly seeping from their countenances, like air escaping from a swollen balloon. In his rearview mirror, Tobias noticed that Brad and Mike were close behind in their cars. Laura Ann went back on the road and moved awkwardly, at a snail's pace. Tobias felt relief that he had caught them. Forced to slow down underneath the hazardous conditions, the two women weren't going anywhere fast. The best that he could do under the circumstances was keep pace. He sensed that it was just a matter of time before something positive would happen. Fortunately, the timing involved only another three miles.

Laura Ann suddenly stopped her car in the middle of the road. Tobias pulled over and turned on his hazard lights. Laura Ann slipped out of the driver's seat and walked from the car toward Tobias. She appeared like an apparition surrounded by the white mists that were illumined by the car lights behind her.

"Brad keeps trying to pull me over." Though she bowed her head to confide in Tobias, she spoke in a booming voice that echoed in the damp air.

Tobias noted that the feigned irritation in her tone. Instead, Laura Ann seemed bewildered by all the concerned male attention. Ignoring Tobias, she returned to the vehicle, remaining motionless behind the wheel until her eyes regained focus. Brad hurried out of his car and stood next to her. As he lightly put his arms on around her shoulders, Laura Ann surrendered her keys to him. Jessica hurriedly popped out of Laura Ann's car and slid into the passenger seat of the Chevy.

"She's lost," Jessica reported. "She can't find her way in the fog, and Brad keeps bothering her."

After watching Mike dive into the passenger seat that Jessica had left empty, Tobias turned back to the car and started the engine. "Let's go home, Jessica."

Leaving Laura Ann in the hands of the two young men, Tobias immediately pulled away, before Jessica could change her mind. Silently they drove down the narrow country road in the enveloping fog, making their way carefully at a restrained speed. Three minutes later, Jessica began crying.

"You are always so perfect," she sobbed. "Always the older, smarter one. Do you know how hard it is keeping up with you?"

This was the last thing Tobias wanted to hear on such a worrisome night. He didn't say a word about coach's lectures, and he kept his vision focused on the road ahead. Only tolerating her lament, he dropped her off without leaving his place behind the wheel. He didn't know how to begin to explain it to her. He had his own pain, which compelled him to soar higher and higher. His flight was something that he wasn't going to ever let go of or stop. Jessica never noticed the tenacious grip of his concealed claws. Perhaps, she'd figure Tobias's reason someday. Meanwhile, he watched her wipe a few tears from her face as she passed through the front door, undetected by the sleeping inhabitants of the house. She knew enough to keep secret the adventures of her night out while she sobered to face her real problems without creating anymore. Satisfied that she was safe within the confines of her residence, Tobias left.

Chapter Three

Be mindful of the way

People spin in and out

Of each other's lives

Like a dreidel

Tune Reference: *Dreidel*

----Don McLean

"YOU'LL HAVE TO go the south end to find a replacement thermostat," the man behind the counter told Tobias.

He tossed the car part between his hands as he closely examined it. Tobias watched the swift moves of his thick fingers with lightly greased prints etched in the skin. His fingerprints told the story of many vehicles and parts. Deftly placing the part down on the counter, the man automatically consulted a thick, heavy reference book and looked up the model of the thermostat. Tobias obtained a part number from the man and headed off for the junkyards at the other end of town. Having left his mother's car dismantled in the driveway, he didn't have any time to waste putting it back together.

Driving past heaps of worn and crushed vehicles, Tobias marveled at the components. It was like getting a glimpse of a creature's insides during a biology lab. Each piece of machinery offered an unbiased testimony to the past, completely devoid of emotion. Some of the vehicles had been silent witnesses to tragedy; others had simply been well used. Parking his car at the tiny shop near a pile of metal rubble, Tobias stepped out onto the muddy lot. A flash summer storm had left small silt puddles scattered around the tin shack where he knew he would be able to find his thermostat. A man behind the wheel of a mini-tractor pushed a few pieces of heavy metal quickly around the lot. He smiled and waved at Tobias. Tobias grinned at him. The collection of metallic possibilities waiting for the right vehicle had a mesmerizing effect. Crossing the threshold of the tin shack, he left the soft clay mud for a cement floor and a wall of bright, shiny hubcaps. Bright fluorescents illuminated the contents of the crowded workspace, making the place look cheerful. This was the place where parts were reborn and given a new life.

"What are you looking for?" the happy man greeted from the front desk.

"I'm looking for this thermostat," Tobias replied as he handed him the part number. "It's for a '73 Ford."

The man thumbed through a thick book, and then he disappeared behind the rows of small packages and various shiny silver components. Within moments, he returned with the proper thermostat. Pulling it from a relatively tiny box, he unwrapped the ball-shaped part and compared it to the notes in the book.

"Ever replaced one of these before?" he asked.

Tobias shook his head, offering the best blank look that he could afford. He wanted the man to tell him everything. Cocking his head from side to side, he scrutinized Tobias for a second. Then he reached for a cardboard cutout plate and a jar of auto gel.

"You are going to need this and this," he said. "Cut out the correct gasket before you replace the thermostat, and then seal it with the gel. It will make a nice seal."

Tobias carefully studied the man's hands as he automatically pointed to the correct gasket on the template and ran his fingers over the edge of the thermostat with pretend gel. In his mind, Tobias compared the man's live demonstration to the magazines that he had ordered from a US government clearing house in Pueblo, Colorado. He had obtained the army's publications on basic car repair for free. Because the military encouraged its soldiers to take responsibility for their vehicles, the documents lacked the convoluted, mysterious air of those manuals found at auto-supply stores. Two do-it-yourself army magazines and a live demonstration at the local auto store was all Tobias ever needed to be able to grease wheel bearings, replace coolant, replace thermostats, change oil, and perform other assorted car maintenance procedures. For him, it was physics in action. His high-school physics teacher had talked about friction, but there was nothing like seeing the effect on the brake pads when he pulled the wheels off.

Respecting the man's time, Tobias paid him for the part without further questions. Soon he was down the road and on his way back to the stilled vehicle waiting for him at home. Usually those who sold auto supplies didn't mind revealing how to use them. They had been educated by experience and passed along information as if it were holy obligation. It was the places that worked for hire that often tried to confuse a neophyte. However, those service places with salaried mechanics didn't mind offering a few hints for an eager mind bent on enlightenment.

"I just pulled the oil drain plug out with vise grips," one Ford mechanic revealed after Tobias had taken the car in without his mother's knowledge. "Just go real easy with the wrench. See, you stripped the threads off the plug. Remember: righty-tighty, lefty-loosey."

Bracing his legs against the tires while under the car, Tobias had overestimated the strength in his swimmer's legs. Luckily, the mechanic had saved him before his mother found out that he had botched the repair job. By the time she arrived home, the oil change had been completed at a nominal price.

As he drove through the south end, Tobias could not help but notice the electronics stores on the strip. There was a lot to be learned from serious, professional supply stores. Despite his schedule, he stopped. He wanted to check out the potentiometers for a radio that he was constructing.

Tobias recently had enlisted the aid of his neighbor, the electronics engineer across the street. This was after he had tied up his aunt's fiancé, a ham-radio enthusiast, for an afternoon last month. Dropping his aunt's boyfriend in favor of his neighbor had seemed the prudent thing to do, especially since he lived several hours away and needed to focus on the upcoming wedding.

The more Tobias delved into the project, the more questions he found. After consulting more books and manuals, he sensed that this store was the place to find the perfect tuner for his project. The result was only as good as the parts, he felt, and he hoped to improve on this ongoing endeavor. After a twenty-minute search, Tobias found a tuning capacitor that resembled the dial on a transistor radio; it was the perfect inspiration for his project.

Two days afterward, he brought his purchase over to the neighbor, who pieced the components together on an electronics breadboard. Then he hooked the breadboard to an oscilloscope, for a closer look at the operating signals generated by the new configuration. The pictorial representation of the hidden dynamics of his electronics hardware never failed to fascinate Tobias. There it was, in blue and white. Hank, his neighbor, clicked through a few dials and changed the shape of the wave. When he had obtained the information that he was looking for, he bowed his head and inserted a transistor and a resistor into the breadboard. Looking up again at the display on the oscilloscope, he smiled in satisfaction at the resulting wave forms that clicked into place with a turn of the dials on the machine. Without a further word, he pushed a few buttons on the side of his desk. Music erupted from the loudspeaker.

Hank rose from his bar stool and faced Tobias with a grin. His eyes twinkled in delight as he watched the expression on Tobias's face change from perplexity to delighted shock.

"I hooked your radio up to an amplifier," he explained.

Tobias blinked and remained speechless for a moment. He slowly moved closer to the workbench for a closer look. "An amplifier?"

The sudden loud noise from the garage brought out Hank's wife. She opened the door from the kitchen and curiously peered at the tangled collection of wires on the workbench. Noticing the breadboard centered in the arrangement of alligator clips, she assumed that Tobias's project was the source of the loud music. A mixture of confusion and amusement appeared on her face as she glanced from Hank to Tobias. Meanwhile, their rounded Sheltie dog darted from behind her and excitedly race around the garage, never daring to go past the florescent lights and into the darkness beyond the opened garage door.

Tobias suspected that he served as the bridge between the worlds of this isolated engineer and this attractive, youthful, socially perceptive woman. It was more than just the time that he and his younger sister had spent babysitting their only child or taking care of the house in their absence. Assuming the role of makeshift interpreter, he explained one to the other.

"It's my physics project," Tobias offered. "It works!"

Slightly taken aback, Hank's wife watched the swerving Sheltie dash behind her for the kitchen. Bending over the racing dog around her knees, she gently tossed her long blonde hair over her shoulder with a laugh. Tobias gave her an excuse to linger at the workbench and ask questions. Meanwhile, Tobias began politely packing his electronics gear for the night. It was time to rest on his laurels, which was almost as important as the work. He required downtime in order to keep moving forward on a project. Timing possessed a social aspect. Years of experience in navigating through high-school halls had also taught him when to leave couples alone.

"See ya," Tobias announced before he ventured into the warm night of a greening spring. He noted that the couple had already engaged each other in a little flirtatious dance that fascinated twosomes often do. They barely heard him, but both shot him a quick glance to indicate that he should come back and not just disappear; they needed him in that strange sort of way that people took comfort in relationships of all sizes and shapes. Nobody wanted to be alone.

The black night that had discouraged the Sheltie did not bother Tobias. He could smell the budding oak leaves and sense the life around him. Nothing remained still, especially in a southern evening. It was just the beginning. Crossing the cement street to his front door, Tobias figured that the next topic for investigation would be the construction of a low-powered amplifier for the radio. It would be another mystery for him to unravel.

For these reasons Tobias could never understand why his graduating classmates were not excited to leave high school. He'd graduated seventh out of a class of seven hundred, and so they had put him on a platform on center stage, along with nine others. Hollering and hooting the entire way through the ceremony, Tobias could have easily led a Southern revival meeting instead of a graduating class. His antics brought chuckles from Connie, the young woman sitting next to him in spot number six. Maybe it was because she took classes like underwater basket weaving to earn her spot on the top ten that she didn't feel as if she had achieved as much. Tobias, on the other hand, had brought up his grade in honors chemistry a whole letter once he'd quit his job at the shoe department. It amazed him and his instructor what a little extra time to study could do. No longer did he have to start cracking the books at ten in the evening to comprehend the incomprehensible in the wee hours. The experience taught him an important lesson about his need for sleep and a fresh approach in problem solving. Simply getting through, day to day, had been a struggle for him. Now that it was over, he could rejoice at his triumph over the difficulties inherent in his life.

It had been a high-wire act, but Tobias remained careful rather than cocky. A year ago, one of his buddies on the swim team had confided in him during practice about the loss of his older brother. Leaning over the rope dividing the two lanes, he'd briefly told Tobias the story.

"He was the perfect kid. Great grades. Popular and well liked by everyone, but he worked hard. He lapsed at the wheel of his car and died in the accident. Being exhausted, he had fallen asleep."

Then the storyteller nonchalantly readjusted the goggles on his forehead and swam off. Stunned, Tobias grabbed a kickboard and took his time to reflect a moment before building into speed. It was another lesson: to keep checking his pace and physical limits. Too many people told him that he worked too hard, but he became his own man in the end. Despite all this, he wasn't near as fast as his buddy in the next lane, and he probably never would be. This he could accept.

Nonetheless, Tobias attended the swim party for the class council given a week after the graduation ceremony, and he was a little disappointed when he became the life of the pool party. Though he managed to enlist a few retired football players in a rousing game of keep-away, the rest of the loungers seemed deadbeat. It was as if their lives were over. The only other animated interaction in the group was from Connie, who was busily engaged in a thought-provoking discussion with the class president. She seemed lighter, for some reason. He did a double take before he turned away, and they took time to wave good-bye to him with a smile before resuming their discussion. Tobias grinned and hurried out. He wasn't sure what it was all about. It became another mystery to ponder.

Two weeks later, Tobias attended Connie's funeral along with several of his other buddies. This time he avoided the various student and class council groups and opted to go with Danny, an old grade-school friend, and a mutual acquaintance from the tennis team, named Sam. Those on the tennis team were loners; they had to have good social skills to be competitive and friendly at the same time. Danny and Tobias had sung for many funerals together in the past. School administrators made funerals a priority for the upperclassman choir, often allowing them out of class to perform for those who had died with a limited social network. Many came from nursing homes and were linked with various church staff.

As they gathered in the car, Tobias recalled another funeral---Danny had suddenly broken into tears when it ended. He had lost his older brother to leukemia the previous summer. An eighth-grade teacher who doubled as a deacon had stayed behind to comfort him. Tobias remembered the expression on the face of the teacher. Although he knew that she'd never lost an older brother, her sincere empathy convinced Tobias that a person didn't need to experience everything in life to possess the appropriate amount of understanding needed to confront the unexplainable. Tobias had packed up his guitar and left with the other members of the choir, relieved that Danny would get the needed assistance for an overdue reaction concerning the loss.

Both Danny and Tobias had been reluctant to attend this particular funeral. Rumor had it that the high-school honors English teacher would be boycotting the experience. Connie had been the teacher's pet for this class; she had done far better than Tobias could ever hope for on any English essay. The teacher required the class to present their book reports in front of the class. The sappy, turbulent romance novels such as *Pride and Prejudice* and *Withering Heights* had been given to the drill-team members and football players, while Tobias had been stuck with the esotericism of *Return of the Native*. Though he was sure he would have botched the essays on these novels about the ridiculous pining of the female heart for unrequited love and designated social standing, he felt overwhelmed by the metaphysical aspects of his novel. He knew that he was too young to determine how much of it was baloney, much less figure out why in enough time to write a coherent paper and pass the course. However, when these members of the class gave their book reports, he could almost understand it from their perspective. There was something to be said for accepting life *as is* without ever questioning some of the fundamentals presented in the earlier chapters. Tobias could always see a bad thing coming and hated to read the affair through. His big questions amounted to *So what?* and *Who cares?* Like the emphatic deacon, the honors English teacher had the advantage of more experience and established opinions. Tobias could sense that she had detected his underlying questions, because she avoided him. This probably was the first year she declined to give her views on the novels. Tobias's debate partner had gone to study at a well-known university on the East Coast. He had told him to listen for these gems of wisdom from the honors English teacher. When the English teacher failed to say much of anything that year besides commenting on what Connie planned to get her boyfriend for Christmas, Tobias felt robbed, and he dug into the matter. While English teacher vicariously lived out the high-school romances in the class, he researched the entire affair on all levels.

Tobias's recourse was to consult one of his buddies on the team who always seemed to take the same day off from swim practice. Out of deference to the women with periods, the coach allowed the co-ed swimmers one day off a month to just take a break. Most often swimmers came back stronger after a break.

"I loved Thomas Hardy," his buddy claimed. "I read all of his novels by the time that I was in fourth grade."

"So, why aren't you in honors English?" Tobias questioned. "You seem more knowledgeable about literature than anyone else I know."

"The honors English teacher taught my third-grade class and had it in for me," his teammate recalled, and he shuddered, with a wry smile. "I can't stand her."

"I can tell that I'm not one of her favorites either, but we get along in an odd sort of way," Tobias admitted. "She sorta avoids me."

"I can tell you about *Return of the Native*," he told Tobias.

"Great. Let's get started. She gave me a B on my essay."

Over time, Tobias obtained a profound version of English literature from his teammate. This proved the honors English class that he'd missed.

There was more about the current of life, expressed in the way words rolled out on the pages than there were questions pertaining to the big picture. Tobias attributed his friend's literary correctness to the fact that his mother was full-blooded French. Because of this inheritance, Tobias trusted the romantic inclinations of his buddy, the only one who could get him to sit through a vampire movie without suffering from the effects of Gothic terror. Tobias became squeamish when it came to inviting horror in his psychic space.

Nothing Tobias could have read would have prepared him for the experience at the funeral home. It proved horrific. Tobias filed past the open casket with the other graduates. Then he stopped to the side and made a brief sign of the cross in the direction of his departed classmate. It all seemed so wrong---one wrong thing leading to another wrong thing. There was nobody around to stop it. All he could do was bless it as he found it and then leave.

A few days prior the funeral, Tobias had visited his friend, Lenny, who was from his advanced calculus classes. Lenny had moved out of his parents' home as soon as he'd finished high school. Another classmate, looking for an escape from an abusive situation at home, would share the apartment. Lenny's circumstances were not as dire as his classmate's, but his mother's recent remarriage encouraged him to quickly move on. Tobias came to help Lenny unpack his vehicle from the parking lot below and carry his belongings up several floors. When the work ended, they discussed the tragedy.

"Calhoun said that Connie had been drinking with her boyfriend when their car overturned," his friend said. Calhoun had been a member of the football team and heard all the locker-room conversations, which had continued into the summer following graduation. "She was thrown from the car and landed in a ditch. The car rolled on top of her. Her boyfriend survived with a broken leg. The honors English teacher refuses to have anything to do with the funeral. She is very upset."

"Yeah, I heard," Tobias responded, backing away toward his car in the lot. He was ready to leave. Suddenly he stopped and faced his friend who was leaning against the stair rail two floors above. He said, "I feel scared."

Lenny smiled and nodded at him.

Feeling encouraged, he continued, "I feel so alone. I've been to funerals before, but this one is different." Then Tobias took a deep breath and walked away from the apartment complex. Another thought came to mind, causing him to pause. His friend on the balcony was still watching.

"She changed at the end," Tobias told him. "It seemed positive, but now I think that her soul had already started to transition at the council party. There was a particular light about her." Tobias pulled his keys out of his pocket as he stood by the car door. "I don't get it. It was like she was saying good-bye in her own way."

Lenny grinned at Tobias with curiosity. Like the stepfather that he was leaving, Lenny also fostered an interest in human psychology. He asked Tobias, "What do you mean by *lighter*? Had she been carrying a weight?"

"No, I did not see that," Tobias insisted. "She became illumined from within, and she seemed to spread her wings toward some sort of enlightenment, as if the internal being was being compelled to turn to an external source."

Lenny smiled through the perplexed expression on his face. He gulped a breath of air before nodding for Tobias to continue.

"It was her compulsion that frightened me, because the end was already in sight before the car wreck. The story is in the passing over of

Connie's soul at that particular moment. No understanding of the situation is to be gained by fathoming the fatal mishap. That is oblivion, and it leads to nowhere."

"So there is more to be gained by examining the situation the month prior," Lenny acknowledged. "Tobias, you always did read between the lines in honors English."

"I always feel like I am in between things," Tobias contemplated. "Maybe that is the real reason for the difficulties I experienced in that class." Then he paused, staring down at the pavement. The surface was the dark, rough stuff that tore the skin off his knees whenever he fell playing in the parking lots. The locals called it *blacktop*. Lifting his head, he recalled, "I did some research on *Little Women* in lieu of that class. The author described a similar type of light when her sister stilled at the moment of death. Alcott died on the same day as her father. John Adams and Thomas Jefferson died on the same Fourth of July."

"Tobias, you read too much," Lenny informed him with a grin.

"I *know*." Tobias emphasized this with an intentional drawl on the word *know* to stretch it out. It was true; he *had* read a lot. "Apparently, the passing of souls was often discussed during the Civil War. The terminology can be found in the book promoted by that speech instructor. We had to learn some of the poems by heart."

Being from New York, Lenny understood the subtlety. Drawls often got in the way of the real stories and hampered communication. For those deep in the South, drawls constituted another inside story. The inner tale held its own in the rhythm of words never amounting to the task of lyrics, commercially used and copyrighted by those on the East Coast. Field hands, sharecroppers, and slaves sang their words, never making the money of "The

Star Spangled-Banner." Through the eloquent employment of the drawl, the South retained its own song, which had never been surrendered to the robber barons who had exploited their Confederate losses. Yankees hit by the ensuing Industrial Revolution were not known to sing during factory labor. In fact, Tobias had not been to a grade-school basketball game where anyone bothered with a production of *The Star Spangled-Banner*; instead, some of the teams would spontaneously break out in freedom songs.

"I never took speech," Lenny confessed, peering down at the blacktop two stories below.

"Well, you missed the art form of the tragedy that we've been discussing. Though, in the present moment, the art is elusive," Tobias rejoined, eyeing Lenny sternly with mock reproach. "Now you've got me drifting into my drawl, which I only reserve for the company that survives two beers."

"There's a lot to be said for dialogue," Lenny insisted. "Tell me the name of the book, before I kill you."

"Yes, I know," Tobias stated, holding his ground by refusing to get straight to the point. "That is why Shakespeare was mostly dialogue. They would have killed him."

"Tell me the name of the book," Lenny said with a growl.

"Lenny, I never knew that you harbored such a manly passion for the literary world," Tobias teased. "In the South, a man is not a man until he kills someone. Even the spider women kiss and kill. They get real creative about their webs, as if they don't want some bug ruining it. Those gals almost become territorial."

"I want the name of the book," Lenny insisted.

"Well," Tobias continued, "if you ever get around to reading Civil War poetry, you might try *Spoon River Anthology*." Then he added, "Like life, the terminology only becomes obvious with the poetry."

"Now I understand the real war between the North and South." Lenny nodded in firm agreement.

"True, that was the scary part of it," Tobias observed. "Spoon River is a place in Illinois, though I think that they are too commercial to talk about it in the way we do here." He explained, "Both sides of my family fought for the Union, though they did not support the industrialists. We are not Yankees who sell their souls for a buck. The ancestors fled to the South to avoid persecution. This is what happens when the next elected president rides a horse called Jefferson Davis. You know how fond generals are of their horses, Lenny. Lincoln had his own team, consisting of those who opposed the human trafficking of the Holy Roman Empire. He sensed that wars were created as distractions from the real issues. We appreciate the South for its free-flowing music, hospitality, and witticisms."

Tobias paused and looked up at Lenny on the balcony. Shading his eyes from the sun's glare, he continued, "There were actually three factions in the Civil War, not two. It was over life, particularly the enslavement of the human form." Waving his arms in the air like a Shakespearean actor, he pondered out loud, "Why is it that when some things get better, other things get worse---really worse? They end before they get started, like a diver in a destined bell-shaped flight. What comes up, comes down. It is the curve that life throws at you, Lenny. They call it gravity."

"Go home," Lenny decreed, straightening at his post at the top of the stairs. Still smiling, he shrugged at Tobias. With a sigh, Tobias hopped behind the wheel and started the engine of the Chevy. He wasn't sure whether Lenny would ever appreciate the finer details in life, especially the ones that led to death. Somewhere he had read that the devil was in the detail. Pulling out of the parking lot, he looked in his rearview mirror and noticed Lenny waving at him.

"I am sorry," Lenny said so that Tobias could hear.

Tobias merely nodded without stopping. Lenny knew that Tobias had heard him and went back into his apartment. Instead of driving home, Tobias turned down the street and drove to a favorite park where he enjoyed watching the ducks.

It was at the funeral where it all played out. Connie's mother and sister were the first to stay by the casket. The face on Connie's mother showed pure adoration. She had chosen a song for the ceremony that, in effect, described their complex relationship: child and surrogate mate. Tobias wondered how one person could be so much to another. Connie's red-faced stepfather stood close to the family. Though about six years younger and half a head smaller than his wife, he composed himself in wired, taunt manner that was almost brutal. Completely ignoring him, it appeared obvious that the mother was playing the daughter against him even in death. Meanwhile, Connie's younger sister sobbed, as did the rest of the congregation.

Next came the boyfriend, hobbling on crutches, unabashed at the tears streaming down his young face. His light, boyish frame surprised Tobias, who'd had the impression that the larger-than-life man would be huskier. Kneeling as well as he could next to the corpse, the youngster determinedly placed a gold band on Connie's wedding-ring finger. There was no sense of guilt on his face, only sorrow and an intimate understanding. Then he swiftly left the scene on his awkward crutches. The rest were compelled to file by; there was no polite exit. Tobias suspected that the mother had planned it that way.

Once outside in the bright sunshine, people regrouped according to vehicles and drove to the burial ground, a familiar one overlooking the highway, near the high school. Tobias and Danny piled in Sam's vehicle, a large Oldsmobile that could have been driven in a roadshow of 1960s antique cars. Somehow they managed to get lost, despite the long line of cars making their way across town.

Danny broke the silence as Sam frantically tried to make his way back into the procession lineup.

"It's quite a lesson for those football players to quit mistreating their girlfriends," he said.

Sam nodded as he swerved the large vehicle around a corner. "Yeah, I hear that Connie's mother and stepfather don't get along."

"He's abusive," Danny added. "Connie would have been in a good place at the technical university in Lubbock. Where are you going, Tobias?"

Tobias revealed that he had a scholarship for a university in Oregon, where he wanted to study premed chemistry. Satisfied with his answer, Danny next quizzed Sam about his plans.

"I leave for the navy next week," Sam said seriously.

Tobias and Danny shrugged and smiled at each other. They had not suspected that Sam was a navy man. The conversation lightened, assuming an almost comical air---which had been Danny's trademark since his older brother had died. Finally arriving at the hill for the burial, Sam carefully parked the Oldsmobile along the dirt road of the cemetery. They stepped out of the car onto yellow grass that was already dead from the summer's heat. Together they navigated the array of tombstones and headed for the covered pavilion where the coffin stood beside a hole in the ground. Tobias stepped closer to the assembly of finely dressed young men and women, who seemed out of place on the prairie. Even the grave markers seemed an anomaly in the brilliant golden heat. He watched one of the large football players carry a female classmate away. She'd been overcome by the looming finality of the closed casket being lowered into the hole below. Her arm dangled limply toward the ground over his elbow.

Where had she gone? Tobias wondered.

Then another well-dressed drill-team member fainted and was gently carried away by muscled young man.

They are visiting Connie, Tobias surmised after he noted the whitish swirls of air drifting in the heat waves. Nobody paid attention to the words of the preacher except the immediate family. Meanwhile, the class was becoming unruly, cutting up and taking advantage of the absence of a stern teacher. Now the typical tension characterizing the Class of '79 was escalating to panic levels. The sense of order was gone.

"Let's get out of here," Danny whispered to Sam. Sam's black pupils widened as he silently nodded his agreement. They both glanced at Tobias for his consent. Tobias readily gave it; he was never one to be still for very long. Now was not the time to be polite.

When they were out of earshot, Danny playfully asked, "Would you like to meet Paul, my older brother? He's buried around here somewhere."

"I'd love to," Tobias replied. He looked forward to a much more peaceful encounter with the other side of the veil, having admired the little he knew of Danny's older brother.

Sam hesitated slightly, but he followed Tobias and Danny over the hill as they skimmed grave markers.

"Here we are," Danny announced. "Paul, meet Tobias. Tobias, meet Paul. Sam, this is Paul. Paul, this is Sam."

Neither Sam nor Tobias answered. Instead, Tobias beamed at the marker, which seemed to glow a little. Danny glimpsed the interaction, and caught himself as he almost fell over the site.

"OK, let's go," Danny said, and he started hurrying down the hill to the Oldsmobile. Convinced that the proper acquaintances had been made, he left before any further light could be cast on the subject. Though life could be fleeting, it was best to not linger in the realm of the dead, no matter how bright it appeared.

After they'd arrived at the vacated lot of the funeral home, Tobias waved the other two off and settled in the driver's seat of the Chevy. He had to get off to one of his summer jobs. There was no time to waste, only enough to switch gears.

The next day, at home, the conversation during lunch drifted to what Tobias's sister had heard about the funeral. His sister was the same age as Connie's younger sister. For a few moments, Tobias stared into space as his sisters and mother chatted.

Lost in thought, he chose his words carefully. It took about three sentences to decisively end the discussion between his mother and sister. He decided to rattle them before he got rattled. "It was an open casket. They only had to redo her face twice. She wore her prom dress," he softly blurted, breaking his silence.

They left him alone after that. Finishing the last few bites of his meal in peace and clearing his place, he moved out of the room like a stealth missile. Out of earshot, he wiped away a collection of tears in his eyes, relieved that he had finally found enough space to grieve and experience the sorrow of Connie's sudden passing.

Chapter Four

Lonesome runner, tired fool,
Why don't you come back to the city
And be cool?

Time makes no allowances
For things you fail to see;
Destiny marches on
And never lets you be.
Lonesome runner, tired fool,
Why don't you come back to the city
And be cool?

Look at what you're trying to prove,
So many things going on;
Look at what you lose.
Did the past hide your integrity?
Lonesome runner, tired fool,
Why don't you come back to the city
And be cool?

Don't let it slip away,
Know who you are;
Travesty is not a legacy.

Flight from Oblivion
Lonesome runner, tired fool,

Why don't you come back to the city

And be cool?

Guess what you try to prove

With too many things going on;

Living with delusions

Will never let you be.

Lonesome runner, tired fool,

Why don't you come back to the city

And be cool?

Come now, sit by my side,

Don't go running off;

Two scared people are happier

Than two who are lost.

Lonesome runner, tired fool

Why don't you come back to the city

And be cool?

Lonesome Runner

----Kim Kacoroski © 1981 with permission granted for respectful, joyous use
in public domain

SHORTLY THEREAFTER, TOBIAS ventured to the Pacific Northwest, where he pursued undergraduate studies. The shedding of tears and his experience of the funeral closed the door on his relationship with his family of origin. It simply could not continue. The incident with Jessica, the sophomore diver whom Tobias had retrieved from the fog that day at the party, had separated him from his siblings. Like Jessica, his younger sisters were always testing the waters with Tobias, purposely bent on bucking his position in the fatherless family. By the time he left for college, he was more than willing to let them have his place, though it surprised him how quickly they took it. As for the whereabouts of his father, Tobias knew not to go down that path. Whatever had transpired between his argumentative biological parents was strictly their business. All he knew was that he wanted out, and he was willing to do whatever it took to jump ship. Again, he felt as though he were just passing through.

Years ago, when his potential was beginning to show, an entity had beamed its way into his life. Tobias had fought hard, but the jealous god had managed to tag his spirit. It had felt like losing an irretrievable piece of himself and being forced to go through life leaving a trail of blood for any shark to pursue. Tobias could beat off the predators, but he could not stop the endless flow of blood that betrayed him and left his spirit forever limp. Unable to staunch the wound nor correct the gait, he remained haunted by this hollow feeling of doomed futility. For his protection, he cultivated a godlike enigma to hide the injury, while he plotted his flight from the alien world.

Meanwhile he continued to collect data and cultivate tools that might provide a safe passage. *Where was he going?* Tobias wasn't quite sure, but he knew that he would recognize it as soon as he landed there.

"So, Tobias, what brought you to the Pacific Northwest?" his college roommate asked him once as he twirled a basketball over his right index finger. "You are a long way from home. It rains here all the time."

"It is because they kiss in the rain here," Tobias told him without any further elaboration. He rose to steal the basketball from his roommate's hand before he was questioned further.

His roommate shielded the ball from Tobias. Stopping suddenly, he placed the ball over his hip and defended it with his free outstretched hand. Then he cocked his head side to side to consider Tobias's response. "I'll have to remember that. Say, how did that date with Olivia go? She's in our chemistry lab? Right?"

"Later," Tobias said, knocking the ball away from his roommate.

The ball bounced out of the room and rolled down the hall. Tobias raced for it before it hit the stairwell. His roommate ran after him. Rushing past other dorm students, Tobias caught the ball and passed it back to his roommate. Tobias became aware of a serious air about the dorm mates who had just ascended the stairwell. Tobias turned and faced them. They were also from the chemistry lab. One of them seemed on the verge of tears. Having finished his lab work ahead of the others, Tobias had cleaned his station and left early to catch up on some calculus homework.

"Did you hear?" one of the young men near Tobias blurted. "Olivia caught fire in chemistry lab. Professor Doogin rolled her on the ground to stop the fire. The ambulance came and took her to the hospital."

Tobias took a deep breath. His roommate watched as his chest heaved with the weight of the news and then quieted. Together they followed the less-shaken young man into his room for more information. Tobias's roommate sat on the orange basketball, while Tobias assumed a perch on a bunk bed.

"How is she?" Tobias asked, deeply moved by the thought of such a beautiful young woman going up in flames.

"Nobody knows. The ambulance attendants wrapped her up in a blanket and took off with her."

"They are collecting money for flowers," the other young man interjected softly. Still visibly shaken from the experience, he sat down next to Tobias on the bed and stared off into space. Tobias watched the man's entire body go limp. His roommate studied the look of horror on the young man's face and met Tobias's eyes. Nobody had any explanation to offer. Tobias grew uncomfortable with the silence, and he left the room. He went down the flight of stairs the basketball had nearly rolled down. Stepping outside in the dark, he started to walk in the rain. People he met on the sidewalk gave him a few more details. Olivia's long hair had caught fire from one of the Bunsen burners, while she was talking with a friend. The instructor had probably saved her life with his quick actions. The rest of the class was stunned.

Women and their faces was a topic that everyone on campus avoided. Recognizing that this was one situation where it was not appropriate to visit the patient in the hospital, the concerned campus waited patiently for Olivia's return. When Olivia returned to Tobias's chemistry class months later, she chose to sit at a desk in front of him. He was relieved that only one ear had the familiar pink hue of a burn victim. Her hair had grown enough to cover most of the scar. Olivia smiled at him. She ran her hand through her hair as she waved off her appearance, making it clear that she was happy to be alive. Tobias smiled at her gesture, rejoicing with her in silence. Watching his response out of the corner of her eye, she nodded in relief at him. She seemed grateful that someone else understood the bigger picture of life.

For the next year, they strolled in and out of each other's lives. Both were too busy with their studies and endeavors to continue seeing much of each other. Tobias finally caught up with Olivia at a college basketball game. After climbing his way over the bleachers to meet her, he gave a light bow and asked if he could sit down next to her. Several girlfriends surrounded her. They were conversing animatedly with the neighboring crowd. With his polite manner, Tobias conveyed the sense that he wished to keep his distance from the crowd. Olivia nodded; she, too, would like a quieter moment.

"How's it going?" he asked; he was startled by the residual shock and fear he saw in her eyes.

"It's coming along," she responded. "I enjoy being back at school. My parents' house caught on fire last month."

"Whoa," Tobias whispered near her scarred ear. "That must have been rough. How did it go after the experience in the chemistry lab?"

"I vomited on the front lawn," she told him as she tossed her head. "I couldn't stop."

"I can imagine," Tobias answered. He shook his head and studied her. "That is an odd turn of events. You've been through two fires in a relatively short time."

"I know," she said. "I went back to talk to some of the staff who helped me in the hospital. Seems that all chemistry majors incur serious burns in pursuit of their studies. They showed me their scars and told me their stories."

"I get it," Toby said. For a brief moment, he focused on the basketball game, and then he resumed his attention on Olivia. "So what are you going to major in?"

"Physical therapy. I want work with burn patients."

A loud roar from the surrounding crowd interrupted their discussion as if on cue. Olivia tossed her head at Tobias and gazed at the court. Tobias had already taken in the play with a well-timed glance; it helped to lighten the heavy topic. Taking a moment, Olivia determined the reason for the uproar. When she seemed satisfied with her guess, Olivia turned toward Tobias with a smile. She appeared very happy that she now knew the purpose of her life. Adding to the emphasis, Tobias rose and hugged her lightly across the bleacher seat. He whispered in her scarred ear, "I think you'll be wonderful in your role."

****

Later in the school year, Tobias went back to Texas. Spring break fell close to Valentine's Day that year, and Tobias went to visit Jerry, a college friend in Dallas. They spent Valentine's Day going to a nightclub with a group of men and women who lived on campus. After a brief group discussion concerning carpool arrangements, Tobias opened the car door for several of the women and then hopped into the passenger seat of his buddy's souped-up hot rod. Jerry steered the vehicle on the back road leading to the downtown streets. This particular street was known for a hairpin turn just a half mile from the college parking lot.

"I wonder what all the traffic is all about," Jerry said out loud, pointing toward the long line of motionless vehicles in front of him.

"Looks like there's an accident," Donna, one of the passengers in the backseat, speculated. She strained her neck for a better look, while Tobias studied the reaction of the women. Donna wore a sporty dress that accentuated her dark hair. She scanned the horizon as intently as a scientist. Unfamiliar with the terrain, he squinted in the setting sun to follow Donna's focus.

Jerry brought the hot rod closer and closer to the scene. As they passed the upside-down VW bug, they spied a young man wandering behind the car. Dazed, he waved the onlookers on while searching for the noisy emergency vehicles that heralded their impending arrival with shrieking sirens.

"I think it is Fred," Donna said. "Is he with someone?"

Carrie, the other woman in the backseat, answered her, "I can't tell. Who has he been dating lately?"

Tobias turned around and studied the curly headed blonde. In contrast to her friend, she was dressed in a flowery, flowing dress. Both women were of equal stature, possessing average height and build. Carrie's manner seemed less deliberate than Donna's, though more comprehensive. She appeared to account for the universe in all her perceptions, as if she had a pipeline to God.

For a brief moment, Jerry and the two women silently deliberated whether to stop or continue with their Valentine Day's plans. The dark outline of a human form remained still in the shadows of the VW's interior. Confidently standing his ground, Fred appeared only slightly concerned--- and perhaps inebriated. He looked almost defensive, as if he didn't want to be bothered. Nobody said a further word. Tobias noticed Jerry make a decision with a firm shake of his head, before steering the hot rod through the notorious turn. In this manner, Jerry avoided any involvement with Fred.

As the car sped down through the lane, the brilliance of the setting sun chased away any problems that were not theirs. Unlike Jerry, his passengers felt shivers run up their spines. They approached the evening with trepidation. Darkness would soon be all around them. Leaving the parked vehicle in the narrow lot between tall buildings, Tobias stepped toward the women and escorted them to door of the establishment.

"Happy VD!" one of Jerry's premed friends announced as he met them at the entrance to the nightclub.

Knowing *VD* was an acronym for Valentine's Day among the cynical, everyone backed away from the tall, skinny, pale student. He ignored their response and whisked a dance partner away to the floor. Tobias watched the man lightly place his long arms on her shoulders. Familiar with his sense of humor and emotional distancing, she accepted him with a grimace, as if they were meant for each other.

Jerry and Tobias danced with various partners throughout the night. Serious on maintaining their swing-dance form, only a few members of the group drank alcohol. Most preferred water or ice tea. All had dressed semiformally, being unaware of the contest for sexiest costume. But it probably would not have made a difference for this crowd. When the hawker interrupted the music for the parade of costumes, Tobias sat down with the rest and watched. It was a woman wearing a long-sleeved men's shirt that won. Those dressed in skimpy, tight lingerie didn't cut it.

Sitting back in his chair, Tobias turned his head and chanced upon an inebriated Iranian man urinating in a corner just a few tables away. The men's restroom was down the hall only twenty feet away. Lowering his head and shielding his face with the hand closest to the foreigners, Tobias snuck a second glance at the men in the corner. He clenched his other hand in a fist as he tried to determine whether they were making an international statement.

These fellows are really hard up. Civility is only a few steps away, and this man can't find the door. He's a Valentine's Day fool. This isn't the desert. He has totally missed the boat on women. It's too late now to change, mister. Your move is not cool---it never even saw the bar. What a state you are in!

Wishing to avoid disturbing the others seated around him, Tobias pretended that he hadn't seen anything unusual and watched the parade of contrasts in the darkness. After resting a moment, he returned to the dance floor when the excitement ended. The drunks didn't last long, and the group soon found themselves alone in the club. At closing time, everyone gathered outside underneath the dulled neon lights to decide on carpool arrangements. Something about dancing the night away had refreshed them, though drops of perspiration beaded on the foreheads of most.

Jerry and Tobias dropped Donna at her apartment off-campus and then accompanied the rest of the group to dorms. As they traded the dim illuminations of the city for the fluorescent lights of the women's dormitory, they were shocked to find the inhabitants in acute grief. Having seen it all before, Tobias took a step back into the shadows. Those who had made other choices for that evening walked away. The scene had already been playing for several hours. Rather than remain in the dorm, the dance party dispersed and journeyed back into the night to maintain their distance from the inevitable posthumous canonization. From the words spoken and the silent actions of the group, Tobias could tell that the dead had not been popular with everyone on campus. There were a few that would have argued with her choices, no matter how lively she appeared to others.

It's quite a Valentine's Day, Tobias thought. Amazed by the mosaic of emotion surrounding him, he acknowledged the intensity of the evening. Chalking it up for another one of life's experiences, he gratefully headed back with Jerry to his place off-campus.

The next day, Tobias and Jerry met several others for breakfast at the main dining hall. As they walked across campus to the cafeteria, they found scores of tear-streaked faces lining the corridors. One striking couple caught

Tobias's attention. Unlike the others, they were out in the open, away from the "madding crowd," occupying some benches outside a classroom. Moving fluidly, they never sat or stood for more than a minute. They appeared the most genuine, and their sincerity pulled them together in a dance that flowed from the soul of one to the other. One partner would reached for the other momentarily, touch, and then flit away, only to rejoin in a soft embrace that dissolved in another flight. The openness of their encounter chased away any fear of pain and sorrow. The free-flowing anguish on their faces radiated the most enlightened expression of love that Tobias had ever seen. Light of the early dawn reflected in their tears like crystals illuminating another path.

Carrie observed Tobias's gaze and offered, "They were very close to the young woman who died. Spent a lot of time traveling together. They knew her well."

Tobias looked at the ground, and he shook his head as if to set free some deadening memory. The bonds he shared with youthful friends in high school had been equally intense, though they'd lacked the mature sexual nature of the interlocking couple driven together in grief. Somewhere along the way, he had burned out regarding family matters. His heart had gone numb to the point where nobody could touch it. Carrie stared at him as he reeled in pain for a moment and then composed himself. Pulling himself upright, Tobias stuffed whatever he could inside himself, as if he were an animated straw man. Without a word, he followed her to the dining hall.

At breakfast, the conversation steered to another matter.

"We are going to visit Lisa in the hospital," one of the more-distant dancers from the previous declared, tossing her hand in the air to discourage questions.

"Who is Lisa?" Tobias asked Carrie in a whisper.

"She has cystic fibrosis, and an episode two weeks ago landed her in the hospital."

After they'd finished their meal, Tobias walked with Jerry back to the car.

"Do you know Lisa?" Tobias quizzed him.

"Most on campus know her. She has an oxygen tent in her dorm room," Jerry answered. "She is premed and studies a lot, so not many see her. She doesn't have too many more years left. It is incredible that she has survived this long."

"Isn't it odd to be spending the last days of your life studying?" Tobias questioned. "I mean, others would be going on permanent spring break or something."

Jerry stared absently at Tobias. Everyone had taken Lisa's existence for granted, never questioning the dynamics. He chose to do the same. "Carrie gives Lisa her calculus notes when Lisa is in study mode. Anna brings her notes also. Anna told me that Lisa had made it to a bonfire a few weeks ago."

"Bonfire?" Tobias questioned.

"Yes, Carrie started roping the inhabitants of her women's dorm for a monthly fire circle. They sing and play guitars. Roast marshmallows and drink watermelon-rind wine."

"Sounds rowdy," Tobias commented.

"No, nobody comes home intoxicated. These are study nerds," Jerry observed. "People find it amusing that these lightweights are breaking the female mold on campus. A few consider it refreshing. It is no easy assignment to get Lisa to leave the dorm for social bonding."

Chapter Five

Every now and then

You wake up

And find that you

Are still alive

And wonder how you managed it

Tune Reference: *Oh Sherrie*

----Steve Perry

LATER IN THE day, Tobias enjoyed lunch with the soft-mannered girl next door from his neighborhood. His mother was busy with a new boyfriend, and his sisters had other activities. Clara, his childhood friend, drove to Jerry's apartment and brought a picnic lunch. Distancing themselves from the campus nearby, they climbed to the top of a hill overlooking the oak woods and scrub brush.

"I ran into Hank's wife the other day," Clara began. "She asked about you. She has fond memories of you and your radio. Remember, the one you brought to life in Hank's garage?"

Tobias grinned as he recalled the memory of a racing dog and loud music on a warm spring night. It contrasted sharply with the latest tragedies on particular campus. However, Clara was about to alter his world forever.

"I had heard about it from a friend, who works with the police. Remember Brad? He joined the Fort Worth force. Hank's wife confirmed the rumor. Dawn Miller was gang-raped and escaped death by driving away. They stalked her at her university apartment.”

Stunned, Tobias leaned back on ground and covered his eyes.

“The Fort Worth paper ran an article on how local teen queens were getting gang-raped. They were blaming it on all the Yankees moving in the area and not respecting the slow-moving culture of the South,” Clara continued.

“It’s the end of beauty,” Tobias commented, opening his eyes to study the billowing clouds in the sky. “They are destroying it.”

“That is not the only thing that has been happening,” Clara noted. “The entire region seems to be getting more violent, as if the entire infrastructure is being attacked to bring in something impersonal and out of control.”

“It’s all about relationships,” Tobias added. Slowly, he rose back from the ground and resumed sitting straight up. He surveyed the calm, stately trees that seemed to beckon him to another existence. “Let’s go for a walk,” he suggested.

They packed away the picnic goods in a cloth bag and headed for the steep edge of the deep ravine, which was lined by a thicket of live oaks. Juggling the bag with one arm, Tobias steadied himself on the incline before peering curiously into the limestone crevasses below. Clara skidded on the soft gravelly surface behind him. The necessity to keep their footing cleared their minds and heightened their focus.

“How’s your mom?” Clara inquired, bracing herself with a sudden stop on the lip of a small boulder.

“She’s dating someone,” Tobias answered.

“Have you seen her?” Clara asked.

"Nope," he replied, scuffing some white, chalky stones beneath his feet. He studied the white imprints on his shoes. "Best I stay away," he said.

Clara shrugged and waved her arms at him. Sensing her disbelief, Tobias decided to provide a deeper explanation. He tossed his head side to side and did his best to assist her understanding. He appreciated her feedback as a double check on his feelings on the matter.

"Before leaving for college, I took out a life insurance policy, one that she would be able to collect on. She watched me as I talked to the salesman in the living room. Seeing so much life going away last year, I thought I might be going too. Mom seemed almost too agreeable about it. I had this eerie sense about it. Things changed once I left Dodge City, so to speak. Up in the Pacific Northwest, I regained my perspective. So I dropped the insurance. If it is money or a man that she needs, she'll have to get it some other way, instead of having it come out of my hide. I realized that she was never satisfied and that I would never be able to please her."

Clara hung her head, studying the dirt around her feet. She murmured, "So that was it."

"Yep," Tobias agreed. "I can't go back." He looked up at the sky. By the distance that the clouds had traversed since the beginning of their outing, he could tell that much time had passed. "It's getting late," he decided. "We should go."

Clara gratefully nodded at his sense of perfect timing. A load had been lifted from her shoulders, and she sprung up the hill like a deer. Tobias smiled as he watched her climb in front of him. He felt lighter too, now that she understood his position. He walked her back to the car, placing her picnic bag carefully in the back so that it wouldn't fall over.

Standing by the car, Clara waited for Tobias to finish. She caught him in her arms when he turned to face her. Taking aback, Tobias wryly grinned at her before gathering her in a full embrace.

"Don't come back here no more, Tobias," she told him gently, with almost-tearful kiss on his cheek. Then Clara stepped away from him. Placing her hands on her hips, she distanced herself as he regained his composure. Clara watched him as he considered her words. Tobias looked down at the ground briefly before casting her a sideways glance. He noticed that she had spoken in a double negative. In the land where they used drawls for emphasis, double negatives hinted at affirmatives. Clara didn't want him to leave her. She loved him enough to have his best interests at heart. Noticing the determined look in his eyes, Clara knew that he had heard her. She abruptly wheeled on her heel and dove into the vehicle.

Tobias watched her drive off, leaving a trail of powdery dust in the air. Then he slowly walked back to Jerry's apartment, where he found a group of medical students rapping around a large bowl of popcorn in the living room. For a few moments, Tobias stood near the front door and tracked the popcorn being tossed in the air, bouncing off open mouths, and occasionally hitting the floor and furniture. Several of the young men had been in his EMT course, where they had trained to become ambulance attendants.

He could remember some of the wise advice from the seasoned instructors. They had won the confidence of the premedical students with their tales. Someone had asked: "What do you do if you see an incident that you are unable to handle without throwing up?"

The answer had been, "Throw up in the bushes, and then get to it. It happens to everyone. We can't control some things that we see or our responses all the time. Some things are gong to move you. You'll get over it."

"I lived in Mexico until I was five," a light-red-haired man told his Hispanic roommate, Eugenio. "My parents had to smuggle me out of the country."

Eugenio smiled. "Why?"

"I was a *rubio*."

Jerry, Eugenio, and Tobias laughed. "A *rubio*? A blond."

"Yes, blond-haired children were often stolen for human trafficking in Mexico," he replied.

Tobias left the room to catch his breath. Clutching his stomach lightly, he refrained from regurgitating after the discourse of the past two days. He returned just as Eugenio was leaving for the library. Eugenio had softened during the discussion around the flying balls of popcorn and iced tea.

"I'll walk with you," Tobias offered. "There's a book I want to check out there."

Eugenio nodded quietly, keeping his head slightly bowed; he was in a reflective mood. Tobias seized the moment to get to the heart of the matter. He bounced on his toes as if preparing for a race and pressed his former classmate from the EMT course for more information.

"Did you get a chance to use any of the stuff that you learned in that class?" he asked Eugenio.

The dark-haired man paused before giving his answer. "Did you?"

"No, I was surprised. My semester has been relatively quiet."

"Not much," Eugenio agreed warmly. Then he resumed in broken English. "Though I went to a racetrack in Mexico. One of the cars ran into the bleachers. A woman next to me was struck. She had vomited. I scraped it out of her mouth and began CPR. I tried to open the airway, but she had a broken neck. She was already dead. I went to another woman who had been hit. She survived."

"Great job." Tobias nodded with a light, encouraging smile. "*Bueno. The training paid off.*"

Eugenio tossed his head and grinned in satisfaction. Reaching the library, Tobias happily waved him off. Eugenio brightened and headed for the other end of the building.

"Bye."

"*Adios, amigo.*"

Chapter Six

Souls don't change

They either evolve

Or fragment and die

Tune Reference: *It's Time*

----Imagine Dragons

TOBIAS WANDERED OVER to the section of the library that provided computers for student use. There were several faces from the EMT course gathered around the screens and even a few from the dance group. He stopped dead in his tracks while still several paces away from the crowd. Something about their manner bothered him, and he hurried out of the library.

"Hey, Tobias!" Carrie greeted him from across the outdoor mall.

Tobias waved in return. "You look like you are going swimming."

"Lifeguard duty." Observing Tobias's harried countenance, she asked him, "Did you check out the new computers in the library? My boyfriend told me that they have a special application for learning how to prescribe drugs. It is very popular. No one else can get on."

"I saw 'em. They turned it into a sadomasochistic ritual. The one who can kill off their patient in the quickest amount of time wins."

"Well, I suppose it beats drinking oneself to death," Carrie quipped. Then she added, "Yeah, my boyfriend told me about the program. He's turning into a computer-science major. He said that the program somehow factors the side effects of the drugs and alerts the doctor if the patient gets too much edema or something."

They watched a young man emerge from the library. He yelled a greeting at Tobias and Carrie. Both waved back as he walked away, having picked up the nonverbal cue not to stop and chat with them.

"He's has been catcalling at one of the woman in the dorm lately," Carrie muttered to Tobias, who also seemed relieved that the man had passed them by. "He gets drunk and yells at her window late at night. My friend, who is her roommate, tells me that she has been finding vomit in the popcorn bowl as a result. Apparently, the stress of the caller has brought on a latent case of bulimia. Her father, who happens to be a doctor, caught on. Even though she is an education major and has a top scholarship, her father is having her transferred to a university closer to her home in Austin."

"I know who you are talking about," Tobias mentioned. "The roommate was in my EMT course. She works part-time as a phlebotomist. They call them vampires because they work the night shift."

"Yeah, she wants to get in some practice," Carrie added. "Last summer she worked at the morgue and dissected an ovarian tumor. She said that they found teeth and all kinds of things in it. It was a real marvel, apparently."

"Well, that's cancer for ya. The cells lose their identity," Tobias said and he grimaced. Another thought had crossed his mind, and he changed the subject slightly. He sensed that he could confide in Carrie. "That fellow and his partners banged on the CPR mannequins so hard that the head fell off the infant. They tried to be comical about it, but something about the sight of an innocent face rolling down the stairs to the next floor convinced me that I was done practicing with that group."

"Yeah, I can't believe Donna dated one of his buddies for a month or two. She gave it up when he wrote her a letter about climbing Mount Olympus and calling it a triumph," Carrie remembered. "Then again, Donna also dated the chief engineer for the library building and swimming pool. After she learned about the heating system, it didn't last long. I think she was bored. They use the hot water from the library's condensers to heat the pool."

"Interesting," Tobias thoughtfully considered. "What bothered Donna about her date's triumph?"

"Hmm," Carrie began. "She said that mountains were not things to be conquered. She's a geologist, you know."

"Oh," Tobias reflected. "It's the mentality."

"She was impressed by the way he had taken his old truck piece by piece, sprayed all the parts green, put it back together, and had it running."

"That might explain it," Tobias pondered out loud. Noticing the bundle of books in her arms, Tobias asked, "What are you studying now?"

"I'm hammering out the next paper for theology," she answered. "The class is required, and the only one that fits my schedule is given by a Protestant minister."

"Odd for a Catholic university," Tobias remarked.

"Nobody comes after him here," Carrie noted. "I can tell that he doesn't like the way I think. He called me a scholar and gave me a B on last paper. He gets off on C.S. Lewis."

"What was it on?" Tobias questioned her.

"He required us to write a paper on Revelations," she related. "I think all the other classes have the same requirements from their professors. I wrote that Armageddon had already come and gone."

"Interesting concept." Tobias nodded as if savoring the notion that oblivion could be sidestepped.

"It was like the English prof who gave me a B for the required paper on Achilles and honor," Carrie elaborated. "I could tell that I wasn't his favorite student. I had a difficult time understanding why men should fight over women. *Honor* is a relative term."

"The native Alaskans share their wives," Tobias piped.

"I wonder how that one got started," Carrie chimed. "The first wife, the first igloo guest."

"Maybe it had something to do with the climate?" Tobias wondered out loud. "What if a blizzard had fallen in Troy, instead of the Trojan horse? And everyone had to stay warm?"

"It ruined any thought of a career as an English major," Carrie said, changing the subject. "I'm too pragmatic."

"That and maybe something else," Tobias ventured. "English majors don't have careers; they just study. I understand that FDR had one of the university presidents write national history. He served on history commissions as well as intelligence operations."

Carrie paused for a moment to reflect on the chaos that could ensue if one were to change history. She rambled on, "There were two women in my dorm room last week who just started crying. On top of their worry over the drunken catcallers, they had heard that sexual offenders were being released at the apartments across the streets. A man was seen in the women's restrooms only days later. He left through a window near the showers. One of these women had transferred to this university after being raped on the campus of a university near College Station. Her parents thought this was a safe place here. The other one cried because she felt that she was missing something by living off-campus. She's a great soccer player and plays on our intramural team. She had experienced just enough camaraderie to feel lonely. I let her know that she wasn't missing that much, and she felt much better. She just had to get it out of her system. Rumor has it that the survivors of campus violence get recruited for intelligence operations, where psychological intactness is not a prerequisite. The rest of the campus transfer, flunk out, or fry out. We had two bomb threats last semester, and last week streakers tossed several exploding devices in front of the doors in the women's dorm. Nobody was impressed, but all were too callous to demand greater security. Everyone blames the bomb threats on the Iranians; it's as if we are being programmed for an upcoming war. People reason that the guys leaving exploding devices in the halls are just people who study too much to have a social life. They say that it is due to pent-up frustration. The women in the dorm feel frustrated that nothing is ever done. Parents and school administration don't take this stuff seriously, and they expect us to laugh it off. During bomb drills, they send all students outdoors. However, there is something about the reality of standing out in freezing rain during finals week that really drives it home, or at least stirs the anger for the next war, or for insensitive naked males and their professors."

"Jerry told me something to that effect," Tobias interjected, stopping her tirade for a moment. "Students have started to wonder. He said that in some courses it seems safer to settle for a C---then they don't think you are worth their trouble."

Carrie smirked and backed away. Distancing herself from Tobias, she said, "Yes, a B means that they are stringing you along, whereas an A means that you might have a chance of escape---but it usually involves you spending your time learning the prof's personal habits and doing a background check as well as a psychological evaluation. If you ask me, it is getting too close for comfort. It is a lot of work to stay two steps ahead of them. Multiply the effort by the number of required classes, and there goes your play time." Carrie paused before redirecting the conversation, "So, when is your spring break over?"

"I go back tomorrow morning," he replied. Approaching her, he countered, "Tell me about your trip. Jerry said that you had your break two weeks ago. A group went to Fredericksburg on a road trip."

"Yes, we went to Luckenbach, a small town on the highway, consisting of two bars and a few houses."

"Like the song?" Tobias said with a laugh.

"We wandered all over the place. First we spent the night at Suzy's house in San Antonio. Then we went to a Philippine restaurant near Hemisphere Tower. Afterward, we visited my grandmother in San Antonio, before taking the highway to Fredericksburg. In Fredericksburg, we stayed with one of Donna's apartment mates. Her father was a pilot for LBJ, and her mother designed their home. Carlos, a senior premed from the Philippines, ran behind the car for track practice, while the eight track played 'Cars.' He is on the track team with my boyfriend. By the time we hit Luckenbach, it was dark on the highway. So we stopped at the VFW and did Swan Lake ballet to 'Blue Eyes Crying In the Rain.' I was surprised at how well it worked together. Meanwhile, Carlos had a beer and kept putting quarters in the jukebox."

Tobias sighed. "Did you see the bluebonnets?"

"And the Indian paintbrushes too. They dotted the fields everywhere." Carrie glanced around and said decidedly, "I'm off to the pool. I don't want to be late for my shift. Nice seeing you, Tobias."

Chapter Seven

Bravery is about

Moving forward

Without knowing why

And why not

Tune Reference: *Brave*

----Josh Groban

"HEY, WAIT," TOBIAS pleaded before Carrie could go. "You've aroused my curiosity. We've touched on a lot of issues in a brief amount of time. I want to finish our discussion. I'll walk with you to the pool."

Carrie stopped and beckoned Tobias to follow her via cement stairs down the hill. She glanced at the Hungarian abbey nestled in the woods almost a quarter mile away. The bombers only bothered the dormitories, never the seminary, convent, or abbey. Then her focused returned to the man next to her. She stated, "You were listening, Tobias." Sensing his thoughts, she mused, "The lifeguards see all."

Tobias laughed quietly. "Tell me what you see."

Carrie nodded in the direction of a family of four making their way to the pool at the bottom of the hill. "See that gentleman over there? He is now vice president of the university. Unlike the other profs, he gives an A to those who can write and don't fall asleep in history class. He says that usually the seniors do the best, because they have learned how to write essays by the time they graduate."

She continued in a succinct manner, as if briefing an astronaut through the stars: "Those who write the history texts would like to have the readers believe that it is all a done deal, but I managed to find some intriguing notions to propose in his class. He caught on. After they promoted him, he solicited my views on a philosophy professor that several faculty and students had reported for various violations. Apparently, the college was in the process of dismissing him---apparently the aggressive fascist from Austria was intent on disturbing democracy, having forgotten that he was in the wrong country. I told the dean that I'd never understood what he'd said; his philosophies had seemed so convoluted. I'd made the grade because I'd learned on my own. Those who had been to East Coast prep schools seemed to understand his implications, whereas the rest of us had difficulty filtering out his fervor for points that didn't make much sense. My classmate, Jerry, occasionally babysat his six to seven children and was convinced that the man was trying to grow his own empire. Jerry sat in a desk behind me and mumbled his complaints under his breath. It became annoying. Just about everything the man said irritated him. Being new to European philosophy, I learned enough about his personal life to be skeptical. As a lifeguard, I had fished his seventh child out of the water several times. He made 'em, but he didn't keep track of them, which created a conflict. He wasn't that comfortable with my efforts to keep his child alive, and so I downplayed all the rescues. You can't miss the sight of a bobbing toddler that resembles a tiny Greek god with cherub cheeks and curly blond hair. Lifeguarding is not just another philosophy---it's my job. In contrast, the vice president took care of his progeny in a gentle, caring manner when he swam here."

"Hmm," Tobias murmured. "Jerry said that one of the former presidents had left to start his own mind-control institute in Dallas. I think he left in '62."

"Yes, that was just prior to the year that the former prime minister of Hungary was seen waving an umbrella at the president seconds before the first gunshot. The sun was out. C.S. Lewis and Aldous Huxley died the same day, but only the occultists make the connection. I think some of the professors were investigated for the obituary the Dallas newspapers printed before his murder. There is the impression that there are different warring factions within the university," Carrie rejoined. "I try to stay out of politics myself. Now I would like to stay out of religion, because it has started to reach occult proportions. The Vatican II pope died five months prior to the assassination. The religious say that it was the Cup of Borgia. A year after the US president's assassination, the KGB exiled the Soviet prime minister."

"Communist Hungary was a decoy for ousting those threatening their control of the Silk Road markets," Tobias told her when they stopped at the entrance to the pool area. "The creator of the Transylvania Land Company worked for the Holy Roman Empire in Hungary. He ran with a reptilian-dragon cult that traced its origins to ancient Egypt. Later, they sponsored Captain John Smith to survey America for their real estate companies."

Carrie nodded in the direction of the Hungarian abbey. "That explains it. The magi of the Silk Road created the illusions. The theology prof told us that the bible says to beware of the Persians."

"It's called dressing for appearances," he said. Wishing to avoid being noticed, under the circumstances, he waved her off. Shaking his head at the scene around them, he offered, "The religious clergy running the place allow the Persians to threaten the dorms with bombs. These descendants of Abel have a penchant for self-destruction. No god supports a suck-up willing to offer anything violently dripped in blood."

Carrie backed away and peered inside the pool area. "There is no such thing as a sacrificial lamb in this country. A few presidents have tried to get the country back since the days following the American Revolution." Dropping the subject abruptly, she stated, "Time for a swim."

Tobias left and began climbing back up the hill. The next morning he took a shuttle to Dallas/Fort Worth airport, while Jerry attended class. The morning light blinded him through the various sizes and shapes of windows that lined his journey back to the Pacific Northwest. He couldn't get away from the sunshine; it broke through every nook and cranny like dandelions in the cracks of a city sidewalk. Despite all this, he felt much better once he glimpsed the first Douglas fir rising from the streets of Portland during the plane's descent.

After the plane landed, Tobias grabbed his bags and took the light-rail train to Portland's largest bookstore downtown. He wanted to get lost in the various stacks of books and papers lining the walls of the huge building, which was divided into sections according to color codes. First he checked out the science area for texts, and then he wandered to the history region, a few winding corridors past the bestsellers. There, out of the corner of his eye, he spied a chum from school half-kneeling before a row of political science books.

"Whatcha finding?" Tobias greeted Donny, who remained fixated on the titles in front of him.

Donny blinked several times. Then he triumphantly yanked a book from the shelf and waved it in front of Tobias, who ignored the title on the book in favor of making eye contact with Donny. Tobias did not share his excitement concerning the book. As a result, Donny quickly tucked it underneath his arm and rose to his feet. He faced Tobias squarely, pausing a few seconds before breaking into a warm grin.

"How was your trip?" he asked.

"Intense," Tobias replied. "It's great to be back. Though it is time to get rid of the accent and my meandering ways." Studying Donny's demeanor carefully, Tobias offered, "Do you have time for lunch? The cafeteria here has some great organic food."

"Yes, it's one of my favorite places too," Donny said. "Let's go. Great timing. You can tell me about your trip."

"Yeah, maybe we could go to the rose garden afterward," Tobias answered. "I think the light rail goes that far."

"Let's go," Donny replied. "I haven't been to the rose garden since I was a child."

They parked their bags at a table and stood in line. After selecting a sandwich-soup combination, they brought their loaded trays to a small table near the huge street windows. Tobias eagerly unloaded his tray, piling the assortment in front of him like stacks of cards. Donny watched him as he slowly sipped his latte. He failed to unload his tray.

Instead he commented, "No coffee, Tobias?"

"No, I never developed the taste," Tobias answered. "I like my steaming herbal teas."

Changing the subject as he got around to clearing his tray, Donny started, "So how's your mom?"

"Didn't see her," Tobias replied unemotionally.

"How did you manage to go back home for a week without checking in on the folks?"

"Well," Tobias began as he reclined back in his chair, stroking his tousled hair away from his face, "it's complicated. She's dating someone who has a son playing the street gangs. It is a scene that I prefer to avoid. Not that I don't like the guy. He's amazing, but lost. I prefer to avoid trouble, especially with black operations."

Donny laughed out loud. "How did you find out?"

Tobias gave a half grin. Taking a quick breath, he explained, "We went on a hike together while our parents were fussing over camping arrangements last summer. This guy starred in his high-school production of *West Side Story* by day and was courted by the mercenaries at night."

"What?" Donny quizzed, dropping his cup on the table and moving his head closer to Tobias in order to hear better.

"They climbed in through his bedroom window and offered him weaponry. If he does well on the streets, then he gets to go on trips with the big boys. He's obviously looking for a father figure and male bonding. This guy is a romantic deer hunter. There is not a malicious bone in his body. He doesn't really fit in with any of the Fort Worth street gangs, but they look up to him. He carries himself well, with a sort of detached air. It's just the kind of disengagement that the relationship-challenged prefer. No strings; no grudges; no emotional baggage---just dissociated disillusionment."

Donny uncomfortably settled back in his chair. "I can see why you would want to disassociate yourself from 'the family.'"

Tobias reached for a sandwich half. Pausing for a few seconds before taking a bite, he added nonchalantly, "You have to understand my mom."

Donny looked down at his soup, chose the correct spoon, and finally started eating. He wanted to keep up with Tobias, who had put down his sandwich for a moment to thoughtfully savor his tea. Tobias stared out the window for a moment as Donny bowed his head over his plate and dedicated himself to finishing his meal.

"I'm looking forward to seeing the rose garden," Tobias reflected. Then he resumed the thread of conversation. "My biology-major friend speculated that the 'mercenary in training' had an extra Y chromosome."

Looking around the room, Tobias nodded a greeting to someone across the tables. The sight of some familiar faces gave Tobias a chance to change the subject. "Hey, look---there's Rhonda and Gail from school. They drug Ed, the guy down the hall, along with them."

Donny turned around and has face brightened at the sight of familiar faces from campus. When he turned back, he saw that Tobias had been watching for his reaction.

"You need a break from academia," Tobias counseled him. Not wasting time in re-establishing college acquaintances, Tobias waved at the trio at the counter. "Want to check out the rose garden?"

Donny quieted, bowing his head over his soup bowl. He murmured uneasily, "The rose garden."

"I wanna go to the rose garden," Rhonda echoed as she put her tray down next to Tobias. She lightheartedly bounced in her chair and nodded at Gail.

"Oh, the rose garden," Gail repeated with excitement. "I haven't been there since I was kid."

Before leaning contentedly back in his chair to watch Ed join them at the table, Tobias nonverbally shot Donny a triumphant affirmation. Then he said, "You're on."

Chapter Eight

Some people believe only what they see

And sometimes they actually see what they believe

They are called fools

The wise use reason to determine whether

Their perceptions make sense

Tune Reference: *What A Fool Believes*

----The Doobie Brothers

WHEN THE GROUP reached the top of the city rose garden, they spread out in different directions over the grounds. Sometimes racing, sometimes pausing to whiff the aromas, they weaved in and out of each other's comings and goings like ships specifically intending to pass in the night. Browsing between rows and circular arrangements of flowers, they eventually met at a clearing, where they rested on the bright-green grass. The view overlooking the city and horizon of ice-capped mountains in the distant east was spectacular. Everyone appeared flushed from their rapid excursion, which was very different from their time under the fluorescent lights of the huge bookstore.

"So, what did you do over spring break?" Tobias asked Rhonda as she dropped down beside him.

"I went Nordic skiing," she replied. "I taught a few classes to youngsters and people with Down Syndrome. Do you ski?"

"No, I picked up some Nordic ski equipment last fall from a place that was clearing its rental gear for the season. The bamboo poles really appealed to me. They seem so grounded, so earthy," Tobias mentioned. "I would like to know how to ski."

"Well, there," Rhonda began. "Come up next weekend, and we'll turn you into an instructor---after we teach you how to ski, of course."

"Is it any different from roping cattle?" he joked, putting his hands behind his head before reflecting on the clouds in the sky. "Not that I know how. It is just that everything revolves around steer control and goat roping where I come from. People practice roping their mailboxes on my street." He relaxed in the sunshine before adding, "I always found better things to do, like swim and play football. It was hard enough keeping my younger sisters corralled, not that I really wanted that job. It just sorta came to me."

"Yes, you are in for a cultural lifestyle change, Tobias," she responded. "Ever see more than three inches of snow?"

"I think that we had some snow in Portland this past winter," he replied. "It came down from the mountaintops so that I wouldn't miss stepping on it. Sorta like cow patties, only it is white, and you can't avoid it at certain latitudes and elevations. Yes, I have met that funny, white stuff."

"What do you mean?" Donny questioned. "Tobias danced with the snowflakes all over campus."

"I couldn't decide which snowflake to ask first. There were so many. Can't get by with only one. Cute little things," he said to defend himself. "I couldn't help myself. They all obliged and danced with me all at once."

People quieted after hearing Tobias's remarks. He sat upright, as if searching the area for a different topic. A book fell from Donny's pack, catching his attention. Deftly Tobias changed the subject from himself and cultural challenges. "I see that they have you reading Machiavelli's *The Prince* in your political science classes," Tobias said.

Donny laughed. "They say that it is the bible for corporate America."

"Reminds me of that Thai restaurant we went to last quarter," Tobias reflected. "The one that discusses the opium wars in its menu. I enjoy studying there and conversing with the waiter at the bar." Tobias lay back down on the ground after he had successfully maneuvered the conversation in an uncharted direction. He added, "They are very aware of the world currents that we must swim, which can be viewed as a typhoon. I like the kindred spirits there---great ambiance for writing research papers."

"Tobias, you don't miss a beat," Gail remarked. She had been quietly tracking the thread of their discussion.

"I'm a musician," Tobias mentioned. "I notice rhythms, especially when compelled to follow the beat of my own drummer."

"Isn't that a paraphrase of a Thoreau quote?" Donny quizzed.

"In Thoreau's better day," Tobias noted. "Though I admire him for his ecological standpoint, he collaborated with those intent on destroying American intelligence."

"How's that?" Donny questioned.

"He ran with Emerson, who said that it was impossible to ever know anything. It's a fine thing to say as long as you don't promote intellectual elitism," Tobias stated, rising from his reclined position on the hillside. "The group had political aspirations. Think about it. Emerson lived down the street from the father of Louisa May Alcott, who was hiding runaway slaves right under Mr. Emerson's nose. Mr. Alcott had to hide them, even in a northern state. Think about it. This tells you where Emerson stood on the topic, or at least his allies. The same ones who sponsored Huxley's drug-induced foray into *Brave New World*. All this ideation rose during the opium wars, which came off the heels of the French Revolution and War of 1812 and ended just in time for the American Civil War. US revolutionaries dumped opium, as well as tea, during the Boston Tea Party. Where China would be today if they had done the same, before the East India Company caught on?"

"I remember the restaurant," Donny piped, interrupting Tobias to slow him down. Taking more time to savor the conversation, he probed the depth of thoughts collecting in his mind. He reflected softly as if coming out of a daze, "We had lunch there after seeing the *Sons of Heaven* exhibit at the museum."

"That's a really nice museum," Gail remarked, picking up speed in the dialogue.

"Yeah, I liked it too," Tobias agreed, continuing to race his words ahead of the others. "Its airy, simplistic design lends itself to clarity in the minds of the viewers."

"Yes, they did a good job with it," Donny affirmed, attempting to slow the pace long enough to process the information.

"*Sons of Heaven*? Sorta reminds me of a local radio reporter and his claims of the alien intelligence surveying our local mountains," Ed interjected, outdoing the rest in timing and the introduction of novel topics.

Everyone looked at Ed, who had been silent for most of the conversation. Then they stared at the mountains in the distance. Ed won. A few sighed in relief that there were no immediate signs of aliens or extraterrestrials in the skies.

"He's not the only one," Donny quipped as he attempted to steal the show. "One of the shadowy intelligence suspects working with the Hungarian vampires in Dealey Plaza says the same thing."

"I heard about that," Rhonda rejoined. She looked around at her friends. "He went from Dealey Plaza to Mount Rainer. We don't want him here."

"Do you think there are connections to outer space in those mountains?" Tobias asked, getting out of the race for control of the discourse.

"And inner space," Ed quibbled. He picked over a clover in a patch of grass. After a mild shrug, he said, "Everyone in the Pacific Northwest has an alien story. I recall being at a concert at the Columbia Gorge, while watching three sky ships soar over us. It is part of the scenery. Nobody makes a big deal about it."

"Speaking of internal flights, the instructor for my Chinese history course talked about the leaders of a particular Chinese revolution," Donny started. Being highly competitive by nature, he turned the topic to his course of study. Making the most of the situation, he paraded an inquiry in front of the intelligent minds around him. He lectured, "This spiritually evolved group was caught between the opium-driven evangelism and the railroads."

"Industry needed their supply lines modernized," Ed said facetiously. Then he pointed something out to Tobias. Raising a figure in the air to outline a distinct change in flight pattern, he said, "See those chemtrails in the sky that are abruptly truncated? These are the marks of interstellar travel."

"Religion is the opiate of the people," Tobias commented, ignoring Ed's direct reference. "As the song says, 'What a fool sees, he believes.' It is like the occult prophesies predicting the deaths of US presidents, which amount to fill-in-the-blanks. I learned in physics that the retina of eye will even fill in color. The rods and cones take in something from the opposite side of the color wheel. I don't doubt you, Ed. The pattern in the sky is highly irregular; such crisscrossing in the sky would wreck typical plane traffic. Obviously, Machiavelli was ahead of his time. He provided the only bedside handbook that Stalin needed to become trustee of Korea, courtesy of the corporate-established UN."

"Tell me more, Tobias," Donny encouraged him.

Tobias sighed as his shoulders raised then dropped them. "Machiavelli was the broker between the aliens and Borgia, who ran the oligarchy of church and state with serpentine heavy-handedness. Da Vinci was drafted initially to protect the government from infiltration by a M33 arachnid guild, which later assumed occult proportions. Meanwhile, Da Vinci and a handful of other Renaissance artists countered and created the Eagles of the American Revolution."

"The conflict became threefold," Donny remembered.

"Most are," Tobias said, retiring to his light dozing on the botanical gardens. "The Renaissance stole the bird that tore at Prometheus."

"The Chinese rebels were known for their spiritual cultivation, which presented itself as a *flight* during battle," Donny elaborated. The populace thought that they could levitate."

"Well, when all else fails, levitate," Tobias jested. "Is that why the anniversary of Stephen, the Catholic saint, is often called Boxer Day? Which came first, the boxer or the Boxer Rebellion? Who came closest to levitation---Stephen or Good King Wenceslas?"

Rhonda turned towards Tobias, and grinned wryly. She told Tobias, "Reggie levitates. He is a professional Nordic skier, who will be your instructor. He flies over the slopes, and everyone complains about having to keep up with him."

"On that note, I'm ready to go back to class," Tobias announced as he stood and shouldered his bags. "Time to grab the next shuttle to the sweet college town of Eugene, Oregon---especially now that I've shook this Texas dust from my head along with my drawl. I'm getting serious. After this, everything is just a matter of fine discussion." Then he stepped away, while managing to squeeze in edgewise a few parting words: "Mighty fine. Mighty fine."

Leaving to the chuckles of his companions, he started walking down the hill toward the light rail.

"Great! Meet me at the dorm parking lot at 6:00 a.m. next Saturday," Rhonda shouted before Tobias was out of earshot. "You can join our carpool."

"See ya," Tobias replied, hurrying to catch the next shuttle. He was ready for some time alone. He wanted to think about what had transpired over the break as well as what was about to come.

The next day, Tobias attended his afternoon organic chemistry lab. The lab assistant passed out the lab instructions. Tobias glanced at the preface at the top of the handout. It alluded to a particular company in Nazi Germany, which had been protected from Allied bombs. The business had manufactured everything from aspirin to the gas used to kill concentration-camp inhabitants. The industrial plant produced the first sulfa drugs used to treat infection during the eventual world war.

"Oh great, we get to make drugs today," Tobias announced to his lab partner, the control freak who was applying to the local medical school. He kept his voice unemotional; Tobias enjoyed keeping the searing sarcasm to himself.

However, his bright lab partner gave Tobias an ominous sideways glance full of trepidation. For the first time in their interaction, Tobias realized that his lab mate might actually own a conscience. Tobias softened a little then and resolved to keep his mouth shut for the rest of the lab.

His decision only lasted a minute. Then he said, "I reacted to a sulfa drug once."

The callous lab mate eyed Tobias and admitted, "I did too. I had difficulty breathing."

"All I got was a rash that last half a day. It got me out of classes while my parents were out of town. I really just wanted to stay home and play with my aunt, who had been a field station nurse at the time they learned how to market this drug." Then Tobias added nonchalantly, "We'll make sure to keep you under the hood."

The hood was the apparatus that hung overhead and removed noxious fumes or gases. Tobias watched his lab mate edge a little closer to the hood. Tobias nodded, nonverbally conveying the message that he would not get in the man's way if he hungered for clean air.

It proved all too easy to make the corporate-famous drug. Tobias offered to stay and wash the shared equipment so that his lab partner could leave early and breathe easier. Promising to return the favor later, his lab mate quickly exited. Tobias remained and bonded with the other students, who were thoughtfully considering the learning experience. As he waited in line to sterilize one of the glass pipettes, Tobias observed that there were two kinds of medical students. One group consisted of the ones who rushed through lab, racing to beat out the next guy, without ever stopping to think about the exercise as if it were a true experiment and not some planned lesson. Then there were the thinkers, the ones who contemplated what was being asked of them and took the time to look their classmates in the eye, at least in acknowledgement.

At the end of the week, Tobias met Rhonda at the dorm parking lot. In the darkness of the early morning, they arranged the ski gear in the car and drove up to the mountains. The sun had risen by the time they reached the summit, and the daylight flooded the scenery.

"OK, beginners come with me," Reggie said as he beckoned them. For a pro skier, he had no qualms about the quality of skier that might accompany him; he seemed to be accustomed to everyone following behind. In fact, he seemed almost humble about it at times. Apparently his wife and buddies had complained on numerous occasions. The objective was not to outdo the next guy. The mode of operation was to learn how to ski together and have fun as a group. Racing would happen soon enough. Unlike most pros, Tobias noted, Reggie knew when to leave the crowd and when to be part of the crowd, which was another art form.

Having been a competitive swimmer in high school, Tobias felt that he could understand Reggie in a way that others around him could not. Sports also assumed a form of self-expression, which portrayed the god-self, the individual striving for excellence. If the athlete turned this into a game, then Tobias recognized the effect as heaven on earth. So did Reggie, apparently. Toward the end of the season, he would often turn around and seem surprised to find Tobias right behind him.

These weekend forays into paradise provided a different outlook on Tobias's studies. Shortly before his last chemistry lab, Tobias turned in his homework assignment to the instructor who was behind all the smoke and mirrors of their chemistry experiments. Tobias subtly confronted him on the preface to the sulfa-drug lesson. "Organic chemistry is like memorizing cookbook recipes," Tobias cautiously commented as he handed the man the written assignment. Though he didn't want anyone to reduce his grade for political reasons, he always fought the compulsion to seek reasonable answers. Figuring that he could take a risk on the instructor, he asked, "When is anyone going to take the time to write up the chemical equivalent of a grand unified theory that explains why we do what we do?"

"There is no money in it," the teacher told him. "All the funding goes into the rush to make the latest and greatest innovation or product."

"That in itself is a recent development," Tobias remarked. "It is not like the alchemists at the turn of the century who questioned *why* and wanted to figure out how it all worked."

"No, there are strings on science now," the lab instructor replied. "Those who ask the questions can't afford to spend the time working on them. They get lost in the demands placed on them. Perhaps someday a group will spend the time to put it all together."

"We aren't that far from putting it all together," Tobias observed. "It might even be easier than developing some of the recipes."

"I know. It would not be that difficult," the instructor said with a nod.

Tobias shook his head and walked away. His latest assignments in class involved predicting the chirality of molecules synthesized in the lab. If you examined the spin of the molecule, no drugs were created equal. Some expressed right-handedness and others appeared left-handed. At least, only two possibilities existed, which would have made the predictive models a statical nightmare. However, the distinction proved lethal. According to the National Aeronautics Society of America (NASA), life on Mars solely depended on the left-handed version. Though NASA remained clear in their search for life, the economic objectives of the synthetics undermined existence.

Chapter Nine

In reality

It is not three strikes and you're out

It usually only takes one

To discourage further human effort

Tune Reference: *Two Out Of Three Ain't Bad*

----Meat Loaf

AFTER GRADUATION TOBIAS decided to stay in Oregon and attend the naturopathic medical college in Portland. Like a cowboy just passing through, he had purposely gathered information without necessarily forming deep ties with those around him. It matched his wandering nature; he believed in one making the most of where one was divinely steered. Naturopathy was not something he would have considered until he took a bad tumble down an icy slope while Reggie wasn't around. Instead, it was a second-year naturopathic medical student who helped him up and asked him if he wanted some homeopathic arnica.

"I fall all the time," she jested, tottering on an icy slope. "So I carry it with me."

"What is a homeopathic?" he asked, ignoring her teetering as he studied the two-dram vial in her hand.

"It is a substance that has been diluted, usually past Avogadro's number and potentized," the student stated. "You know Avogadro's number?"

"Oh yes, something like six to the twenty-third power. It is the magic number that defines the point when a substance becomes a shadow," Tobias reflected. Though his countenance assumed a more studious expression, he seemed more steady on his skis than ever. He eyed the student with one brow raised. She had been watching him play with the disabled children who were learning how to ski. He queried, "Potentized? Is that sorta like imparting kinetic energy to give a substance potential energy? I can relate to quantum physics. Here, let me try it."

After placing four little white sugar pills under his tongue, Tobias realized the effects immediately. It all came with being an athlete and feeling that constant drive to remain within one's godliness. He felt lighter, and his vision became clearer, "Gosh, I haven't felt this good since before I landed on my head when I was three. What is this?"

"Just an herb that the Roman soldiers used to carry with them when they went into battle," the naturopathic student answered.

"But if it is diluted past Avogadro's number, then all the chemistry books say that there is nothing in it."

"That's just a technical term to divide the real substances from the shadows," she repeated.

"So I just savored the ghost of arnica to get back on my feet again," he said decisively. "Or was it the shadow of arnica?"

She shrugged. "It doesn't matter, as long as you recover from shock. A homeopathic has a unique electromagnetic frequency, which can be mimicked and reproduced with machines." She smiled as she retrieved his fallen ski pole and handed it to him. Then she slid down another trail. "Good to see you back on your feet again. It is the light that defines the shadow."

"Sold," Tobias said, racing to catch up with her and hear more of her philosophy. "It beats waiting around to watch someone's blood pressure and pulses go awry. I like solutions, especially ones that seem to work."

Afterward, he went back to the college and began voraciously researching and studying homeopathy before he enlisted in the ranks of those nature doctors who did everything a little bit differently. The naturopathic student who had introduced him to this path took Tobias under her wing. They continued their lighthearted play during their studies and collaborated on further intense, scientific pursuits. Meanwhile, Reggie left for Korea to pursue ghosts from the war. Having been in Vietnam, Reggie said that he wanted to pay his respects to the boys who had been sent to the previous war.

"Why Korea?" Donny asked Tobias one day during lunch at their bookstore haunt.

"Initially, Reggie told everyone he wanted to take some time off work to teach English in Japan. He had been an engineer with the power company for almost twenty years and wanted to take some time off. Nobody, not even his wife, wanted to go with him," Tobias explained. "He's a Vietnam vet. Something about his experiences in Japan and Vietnam compelled him to seek answers in Korea."

"I think that it has to do with C. S. Lewis," Donny speculated. He nervously bounced his feet underneath the table. Gathering his things, he prepared to leave.

"Why? I never cared for his novels, too much pomp and circumstance," Tobias confessed. "I think that I've been in physical shock all these years. I'm only just beginning to see the things that you do. I don't understand the connection with Reggie."

"The relationship goes as far back as the Church of England and the sons of heaven," Donny related without further elaboration.

"I see your point," Tobias responded, and then he spied a friend at the counter. "The sons of heaven were the monarchs of the East." Leaning his head on his fist, he thought a moment. "What do the East-West oligarchies have to do with Reggie's path?"

Appearing impatient, Donny didn't answer Tobias directly. Instead, he rechecked his assignments concerning the texts in his collection. Bowing his head over an open book, he lapsed into silence. Rather than dwell on the subject, Tobias decided to entertain some new company. He nudged Donny and directed his focus toward the appearance of a familiar face. Immediately, Rhonda came and joined them at the table. No longer did she wait for an invitation from the young men to join their table. She was carrying an armful of recently purchased books.

"I see that you are reading Sarah Breathnach on authenticity," Tobias remarked to Rhonda.

"Authenticity in history is the next topic for a paper I'm writing," Rhonda stated. Having overheard Donny talking to Tobias, she asked, "Speaking of C. S. Lewis, did you know that he was a contemporary of Virginia Woolf?"

"I'm not surprised, given the types of books that they wrote," Donny said.

"Breathnach says Woolf described a sexual assault in one of the English countryside manors associated with Lewis's groups," Rhonda pondered out loud. "It changes everything."

"What does it change?" Donny asked in a direct low voice.

"It helps people understand her writing," Rhonda replied. "There is nothing to fear."

"Was there someone afraid of Virginia Woolf?" Tobias asked. Removing his head from where it leaned on his fist, he sat upright. "Now that might explain Lewis," Tobias commented. "Like the ghosts of the wives of Henry VIII, they perpetually avoid the Church of England, along with its bloodlines tied to corporate oligarchies." Dropping one arm down to the floor with an air of resignation, he added, "They were the ones who pushed the religious opiates on the sons of heaven."

"Did Henry VIII's wives avoid him, while they were alive?" Donny asked rhetorically, shifting uncomfortably in his chair.

"Good question," Rhonda announced, shaking her head decisively.

"If they were as smart as his daughter, they did," Tobias said, thumping his hand down on the table.

"So England's religious corporations sent traffickers to China instead of missionaries during WWII, which ignited a civil war after Japan lost its hold," Rhonda surmised. Then she added in a quiet voice, "Japan lost as a result of the same industrialists who supplied the traffickers."

"The nuclear industry is associated with the drug trade," Donny rejoined.

"Next thing you know, they'll use radiation like a drug," Tobias observed.

"They do. It is called chemo," Rhonda quipped.

"It is like the aspirin and the headache, the industrial chicken-versus-egg question. Which came first?" Tobias asked rhetorically. "We studied this in chemistry class."

"Like the war and nuke?" Donny questioned, stretching back in his chair and browsing the pile books around him.

"The result is domination through a yin- and yang-like dynamic. There is someone pretending to be a wizard behind the iron curtain," Tobias remarked.

"It is not all smoke and mirrors," Rhonda asserted.

"The *Wizard of Oz* was written around the time this was being set up, at the turn of the century," Donny said. "I know, because my grandmother used to sit in Baum's lap as he read. She was a runaway Boston Brahmin, who later came out west and ran pony clubs."

"I can see why authenticity comes into play here---it is used to get around the smoke, mirrors, and curtains," Tobias chimed.

"So we have the fake wizards and the wicked witches to contend with in this semiconscious opiate-like dream state. What next? We can't just click our heels and say there is no place like home," Donny insisted.

"True," Rhonda acknowledged. "Woolf attempted to bring in the divine feminine in her writings, but she got lost. I think that she meant well, but the truth was out of her reach, for various reasons."

"Like General MacArthur, who meant well, but the truth was out of his reach," Donny noted. "Washington, DC, forced him to let go of the communists, who were also sponsored by the industrialists."

"So the railroad industry removed both Lincoln, the Boxers, and a few cowboys," Tobias gleaned.

"Corporate oligarchy," Donny announced. "This is the connection to Reggie, and perhaps why he is lost in Korea."

"Why didn't you tell me outright?" Tobias asked him.

"By the time of WWII, the gurus of the East India Company were Nazis," Rhonda remarked. "He didn't tell you directly because of the implications."

Donny rolled his eyes. He continued, "The Church of England separated from the corporate oligarchy, inciting the American Revolution. The church and corporation will soon be allies again, probably when the grandson of the British throne marries. The alignments will be in the puppets strings surrounding the relationships surrounding the marriage. The puppeteers will pull and jerk so that nothing stays on course."

"Call them the *nadas*, which means nothing in Spanish," Tobias concluded.

Donny asked Tobias, "Are you sure you want to give up aspirin for arnica, Tobias? It could be a dangerous path. Reggie's sojourn may come back to haunt you."

"Oh, Donny, we all must grow up sometime," Tobias responded. "It isn't pleasant seeing the underbelly of my life, but I am on a more poetic pursuit. It is an opportunity to leave the negativity behind."

"Keep talking," Rhonda told Donny. "I want to move forward."

Chapter Ten

There's is nothing like chaos

To make a person feel nonexistent

Tune Reference: *Too Much Time On My Hands*

----Styx

"SO HOW DO we break the gridlock?" Tobias asked. "Sounds like we have too much time on our hands."

"Cherry Blossoms," Donny said. "Let's go to the museum and see the cherry blossoms. It is a custom in Japan to spend time viewing the cherry blossoms every spring."

Grabbing their bags, the threesome hopped the light rail to the museum area of town. Over ten years had passed since Tobias's trip to Texas. He was glad to see spring again in the Pacific Northwest. The brilliant, soft, pinkish-white petals showered the ground lightly with an exquisite sweet surrender, embodying the refinement of nervous system and spirit. Although the verdant carpet of flowers lasted several days, the total effect caused the viewer to experience sorrow that the petals had ever left the tree initially.

"According to history, this is what the kamikaze pilots saw before boarding their planes. The tradition of connecting with the cherry blossoms goes further back than the beginning of the samurai," Donny commented.

Tobias savored the delicate scent of a petal between his fingers. A flash of recognition crossed his face, and he acknowledged, "It is about openness and composure, attributes the pilots would have needed before diving in."

Standing erect with a few petals clutched in his hand, Tobias imagined himself taking the path imparted by the essence of the cherry blossoms. He didn't go with Donny and Rhonda into the museum. The grove of flowering trees called him to a world of molecules and essences that was underwritten by the interplay of light and shadow. Like the chirality of a molecule, individuals could roll a *Dreidel* with a self-destructive spin on it. Some people like the Hindu goddess, Kali, just danced with the outcomes. Others, like the whirling dervishes and spiders simply spun. Did anyone know where they were going? Researchers determined that positive thought influenced the molecular arrangement of water molecules, but Tobias had not seen the evidence on the chirality of the matter. The best healing results had been obtained with the use of the word, natural. Tobias imagined the Asian block design for 'natural', in a language which corresponded to the way they communicated in parcels of information, sorta like bytes in a computer program.

Unlike Reggie's, Tobias's journey in life had not been an easy undertaking. The student homeopath had taught him well. Serving as a beloved authority figure, she had led him away from groups that didn't really care for him. Reggie had honorably left everything that Tobias valued, and yet it had been Tobias's values that had propelled him toward a historically dangerous road in life. His broken heart had told him that he didn't need to go around the world to find trouble. Instead of competing with Reggie, Tobias forged his idea of a win-win situation as he armed himself with the intentions of the cherry blossoms.

****

"I dreamed about Reggie last night," Tobias confided to Rhonda. He could hear her light breaths on the other end of the phone. Although it had been several months since they had talked, she had contacted him about Reggie's sudden hospitalization. She told him that he had been teaching English in Holland and had suddenly come down with a lung infection. The drugs that they had given him were not working. Now that he was experiencing kidney failure, the end seemed imminent.

"In my dream, I was scrambling behind Reggie on the ski slopes again. He was leading me up and down over hill and dale. We moved so fast that when I awoke from the dream, I felt dizzy, almost nauseated," he admitted. "It is like I am racing him." He took a deep breath, before he uttered, "Do you think someone killed him for asking too many questions in Korea?"

"I don't know." Rhonda sighed. "I've been out of town at a Linux conference," she told him. "I threw up in the hotel lobby this morning. My colleagues blamed it on the corporate microcomputer conference next door. They know how I feel about those."

At Reggie's memorial service several weeks later, Tobias drove with Rhonda and some others to the cabin in the mountains. They had often stayed there during the weekends they taught Nordic skiing. Tobias took responsibility for whatever crossed his field of view. He had learned when to close his eyes to avoid being pulled away from distractions. Reggie's demise was a confusing, serious matter. Tobias probed deeper and addressed the relationship Reggie had with the divine scheme. He wondered what had taken Reggie away from them in such a profound manner. He didn't think that it had much to do with Reggie, his wife, and friends. They had only refused to follow him in his soul-searching trek.

"We were too busy studying," he told Rhonda.

Tobias walked outside and joined the gathering of old friends. Reggie's wife held his urn as tightly as she had once held him in his final moments. At times she squeezed the metal urn as if he was still there, as she listened to everything spoken at his service.

One of Reggie's close friends, another Vietnam vet, wielded the microphone in his hand and began, "We are here today to commemorate Reggie, who left us. Does anyone have anything to say? Please do so."

As he passed the microphone to someone nearby, the group silently groped for a meaning or an understanding of his death. Perhaps Reggie was also wondering. People were encouraged to speak their minds or try to provide some sort of explanation.

One of Reggie's close friends took the mike.

"I will always remember Reggie taking away my three-year-old son's favorite stuffed bear and tossing it around on the sailboat. I protested, but you know Reggie. He kept teasing and entertaining the child, who was laughing under duress. We were all laughing until the bear went overboard. I can't even remember who missed the catch. Now it is Reggie who is gone."

More anecdotes were revealed with a similar theme.

"We found ourselves in a place called Vietnam...we asked where the waterways were...it took us awhile to realize that we were not there to kayak...we didn't get it..."

Everyone walked slowly away from the gathering. All Reggie's former students from around the globe, whether it involved skiing, kayaking, or speaking English, remained puzzled. Their time together had not yielded immediate answers; they only knew that there was more to learn about Reggie's leaving it all behind and going to Korea. And they all wondered what he had found there that had affected him so much.

Tobias returned to his residency at the naturopathic clinic, where he could not take any time off to grieve his friend's passing. The situation mirrored his naturopathic medical studies, where grief manifested *in situ*. Instead of later swallowing the sorrow down with a glass of alcohol, the emotion served as a sign or symptom. The grief became part of a patient's case. In order to understand where a patient stood, it became important for a physician to know their own position. The process often yielded valuable insight that could be used for healing. Grief could be examined, experienced, and addressed. Feeling isolated from the community on sea and mountain, Tobias left the shift early for some fresh air. He found that his colleagues and the interns didn't get it. Reggie's death really bothered him. Though moved close to tears, Tobias understood that he seldom cried at transitions, untimely or not.

As he was leaving the building, he encountered an associate from the midwifery program. Michelle was a singer with one of the bands among the naturopathic physicians. Though she had already graduated, she still sang with the group of musicians. She recognized Tobias from some of his performances at the annual talent shows. Music held a special bond on campus. It pulled the musicians together unlike anything else. They supported each other as they strove to express the unspeakable thoughts pulsating through their intense lives.

Noticing the tears welling in Tobias's eyes, she stopped him. She gently asked, "What happened?"

"My friend died," he revealed. "It is a real loss. I suspect foul play. There aren't many people like him."

"Oh." She smiled and nodded at Tobias. Before letting him go past her, Michelle summarized, "He was one of the good guys."

"Yes, he was one of the good guys," Tobias echoed. His face brightened with her consolation. She appeared as the only one who understood. Acknowledging her insight, he looked at her and said in heartfelt gratitude, "Thank you."

Then he exited through the glass doors to the refuge of the fallen cherry blossoms on the spring turf. He kept her words with him as he touched the petals on the ground. Bringing a flower to his face, Tobias sniffed the aroma. Reggie's untimely death had taught him much. Savoring the bouquet in his hands, he made peace with Reggie. The creation of a win-win situation steered him on the path of intrigue and love.

Chapter Eleven

Ruby Tuesdays are only

For rolling stones

Tune Reference: *Ruby Tuesday*

----The Rolling Stones

SHORTLY AFTER THE memorial service, Tobias consulted his homeopath friend for help in dealing with secondary trauma associated with the deaths of several close relationships. She was the same one who had given him the arnica on the ski slopes. In the meantime, she had graduated and set up her practice. The patients that he saw in-clinic were bringing heavier and heavier cases, and she could offer him help from her own experiences. In addition, world events appeared particularly violent that year, and his services were in even more demand. Wishing to stay on top of his workload, Tobias sought a boost from another therapeutic modality, rather than take an overdue vacation.

"True, my mother did threaten to tear me limb from limb," Tobias mentioned. "Now that I am older, I feel like I have been poisoned. I don't think I did anything wrong to merit such a threat. I mean, I haven't seen her in years. The thought has started to haunt me as I work with my patients. Maybe it started in cadaver lab. Maybe my life is too compartmentalized--- you know, a hazard of the profession. I have this compulsion to put things back together. I was the only one in kindergarten building complete cities with fire stations and hospitals, and forming diplomatic relations with the other kids playing with building blocks."

The homeopath leaned back in his chair and thumbed through a book that resembled a bible. Silence ensued as she studied the rubrics in the little black book. She peered at Tobias and asked a few short questions.

"Do you feel like you've been hibernating? Do you easily get chilled? Do you like wearing things around your neck?"

Tobias mildly nodded in affirmative to the first two questions but shook his head at the last one. He elaborated, "Sometimes I get chilled when I am encounter something chilling, like a traumatic case, or something. My hands either heat up or chill out, depending on whether the patient needs a hot water bottle or an ice pack. I don't like wearing turtlenecks for warmth, because I feel suffocated."

After more pregnant moments of quiet, the homeopath pulled a vial from her desk drawer. Offering it to Tobias, she said, "Healers tend to be empathetic. Take this in sympathy. Like heals like."

Tobias studied the vial in his hand. He wondered what spin on the *Dreidel* had brought him to this point. "What is it?"

"I'm not going to tell you. You'll think about it too much. See you in two months."

****

"It is the oddest thing," Tobias began, two months later. "I think I'm losing my mind with this latest research. I find myself drawn to the theosophical library in downtown Seattle. Sometimes I go to Seattle for seminars. At first I was scared to be in that part of town. I have never had a fascination for the occult; it sorta scares me. Somehow I mustered the courage to spend an afternoon at this library and read Dion Fortune's *Psychic Self-Defense*. I've always been afraid of witches. Back in the '60s, when women teased their hair like the movie *Hairspray*, I ran out of the house because I was afraid that my aunt had turned into a witch. Of course I ran out of the *Munster House* in Hollywood studios---I never forgave my father for carrying me through the place, but he convinced me that it was the only way out of the amusement park. Everyone else ignored me. They thought that I was just a scaredy-cat. Something about the vampire that popped out from the basement lab freaked me. I never thought that that the *Addams Family* was funny. Even when I was five-years old, I thought that this stuff was pathological rather than entertaining. In fact, I don't like associating with people who get mesmerized by such shows, which is another reason why I didn't hang with my sister. Now I know that it is a homeopathic fact; the texts document such cases as suppressed gonorrhea or syphilis---the stuff that conquered the Hawaiian Islands. Streaks of white in colored hair, like the ones in Herman Munster's wife had, express a homeopathic miasm of serious proportions."

"Sounds like you are on the right track, Tobias," the homeopath said soothingly before he could exhaust himself with a soliloquy. "I gave you Lachesis." Pausing for a brief moment, she looked down at her notes and grimaced. "It is for repression. Follow your instincts. When you are ready to study homeopathy, give me a call."

"But what is even more weird about the whole situation is that I find myself refuting Dion Fortune almost line by line," Tobias rambled, ignoring the homeopath's offer. "The book annoyed me," he stated as his eyes grew wide. "I realized that I wasn't the only one who saw through her, though for different reasons. At the end of one of her books, an authority says that she had essentially lost her soul due to sentimental attachment. I didn't know that sentiment could be such a crime. I haven't thought about it long enough. I'm not sure that I want to. It's chilling."

"Don't worry about thinking so much, Tobias," she said. "Possibly they are referring to the lack of real emotion or heartfelt warmth."

"Sorta gives me a headache," he said. "It is like she got lost in her rituals. Researchers say that she worked as a Freudian psychologist by day and a witch by night. Many of the rituals described amounted to sexual orgies, involving much of England's daytime labor force---even taxi drivers. Supposedly they were fending off Hitler and the Nazis' occultism during WWII. Now I think that it is deeper than that. For some reason, this group targeted US Naval Intelligence. Nobody knew that England had switched during WWI. The monarchs of Britain and Germany are cousins. You'd think that they would be on the same side as Allied Forces, but these were just the rough kids on the block providing another distraction that couldn't be ignored."

Tobias paused a moment as his thoughts drifted into a sunbeam that had risen across the wood floors of the extensive room. The homeopath followed his gaze and marveled at the brilliance of the light, which seemed to elevate the space, bringing peace and inner calm. Feeling blessed by the warmth of the sun, both savored the experience and the insight shared.

"Lachesis was one of the Fates, a Greek goddess. Her task was to measure a lifetime," the homeopath commented. She laughed as she slightly deviated from the subject. "Even though we aren't on the snowy slopes, I still feel as if I am skiing with you, Tobias. Our conversation pursues paths that go up, down, and all around."

"And on slippery slopes. Lachesis must have understood relativity," Tobias remarked. Finally responding to the homeopath's offer to consider studying this therapeutic approach, he added, "I suppose the Greeks characterized fate as a cold-blooded fatality, like the bite of the bushmaster snake. There is another name for you---bushmaster. The master of the bush is master of the understory. I feel that I am looking at life from the bottom up. It is a colder commentary when one peers through the shadows into the light. I can see the connection to the action of the homeopathic remedy."

"Do you suspect that British Intelligence was also aware of Fortune's activities?" the homeopath questioned further.

"Yes, and it had to do with the difference between fate and fortune," Tobias stated, before lapsing in a lecture. "She and her mentor were trying to counter the Nazis' version of the Philadelphia Experiment. They ignored covert US military operations. Likewise, British Intelligence only knew as much as Fortune's group did, which provided the front for them in this arena. Meanwhile, US Naval Intelligence watched them for specifics on telekinesis, astral projection, and telepathic communication. They were trying to anticipate the maneuvers of the powers funding corporations like Bayer and IG Farben as well as the Manhattan Project. Various occult lodges also participated. Some of the lodges, like the Fortune group, became corrupted by various masters."

"Do you see the connection to Lachesis?" the homeopath asked. "One of the themes of the remedy is repression."

"Yes," Tobias answered. "My days are filled with tuning into patients. There isn't anytime to dialogue the findings."

"The resonance of your work with Reggie's death is not accidental," the homeopath observed. "Lachesis is energizing you to connect the dots of your experiences through dialogue. The emerging pattern is clear. You sense peril. Did you ever suspect that Reggie was targeted for the knowledge gained through his travels?" Pausing briefly to stare again at her desk, she informed him, "Tobias, you have been paralyzed by this poison. You need to run. This research helps you find safety. Keep in communication. Perhaps, we *all* must make a run for it."

Chapter Twelve

Never try to stop a moving boat
Steer the drift of the craft instead

Tune Reference: *Abracadabra*

----Steve Miller Band

A FEW DAYS later, Tobias lingered late at night after the clinic had closed to finish looking at some patient charts. He noticed a soft light seeping out into the darkened hall from a door left half-ajar. As he approached the exit, he checked to see if someone had left the light on.

"Oh---hi, Michelle," he said, peering from behind the opened door. "I thought that I was the only one here."

"I am just returning from a birth," she answered as she slowly unpacked some of her bags. She questioned him in a voice that reflected her mild concern, "How are you doing?"

"I'm getting over my loss," he told her. "His death is awakening me to the threats on my own life. I am still putting the pieces together."

"Interesting," she said. Then she sighed. "If you are at risk, then so am I. Midwives have a long history of persecution. We just don't talk about it nowadays."

"Yes, I know," Tobias said with chagrin. "The homeopath gave me Lachesis to get the dialogue going. Tell me about the birth. "How did it go?" he asked her.

"Very well. The new family is resting peacefully now," she answered.

"Do you need any help?" he offered.

"Yeah, sure," she answered, studying Tobias closely for a few seconds. Then she thoughtfully said, "You can sterilize some of the equipment. The autoclave is in the far-right corner on the shelf."

Tobias set his gear down on the hallway floor. As he placed the stainless-steel instruments in the autoclave, he observed an ink drawing of a single stately tree hanging on the wall in front of him. The tree lacked the usual natural appearance, having been created in black on a copper background.

"It took me awhile to realize that I could see the auras of trees. I've always painted them in hues of purples, reds, and pinks. It wasn't the usual seasonal colors, though I liked those too. I saw trees like people. This one seems different. What kind of tree is this?" Tobias inquired. Animated by this sign of life, his understanding flowed through him like sap running its way through branches. Glancing at Michelle, he added, "The homeopath encouraged me to keep gathering information."

She chuckled when she heard about the homeopath's instructions. "It's the Kabbalah Tree of Life." Then she stopped and answered, "It's the Kabbalah Tree of Life."

"It is fitting for a naturopathic midwife," he commented. Then he lightly jested, "I want one. What makes this tree so special?"

"The Tree of Life serves as a cosmological representation of how the universe came into being," Michelle answered as if she was being briefed at a medical case study.

"Wow." He sighed. "There's the Tree of Knowledge in the Garden of Eden, and now there is this one for the creation of an even bigger picture. I am from the Bible belt, so my knowledge on sacred trees is somewhat limited."

Michelle stood next to Tobias and gazed at the drawing with him. "They say that the Tree of Life was the second significant tree in the famed Garden of Eden, but I think that it existed in North Korea."

"Perhaps," Tobias considered. "*Korea* was derived from the term in ancient Greece for 'insect.' *Snake* is to the Tree of Knowledge as *insect* is to the Tree of Life. No pun intended, but how does that bug you?"

"A snake speaks with a forked tongue, whereas a bug eavesdrops. One is projective, while the other is receptive. It is like a yin-yang arrangement."

"Do you mean sorta like a radio? The snake is the transmitter, while the bug is the receiver. What do you think they were connected to? The Eye-in-the-Sky?" he quizzed her.

"Why, yes," she speculated. "Which brings us back to Gondwanaland, and the eye on the Eye-in-the-Sky."

Tobias smirked. Becoming his own witness, he provided an observation, "This is very ancient stuff that we are talking about." As he broke the focus of the conversation, his countenance softened into a more serious aspect. His gaze returned to Michelle. Tobias asked, "Would you like to get together for lunch sometime?"

"Next week would be best, when I am not on call. Lunch sounds great!" she answered.

Tobias watched her quickly finish repacking her supply bags. They remained quiet as she concentrated on completing her task. After she had lifted her purse to her shoulder, he offered, "Here, I'll carry a few bags and walk you to your car. We can talk along the way."

Michelle appeared relieved. Her face brightened. "I appreciate your help. I've been up since two in the morning," she said, almost apologetically.

"Figured as much by the looks of the equipment." He smiled.

Michelle laughed and led the way out the building to her car parked outside. It was as if a weight had been removed from her shoulders, and her steps seemed lighter---she was playing again. Tobias watched her toss away her workload, admiring the change and how quickly she did it. They emerged like two kids embarking on a fun adventure.

Though dusk had already faded into night, a spring mist rose from the verdant grasses and trees around the parking lot. It felt warm and inviting, signaling a beginning rather than an ending. With a light inhalation, Michelle relished the soft breeze on her face and glanced at Tobias. He blushed slightly with the attention, as if accepting congratulations for doing the right thing at the right time. Transformation of a professional relationship into a friendly one with romantic potential wasn't always easy. In fact, it became very awkward after one was established in the profession. Placing Michelle's bags in the back seat, he felt her hand brush his arm while he pulled away from the car. Once he had collected himself, she politely drew back, as if denying any sense of affection. Instead, she turned and faced him as if in confrontation.

But it was too late. Tobias grinned softly at her before stepping away. Without causing her to feel awkward, his demeanor remained neutral, as if he wasn't going to let her forget what she had just done.

"How about Tuesday evening at seven?" His proposal jumped over lunch in favor of dinner. In the rapid growing seriousness of the relationship, he offered a wave of his hand before heading down the street. He turned around for a brief moment to await her reply, while adding further details, "Meet me at the Thai restaurant on the main street."

She beamed at him. Expressing relief that he wasn't going to encroach upon her, she responded, "Yes, Tuesday it is. See ya there, Tobias."

He smiled again and walked away with almost a slight skip. As he unlocked his bicycle from a nearby rack, Tobias watched her pull out of the parking lot. She glanced up at her rearview mirror and waved at him before turning onto the street. Tobias wrapped a band around the legs of his pants, so that the hems would not get caught in the greased gears. Having already changed into casual clothes, he leisurely navigated his way through the side streets.

A good day is when I get to ride my bicycle and a bad day is when I get to ride, he thought to himself as he sped past newly budded trees. He continued to paraphrase the quote from a professional baseball manager. *Either way, I get to ride my bike, which makes it a great day.* In this frame of mind, he reflected on the quickening of his relationship with Michelle. He fell headlong into a whirlpool of curiosity and desire. Feeling the wind lightly whip his brow, Tobias calmed as he entered the eye of the storm inside himself. Whatever he was presently doing harmonized with his spirit, providing a wellspring of confidence in his latest pursuit.

Finding that Tuesday evening arrived only too soon, Tobias entered the restaurant moments ahead of Michelle. He opted for a cozy table for two with a window view. He sat down comfortably, daydreaming as he gazed out the window for a few minutes. An elegant tree across the busy street reminded him of the Tree of Life in Michelle's office. Something drew his attention back inside the restaurant, and he looked for the source of the distraction. As if on cue, Michelle appeared only a few steps away, as if she had stepped out of nowhere. She wore heels, dark hose, a black leather skirt, and a tight-fitting cotton---probably organic---shirt that hugged the curves of her arms and torso. Tobias rose, somewhat mesmerized by the obvious change from the world of white lab coats and professional dress codes. Michelle paused, reveling in the obvious effect on her date. She smiled slightly at Tobias. A slight sense of relief flooded her countenance, mostly because she had successfully communicated the terms of tonight's encounter to the world. Practically jumping to attention, Tobias held a chair out for her and edged it close to his position at the table.

They began by ordering red wine, which they sipped over candlelight, with heads slightly bowed in each other's direction. Minutes passed as they made small talk and decompressed from the cares of the day, week, month, and year. Pretending to be busy behind the counter, the waiters and waitresses seemed not to notice the couple huddled over the distant table.

Then Tobias made a subtle play, edging nearer Michelle. "Tell me more about the Kabbalah Tree."

Michelle looked down at the dark wood of the table and quieted. A waitress suddenly stood before them to take their order. Tobias abruptly sat back in his chair and perused the menu. After watching him respond to the interruption, Michelle decided to do the same. Like two dancers in a chorus line, they hurriedly placed their orders so as to chase away the intrusion. Michelle seized the advantage of having taken the same classes as Tobias, and resumed answering Tobias's question as if he had been a long-term study mate.

"It is about transformation," she began. "Last year, the president of the national midwifery association started his presentation by saying 'Babies die---babies die.'"

Tobias looked at her with an understanding smile. "You don't just get over it. Do you?"

"No, but the Kabbalah helps me keep the perspective."

"What perspective do you have as a master of midwifery?" Tobias queried. "By the graduation, if not by the end of first year, we all come to our own code or key to unlock the doors of life and death before us."

"Unlike in the Greeks' fatalistic view of fate, the Tree of Life depicts death as an agent of change."

"Almost sacrificial," Tobias reasoned as he studied the plate that the waitress placed in front of her. Then glancing up at Michelle, he continued, "Even the Native Americans have their sun dance, a mirror of the Western ritual of the sacrificial lamb or the hangman."

Michelle paused for a moment, and then she stared down at the table to conceal a chuckle as she thought about their conversation. Then she quickly composed herself. Grinning, she raised her empty glass with a toast: "Here's to sweet surrender, Tobias."

Tobias almost laughed at her gesture. Meeting her toast, he fingered the glass in his hand a few seconds before taking a gulp. Then he put the glass down firmly on the table and announced, "Let's eat."

Chapter Thirteen

In the year 2525

The planet may still be alive

If we can survive the present

Tune Reference: *In The Year 2525 (Exordium & Terminus)*

----Zager and Evans

THEY FINISHED THEIR meal in near silence. The conversation consisted of abbreviated sentences that mimicked sporadic, melodic hums. Tobias's appetite had disappeared, and he swiftly intercepted the check the next time the waitress came over to see if they needed anything else.

Steadily savoring small spoonfuls of soup, Michelle glanced at his lightly touched plate and rapid movements. She said, "I've had a long day. I'm still dazed from the last birth. Give me a moment."

"No rush," he assured her like he was making a lifelong promise. He nibbled at the remains of the appetizer. "Take your time."

Taking him at his word, Michelle slowly finished her meal. When she was done, Tobias suggested, "Let's take the rest home and check out the lake."

After tucking the huge untouched portions away in several doggie bags, they stored the food in their car. Then the couple crossed a busy street and went for a walk around the lake just a few streets to the north. Familiar with the concrete path leading down the hill to the water, Tobias surveyed the territory as if welcoming an old friend.

There was bakery up the hill, where he passed hours reading, writing, and socializing. Often he would grab a bowl of chili while watching acquaintances come and go in the establishment. Generally someone would say, "Let's take a walk along the lake," and he'd go. Very seldom did he turn down an offer to walk around the lake. Only the occasional looming deadline detained him, though he always demanded a rain check. Once he had found his way down the hill in a blinding downpour in which visibility was limited to two feet. It had been after playing Ping-Pong with several other clinicians, who were passing time before an important state professional meeting. A series of thoughts had crossed his mind, and he'd decided that he needed some fresh air. So he'd raced down the hill in the pouring rain to deflect the intensity of his feelings about life. Then he'd ducked into the bakery to dry off---in his suit with flamenco-dancer flair.

He could not even remember what had concerned him at the moment, only its intensity. Unlike the others, he had been all dressed up, and the company at the Ping-Pong table appreciated the look. One young woman had planted a kiss on his lips before he left. It was the start of an intimate relationship of sorts. Like an engineer with a calculator perpetually hooked to his back pocket, Tobias was always ready to be genteel and debonair. It was part of his conservatism---perhaps it was performance art. Though he never looked for the kiss, it reminded him that he was being watched. His audience sensed that he was from somewhere else---more than just his own head and not just the Southwest---somewhere definitely old-fashioned and anachronistic. By the time he graduated, even straight men kissed Tobias, as if welcoming him from a long flight. The straights excused themselves by claiming Italian blood in their souls. On the other hand, the numerous homosexuals in the profession never kissed him, though he was often invited to their closed parties. These tight-lipped encounters dotted the chaos of pathology and disease that coursed through their lives. Somehow this grounded and centered them, reminding them what was meaningful. On the other hand, his friends in engineering *never* kissed him; they always told him K-I-S-S: Keep It Simple, Stupid.

He could remember another time, when he'd been sipping warm cider while watching the raindrops splash the picture windows of the bakery. Two other men had entered the bakery and approached the counter for their order. Like Tobias, they were somewhat eclectically dressed with a plaid cap, a Greek sailor's cap, vests, and beards. They'd even started to dance to the slide-guitar rhythm of an Eric Clapton tune. With a little skip in their stance, they'd accepted their mugs and chosen seats in the empty room next to Tobias, who smiled at their light jig.

They were social workers, counselors of teenage street children. Tobias recognized the perspective that he shared with them: "It's life. If you are going to be here, you might it as well live it." They complained about how the medical students in the area, conventional and alternative, chatted with them until they graduated and became gods. Once they became docs, they quit talking to them. Tobias laughed at their analysis. He didn't have to prove that he was different from the others, nor could he predict his availability in the future. The sun broke out into brilliant beams through the window, and the men invited him for a walk around the lake. Tobias noted the twinkle in their eye as he agreed to join them on their merry adventure. Hopping over puddles and torrents, they made their way to lake like a trio of frogs preferring a large body of water to the heated cement. After a few yards on the lake trail, Tobias felt bonded, having won acceptance of the social workers. He might need to consult with them over a patient someday. Tobias didn't leave them until he glanced at his watch and suddenly recalled that he had a meeting to attend. He would have preferred staying with these lighthearted, seasoned fellows, but he had his own mission to fulfill. Now that his suit was dry, he climbed the hill, and vowed to never be a god-doc.

This evening with Michelle constituted the first time that he ever brought a date to this rather large frog pond. Tonight was the night to be a prince, instead of a frog. *Well, maybe,* he thought; you never knew what some women wanted.

The damp night air enveloped Michelle and Tobias in shadowy patches, disrupted by hues of neon lights, which eventually gave way to a soft moon hovering over the water. Several disjointed groups of people appeared on the three-mile trail, where occasionally a single, focused jogger would overtake them and pass in front. Tobias took Michelle's hand in his once they had reached the trail surrounding the lake. She hesitated at first, but there was no mistake about the hot, small grasp underneath that reminded him of a child.

He had been to this lake so many times before---sometimes in the rain, sometimes on a sweltering summer's day, and sometimes on a blustery autumn eve or a bitter-cold, windy night. Kayaking, running, cycling, rollerblading, picnicking, Christmas caroling, performing at the local theater, or swimming in the city pool had brought him here. No matter what, his mood was always the same; he was never sad though never ecstatic. The water and breezy air took everything else, except for a feeling of almost numb, curious, perplexed amazement that compelled him to take a deep, deep breaths when viewing the area. The intermittent, varied chorus of crickets, frogs, and ducks seem to help him keep his feet on the ground and keep from blowing away with the subtle lacy tide. The tide brought in a powerful misty vapor that provided an invisible push, yet held him firm in an embrace.

Yes, he thought, *this was the perfect place to take Michelle tonight.* Many naturopathic students and clinicians had their most serious discussions while trekking around the lake. He slowed his pace, realizing that Michelle would probably not wish to walk the entire three miles in heels. She sensed the change in him, and she seized the opportunity to stop in front of some tall reeds and gaze past the shore at the moon's reflection. Tobias paused with her, still holding her hand decisively. This was the type of trail that hikers could take in bits and pieces without feeling that they'd missed anything.

"The sons of heaven never had a hangman archetype," Tobias resumed.

Michelle let go of his hand for a closer look at what was making an interesting swooshing sound in the reeds. She peered between the blades of grass and her head bobbed up and down. Without giving him a second glance, she acknowledged, "Why do you think that is, Tobias?"

Tobias smiled. With a bounce in his step, he lifted her up to a nearby rock so that she could see over the reeds. Then he stood back. "I think that it is just another corruption of a cultural myth."

"I agree, Tobias," she said, fixing her gaze on the shadowy glimpse of the water past the vegetation. "Which myth was tinkered with? The sons of heaven in the east, or the son gods in the west?"

"Probably both," Tobias replied, hopping on a rock beside her.

"Probably," Michelle rejoined. "It keeps the balance if everyone is wrong at the same time."

Tobias laughed and teetered on his rock. Michelle jumped off hers and offered her hand to Tobias for balance. Tobias accepted her hold and then leaped to the pavement beside her.

"Let's head back," Michelle suggested, wrapping her arm around his. "Some cultures are big on sacrifice, while others party. The Kabbalah emphasizes life rather than death. It is not the Tree of Death."

"We wouldn't have a live tree, then." Tobias chuckled. "Even death is encapsulated in the framework of life."

"You've been doing your homework," Michelle commented.

"I study up for all my serious dates," Tobias quipped. Without pausing further, Tobias asked the next question. "So, you tell me, how did the Tree of Life get to Korea from the Garden of Eden?"

"People," Michelle said in a voice reserved for clinic, "A relatively large group foresaw the inevitable destruction of the Tree of Life and decided to embody the principles that drove its existence."

"That's heavy," Tobias reflected as he examined the ground underneath his feet for stable footing. In the night sky, the pavement appeared like a winding, black path. "Why Korea?"

"It has to do with the breakup of the earth's motherland that resulted in the two supercontinents, known as Laurasia and Gondwanaland. The landmass that gave birth to these two continents was called Rodinia. After Eden fell, the Tree of Life began decaying. Lilith, the first human female, had taken the apple from the Tree of Knowledge to propagate another lineage. The sons of heaven helped the survivors of the human family---who came to represent the tree---immigrate to the portion of Laurasia that was later called Korea."

"Were they attacked by bugs there?" Tobias asked.

"Most likely there were rather large insects," Michelle added, lapsing temporarily out of her flat, clinical assessment. "Obviously, the human race survived, but the DNA has been tampered by bacteriophage-like entities carrying out the mission of the intergalactic insect race."

"The story reminds me of the book *Starship Troopers*," Tobias remarked. "They are making a movie about it. The Arachnids felt that the humans were encroaching upon their turf."

Michelle raised her brow, eyeing Tobias carefully. "Consider it another excuse for an out-of-control population with the motto Live to Die."

"The live-to-die syndrome is in sharp contrast to the harmony found in Eden," Tobias commented. Now he became clinical. "I can see why the Asians came to emphasize balance in their religious structures. It parallels the demands of the sun gods for human sacrifice on another continent. Imagine the Aztec rite of breeding victims for heart carvings."

Michelle matched him with a clinical commentary, "The scene sorta reminds me of a former classmate. She remembered her deceased father by the books of his library, not that she ever read them; they were just there. The classmate had an interesting way of detaching herself from relationships, even leaving her spouse to pursue studies in another nation. She told him out of the blue as she rolled over the back of the dock and into the lake. That was it. The student hopped from friendship to friendship without ever really being a friend to anyone."

Switching from her detached perspective to a more personal observation, Michelle said stoically. "By luck of the draw, we were partners in massage class once. I always felt that she was going to tear my heart out. She went back to Canada, fortunately."

"Do you think the high priests performing the Aztec ritual envied the hearts that they tore out?" Tobias questioned, pondering the implications of a massage without heart.

Michelle shrugged. "Most likely they were living out their own trauma and chose to fuse it with their cortex."

"Do you think that is how gonorrhea came about?" Tobias asked, jumping to another conclusion. "Sexually transmitted diseases are a relatively new phenomena in the evolution of the human race. They became a health issue during the industrial colonization of the 1700's, which was generally corporate sponsored. It resembles the AIDS epidemics that we are seeing now, though the medical community disagrees about the sociopathic implications."

Michelle silently laughed but then grew concerned. She turned and faced Tobias, who stopped under the weight of her stare. Together they took a few steps off the trail for a better look at the lake. Underneath the subtleties of their conversation, the two physicians were sizing each other up.

"As both a naturopathic physician and midwife, I get to see new families grow and develop," she began, fathoming a future with Tobias. Philosophical alliances brought naturopathic physicians together and held them there. "I have the opportunity to treat *miasms*, or inherited diseases, that seem to go back seven generations. The old medical texts are full of case studies from the days when most practitioners were homeopaths. Then there are the old medical texts from the pre-pharmaceutical days, which give the background on the crude forms of substances that were later used homeopathically by the time of the American Civil War. Lincoln sponsored a homeopathic college before becoming president, however, the Civil War benefitted military medicine."

Michelle studied the silvery waves dancing under the moon's glow, and she sighed. Then she continued, "I see the cutest young families who celebrate Halloween in the most horrific way. Once I've started treating them homeopathically for suppressed gonorrhea, they naturally turn to celebrations of harvest. Symbols of horror and fear give way to connotations of gratitude and contentment. Their Halloween costumes and home decor change dramatically. They spend less time in spook houses and more time in corn mazes."

Tobias nodded. "Yes, it is in the texts. Those thick lips that professional models buy belong in the realm of suppressed gonorrhea, at least several generations over. Whereas measles, the communicable disease of childhood social development, is successfully treated by the same rubric of homeopathics for gonorrhea, regardless whether the parents are carriers."

"I use the same rubric for stubborn cases of diaper rash in the pre-social child," Michelle confessed. "It works well."

"Pre-social age? That's zero to three years old," Tobias commented. He put his arm around Michelle's waist and led her back to the paved trail.

Michelle rejoined, "Look, I know that I don't have all the answers. I just have a sensible approach, a methodology that is reproducible, with consistent results for the past two hundred years."

As they neared the parking lot where they'd left their vehicles, Tobias stared into the starry night. "Michelle, I can see where this is going. I want your latest blood work and chart notes."

Michelle stopped at her car and hugged Tobias. Then she pulled away, smiling her understanding of his deeper meaning. She added, "And an agreed form of birth control that both approve."

Tobias grinned. "My sentiments exactly. No telling where this relationship may go."

Then he planted a quick, closed kiss directly on her lips and immediately drew back. Michelle blinked.

"How about going dancing next week?" he asked as he turned toward his car.

"That sounds fun. How about going to the club Neighbors?" she asked. "I'll call you after I check my midwifery schedule tomorrow morning. I may have a few babies to 'catch.' The mom delivers; the rest of us just stand around and wait to catch the babies."

"Sounds like a plan." Tobias waved. Then he stopped in his tracks and confronted Michelle. "That's a gay bar."

"They take everybody," Michelle told him. "A group of us went there after a bachelorette party at the male strip-tease club. I went with the married women to Neighbors, while her sorority took the bride bar-hopping downtown."

"I heard about that one," Tobias confessed. "Several of the women interns go there because they feel safe dancing there. They don't want to get picked up. The gays adore them."

"If I had not gone that night, I never would have been able to dance with one of my classmates before she died."

"I heard about that too," Tobias confronted her. "She underwent cardiac surgery after graduation to correct a congenital defect. She died on the table." Then he paused for a moment, before adding, "She always preferred conventional treatments, rather than the more quantum physical ones. I'm glad she was out dancing and got around to having a daughter." Taking a deep breath before continuing, Tobias remarked, "I have another one for you. Do you know that the successful treatment for cystic fibrosis is minerals? An animal doctor did the research for the Smithsonian back in the early sixties. I know the case of one young woman in the eighties who spent the few remaining years of her life looking for a more complicated solution. Of course, the oversight may have been due to the religious-political-corporate view of her family of origin as well as collegiate setting. *Diablos*."

"OK, Tobias," Michelle began. Her shoulders dropped and her eyes watered with tears as she related, "Life is precious." Waving her arms at him, she almost chased him away. "*Diablos* is Spanish for 'devils', otherwise known as derivatives of the Holy Roman Empire. It is a term used by those who wish to keep their lives. I know what you are getting at here. The constructs of diablos are based on fear rather than other brain functions. Their lives assumed serpentine patterns, becoming convoluted, meaningless paths going nowhere." Taking a deep breath, she caught herself before looking at Tobias. A sense of relief filled her and she smiled at him suddenly.

Tobias did not interrupt her soliloquy. Instead, he waited for her to finish and gazed at the starry night. The effect seemed to center him as he listened to her reasoning.

Michelle questioned, "Your place or mine?"

Chapter Fourteen

A friend is someone

Who hears you

When you need them the most

Tune Reference: *Urgent*

----Foreigner

FOR A BRIEF moment, Tobias considered the state of his condo. Although it wasn't shipshape, it was close to being as clean as he wanted it for this moment. He had seen Michelle's office, and he reasoned that her place would be similar. Sidestepping cluttered, cutesy feminine decor tonight, Tobias opted for a place where he could man the ambiance.

"Mine," he answered. "I have candles, sparkling wine, and a room with a massage table. Let's make it as unprofessional as possible."

"Great. I have an IUD," Michelle offered. "Change of clothes in the car for births."

"Plenty of condoms here," Tobias said as if not to be outdone. "And in case, you're wondering---clean."

"Clean here," she admitted with an innocent shrug, almost in regret. "I'll follow you home in my car."

"Sure thing." Tobias grinned as he pulled his keys out of his pocket. He gave her some general directions before he unlocked his car. Sitting behind the wheel, he waved at her before swerving out of the lot.

Michelle followed behind. When they reached Tobias's condo, Michelle parked in the adjacent lot. Tobias met her at her car, waiting patiently while she found her overnight bag and gathered a few things. Quietly, he took her bag before putting his arm around her. Together they walked toward the entrance to the condo. Shouldering the bag briefly, Tobias unlocked the front with his freed hands. He directed Michelle inside as he quickly flipped the light switch. Light flooded the room before he immediately dimmed the ceiling lights.

Placing Michelle's bag near the kitchen window-bar, he told her, "Bathroom is down the hall to the left. Make yourself comfortable."

Michelle glanced at her surroundings. Tobias sensed her impatience and decided to act immediately, instead of being a proper host. The harsh light from the opened refrigerator briefly distracted Michelle. Tobias seized a pitcher of water and placed it on a tray with two glasses.

"Would you like something to drink?" he asked politely.

Michelle shook her head.

"Follow me," he said, taking her overnight bag with him. He carried the tray with the water on his other arm, despite her refusal. Tobias knew better than to let a lover get dehydrated.

Ushering her in the room with the massage table, he left the bag on a nearby chair and set the tray down on the top of a bookshelf. He lit a candle in the room before lifting Michelle onto the massage table. His hands never left her body as he simultaneously kissed her and ran his hands past her thighs, removing her skirt from the inside out. Feeling his hot hands smoothly caressing her skin, Michelle took his breath with hers while unbuttoning his shirt.

Tobias lit another candle. Michelle persisted, tugging gently at the button on his pants. He forgot about lighting the remaining eight candles as Michelle helped him climb out of his clothes. She drew him near to her in the semidarkness, holding him with her mouth as she undid her bra. Kissing her gently, Tobias removed the rest of her garments with a sweep of his hands. Soon he was partially over her on the table. He sensed her leaning back while he entered a void connecting them in a swirl of formless thought. Their senses stilled, then they entered it again, holding hands while they found each other. Again. Again.

Submerging from the depths, they gasped for air only to go back under. Nothing below seemed to content them, until one last final grope, not in unison, but within confusing seconds of the other, finding something that they hold on to. Michelle, who was on top of Tobias at this moment, gasped and dropped her head on his chest with a sigh. Tobias felt her release and smiled contentedly. How many and who came first didn't matter. All was lost, including the track of time.

They awoke as early morning light flickered from behind one of the shaded windows next to them. Tobias moved his head, squirming slightly under Michelle's weight. He was delighted to find that she was such a good sleeper. She gave no hint of being disturbed by his motions. Meanwhile, he realized that he was starving. He wiggled out from underneath her, tucking her back in place under a sheet.

Noticing a small smile on her face, he explained, "I'm going to fix some breakfast. Hungry?"

Without opening her eyes or saying a word, she nodded affirmatively.

"Great," he said. "Don't get up."

Donning his bathrobe, he went to prepare a feast.

Flight from Oblivion

Chapter Fifteen

Accusations have a way

Of reversing on themselves

Whereas understandings do not

Tune Reference: *Before You Accuse Me*

----Eric Clapton

"WHEN DO YOU go into work?" Tobias asked Michelle when she wandered into the kitchen area. He placed a fruit plate in front on the counter as he pointed to a nearby stool.

"Never," she replied. "Just joking. I have a full day, and now I don't know how I am going to make it.

Michelle stretched and yawned before sitting down across from Tobias. She was wearing only a nightshirt and underwear, matching Tobias's casualness. After taking a few sips from a cup of rose-hip tea, Michelle shook her head to regain her waking consciousness.

"Luckily, I don't have any patients scheduled," she admitted, savoring the brew in her hands. "I've been invited to a meeting at a local hospital."

"Sounds intense," Tobias said as he opened the refrigerator to retrieve fixings for an omelet.

Moving the stool closer to the counter, she explained, "Almost a year ago, I referred a two-month pregnant woman to their care after she developed eclampsia. She became even more toxic at the due date, and there was an emergency. The baby was stillborn. The hospital wonders whether something more could have been done on their end. We are convening behind closed doors so that the caregivers can learn from the experience. No one from the press or family is allowed. No lawyers either, though there isn't a lawsuit involved."

He remarked, "Sounds heavy."

Rising from her stool, she took a few steps around the counter as she became more animated. She told him, "The head doctors want to learn what happened for educational purposes. They asked me to come along for the ride."

Tobias cracked a few eggs in a bowl in front of Michelle and began stirring them vigorously. He commented, "Good for you. It's a nice gesture on their part; however, both you and I know that the mother should have started on a detox program at least one year before getting pregnant."

Michelle confessed, "I like to get them two years before they get pregnant, dad and mom." Then she added, "I think the hospital did the best they could under the circumstances."

Tobias observed, "The legal world sometimes obscures truth."

Fully awake now, Michelle continued her narration, "Most hospitals roll over on lawsuits to avoid lengthy, disruptive legal investigations. They figure that it is more cost effective to pay out front than hire lawyers. Even if they win, people lose out in quality of life."

Tobias poured the egg mixture into a hot skillet. The pan sputtered as the cold substance hit the hot metal. Quickly waving a spatula over the contents, he added, "Unfortunately, nobody addresses the parents from the medical standpoint."

Michelle leaned over the counter and watched him. She rejoined, "Most think that it is okay to break an arm because insurance will pay for it."

Tobias smirked. Michelle's posturing over the counter distracted him as her shirt rode up over an exposed thigh. Instead of addressing the half-naked woman in the kitchen, he lectured, "The average American attitude is lackadaisical when it comes to self-care. They are like overgrown babies who cry when their lollipops are taken. Forget about asking an obese person to diet, exercise, or seek addiction counseling; they would rather get a tummy tuck, paid by insurance---then they wonder why their newborn exhibits neurological damage associated with malnourishment. Autism is becoming epidemic. Unfortunately, we all bear the cost of their neglect. People need to avoid doing the things that insurance covers, rather than take risks because they are covered."

"Yes, most would rather eat junk food and get shots. Junk food lowers immunity," Michelle stated, handing Tobias a potholder so that he wouldn't burn himself. "For the pioneers, it was do or die. Records show that they practiced self-care like a seasonal ritual. It may not have been the correct thing to do, but they were often on the right track by today's knowledge."

"I don't do abortions, and I don't do vaccines, either. These are complex decisions, and I prefer to keep my focus on life-supporting spins in life. Instead, I refer the high-risk patients to people like you for evaluation." Changing the subject slightly, Tobias noted, "I just heard on the radio that fifty-four neurologists walked out of the university hospital because of the soaring malpractice rates."

"At least they could afford to retire. Unfortunately, there won't be anyone left for my obstinate, high-risk patients," Michelle mused. Then she walked away from the counter and checked her nails to determine whether they were too long for her work. Dropping her arms at her side, she came around the counter to gather eating utensils. She mentioned, "I met a few early retirees at a party last week. Imagine leaving behind all that education to go on bicycle trips. They already seem bored."

Tobias smiled, turning his head to track the assistance. "It is a balance." He added, "What a drain of resources! I shudder at the replacements. Lately the clinic has been noting how many of the new clients seem to be covert intelligence agents. Coming from all over the world---Russia, Israel, the software industry---they get caught rifling through desks with their small children. They blame it on their children's curiosity, but we know better, though few of us are parents yet. I learned that one patient, who is from the former Nazis-German portion of Czechoslovakia, directs the regional vaccine manufacturing company several miles away. The interns give her a homeopathic, hoping that they have determined the correct one."

"What remedy did she get?" Michelle asked, rattling the forks and spoons against each other as she collected them from a drawer.

"They decided on Hydrophobinum 200K for the dog-eat-dog world," Tobias told her.

"That's homeopathic *rabies*. The dose is considered safe enough for pregnant women," Michelle observed.

"Yes, hopefully there will be one less angry dog in the world," Tobias announced. "I am more concerned about the patients who come from the university hospital. After the latest turnover of neurologists, they all seem to have psychiatrists from South America."

"Do you think that the retirees are being replaced with physicians from Nazis Germany?" Michelle pondered out loud.

"It appears that the Nazis from South America bring all their medical research," Tobias quipped. "Although homeopathy originated in Germany, it presents a conflict for Nazis Germans. Like falun gong, they have a different spin on the Chinese symbol for good luck, and it is called a swastika."

"They don't want to empower their people," Michelle speculated.

"Or teach them social skills," Tobias observed. "The clinic has learned to spot agents by their rudeness. They usually get referred back to the Nazis doc, who will give them mind-controlling drugs---which in their case isn't always such a bad thing. However, we usually scare them off first, because they freak when the intern sees right through them."

"Congratulations to the interns for identifying good health and being discriminate," Michelle said.

Tossing some finely diced potatoes in a skillet, Tobias used a wooden spoon to keep the hash browns from burning. Then he nodded in the direction of the warming oven. "There are organic muffins inside. Help yourself. I don't have any coffee around the place, only green tea if it is caffeine that you need. No juice; it has too high of a sugar content."

"I'm fine," Michelle insisted firmly as she slipped to the other side of the counter. She pulled some muffins out and called to Tobias, "How many do you want?"

"Two," he answered as he scooped the scrambled eggs onto a platter. He noticed how well Michelle found her way around the small kitchen, almost as if she belonged. He continued, "I've also noticed that my favorite Thai restaurant went out of business, almost overnight. My friend from college thinks that they were pushed out for similar reasons as the neurology walkout."

"Yes, I started to refer my emergency cases to a Swedish hospital. They are more neutral. This is like WWII all over again," she said. Glancing at her watch, Michelle announced, "I gotta run. There are some papers I can gather for the hospital meeting."

Tobias offered, "I don't go into clinic until ten. You can have the shower first."

Remaining in his robe, Tobias cleaned the kitchen and checked the messages on his phone's voice machine. He noticed there was a call from an acquaintance he'd made during a kayak trip around the San Juans. Curious, Tobias mused over the reason for the call. Without leaving much information, Joe had simply asked Tobias to phone him. It has been almost two years since he met Joseph O'Connor and saved him from a visit to the emergency room. Tobias's collection of bandages, homeopathics, and herbal ointments had worked well in the backcountry where the closest medical facilities were two days' paddle away. Intent on finishing his trek, Joe had been extremely grateful for Tobias's assistance. Joe kept his focus despite the odds. Though they had not talked at any great depth, they maintained some contact. Until this moment, their relationship had involved Tobias serving as a resource for Joe while Tobias watched Joe's lifelong journey like a hawk.

Tobias looked up from his notepad near the phone as Michelle entered the room. Showered and almost fully dressed, she tossed her hair from side to side as she towel-dried her long black hair. She smiled at him before searching for her heeled shoes. Having donned a fresh white blouse and blue skirt, Michelle seemed radiant as a sunbeam emanating from a window. Tobias watched her appearance transform from slightly disheveled to kempt and professional as she prepared to face the world, which she greeted like a new dawn. It occurred to him that it *was* a new world, one built on the ashes of the old. He rose from his sitting position near the phone to kiss her good-bye.

Despite being on the threshold of a new beginning, Tobias felt the warm grip of Joe's call. It pulled at him in an invisible energetic hold, almost holding him back. Curious, Tobias contrasted the formless pull from Joe as he approached Michelle. Another thought crossed his mind. Rather than yield to one or the other, Tobias merged the two people in his consciousness, and he asked, "Ever read *The Starship and the Canoe*?"

Then he softly kissed her before drawing away to await her reply.

"Funny, you should ask," Michelle began, still savoring Tobias's affection. Smiling again, she revealed, "I ran into the author's father at the organic cafe. It was the day after a girlfriend and I attended the father's lecture at the university."

"Yeah, I went to the presentation too, but I didn't see you," Tobias mentioned.

"My girlfriend got his autograph on a twenty-year old article in *Scientific American*. She has an undergraduate degree in physics and wanted to hear the author's lecture. He is the nicest man." Then she shouldered her overnight bag, pausing briefly to eye Tobias before leaving. She added, "He spoke about going to Mars, though his article was on grand unified theory."

"GUTS," Tobias murmured softly as his gaze fell to his bare feet.

"And we know all about guts," Michelle told him with a wink. "I'll see you at the clinic, if you don't hear from me earlier."

Tobias grinned a little as he closed the door behind her. He appreciated the fact that Michelle had rather permanently walked into his life and condo in so many words. There wasn't anything more he wanted to tell her at the moment.

Flight from Oblivion

Chapter Sixteen

Let the space-nut heroes

Do all the overachieving for us

Then let them go fly off to oblivion

It's a free world

Tune Reference: *Space Oddity*

----David Bowie

AFTER MICHELLE LEFT, Tobias returned Joe's call. "Hey, what's going on?'

"Seems we have some mutual acquaintances," Joe told him. "I have two friends who have been hiking around Mount St. Helens. One of them twisted her ankle. Can you help them?"

"Yes, I am good with ankles," Tobias said. "Who are they?"

"Donna and Carrie said that they met you during spring break in college," Joe responded.

"Yes, I recall dancing with them on a Valentine's Day in Dallas many years ago. I had an interesting discussion with Carrie the next day. It sorta sent me on my path to the Pacific Northwest."

"I can't talk much. My lines are tapped," Joe informed him. "Check with the ranger station at Ape Cave for the location of their campground."

Late in the afternoon, after finishing his work in the clinic, Tobias told his colleagues that he was going on a search-and-rescue operation at Mount

St. Helens at the request of old friend. He mentioned the brief, wiretapped phone call, and suggested measures to protect their own lines. Then he showered and changed clothes in the facilities. After refreshing himself, he placed his doctor's bag in the car, grabbed a sandwich, and drove to the station. Enjoying the drive past tall cedars and hemlocks, he arrived at the ranger station shortly before dusk. He caught a view of the mountain as he slipped out of his hybrid vehicle. The snow-capped active volcano loomed in the distance, glistening visibly in the rapidly disappearing sunlight. Looking around, Tobias surveyed the region carefully before taking a deep breath and allowing his shoulders to drop. The Neanderthals were around for his protection from the ivy-league occultist landholders in the area. Ever since the collapse of the high-rises in New York, they'd run the higher levels of security for the national park, where the energy became polarized between the light and the dark. They targeted tourists by the brightness of their aura and other aspects. Maintaining a low-profile attitude, he donned sunglasses and a hat. Tobias turned toward the ranger's office, while eyeing the woods and the parked car as if he might decide to make a run for it.

As he entered headquarters, Tobias was approached by an officer in uniform. She smiled cheerfully when she saw him. With a nod, she encouraged him to speak his mind.

"I'm looking for a message from someone named Joe O'Connor," Tobias said.

Rising from her seated position, she recovered a map from a nearby drawer and began marking it. She told him, "I don't know about Joe, but I can tell you where you can find his two friends."

Tobias removed his glasses and hat. With a smile, he said, "Good deal."

Grabbing the map, he left for his car and drove to the trailhead. There were a few cars in the lot with backcountry stickers. After parking in a slot where it would be difficult to slide another car next to his, he hiked up the trail with his pack. Several miles upstream, he found the two women camping near a waterfall.

"Long time no see," he said to Donna and Carrie.

Donna rushed toward him to give him a hug, while Carrie waved at him from her position on the ground. Then he went over to Carrie and began examining her left ankle, moving the soft tissues into place. They both heard a soft click as the joint moved into alignment with the rest of her body.

"You got triggered," he told her. "I'll need to check the vertebrae in your neck. I bet those are torqued as well."

Carrie lay flat on her sleeping bag as Tobias slid the vertebra into place. He coached her as he worked, "This ankle mishap is providing you cover. Do you hear the subterranean explosions? You are not walking on firm ground." Offering her a homeopathic remedy before working any further, he explained, "You need to be grounded before *being* in the world."

"*Being*?" Carrie echoed as if contemplating his words deeply.

"You must apply yourself to save your soul. The situation reflects the injury. You chose a very arduous road test in venturing to this particular mountain. From our conversations in the past, I know that you should know better."

Crossing her arms, Donna listened thoughtfully to Tobias's assessment. He tossed her a quick glance but then resumed his focus on Carrie. Ignoring Donna's obvious consternation, he continued, "It is time for a little re-parenting before you get tripped up by those dynamiting a tunnel beneath your feet."

"Why are they building a tunnel?" Donna asked, dropping her arms to her side.

"Human trafficking," Tobias replied, checking Carrie's head for alignment and cranial-sacral rhythm. "The traumatized youngsters are exploited for innovations in various electronics industries. There is no escape now. The higher one strives, the stronger the spotlight. They pursue all the fish that run away."

Tobias removed his hands from her head, while Carrie sat up and ruefully rubbed her ankle. "I understand," she said. "I get to grow up."

"I am not going to ask you about all the hows and whys about why you failed this latest road test. It's a privilege and a honor," Tobias said. "Being lucky and strong doesn't cut it. Not anymore. It is a different world. Your task is to fly away from your attackers and return to peck out their eyes."

Donna sat down on a log next to them. She excitedly nodded her head at Carrie when she heard about the latest mission. Carrie laughed.

Tobias rummaged through his bag and pulled out an Ace bandage and some rice milk. Breaking open a capsule into a camper's cup, he mixed the milk with the anti-inflammatory botanicals from the capsule. Then he made a paste and dunked the bandage through the brilliant-yellow substance. "It will make a mess," he said, offering to bandage her ankle. "But so does surgery. You'll be able to walk out of here tomorrow morning. That I know."

Donna stared at the amethyst bracelet around Tobias's wrist as he worked. "Before you leave, you must tell us the history of the bracelet," she said.

Tobias stopped in midair and momentarily turned toward her. "It was given to me by a mechanic at the airplane museum. He worked with

Interpol." Facing Carrie again, he finished his work. "The bracelet belonged to a French fighter pilot in World War I."

"How did he die?" Donna quizzed him as Tobias sat down on a nearby log.

"He was killed escaping the horrors of experimentation destined for POWs," Tobias answered. Resting on the log, he dropped his hands and related, "It wasn't like Snoopy fighting the Red Baron. The Red Baron associated with the robber barons. The oil barons later imported his operations. By WWII, the French intelligence network superseded the parlors of the French Revolution." Wiping his brow, he continued after glancing at his audience, "Through their connections with the ratlines governing Italy, French social networks convinced the Black Prince to not bring his Italian submarines to New York."

Donna bounced on the log where she had been sitting quietly. "I heard about that fascist plan. As Joe will tell you, the prince came from the same family that stole Da Vinci's engineering work. Like Joe and his company, Da Vinci established a knighthood to protect commerce on the Silk Road. They called themselves the Eagles."

Tobias looked at her. Ending, his story about the bracelet, he said, "The French were in Dallas on November 22, 1963, for social reasons. Fortunately, someone lowered their gun and saved us all from World War III. By the time the president's motorcade arrived in Dealey Plaza, the Nazis stranglehold on France and the United States was equal."

"The planet died in Dallas," Donna murmured.

"Yes, but all hope was not lost," Tobias said.

With a few more instructions for the care of Carrie's ankle, Tobias packed his gear and left. He smiled and waved at the overnight campers before heading back down the trail. By the time he returned to his car, there was a couple from the local military base checking out his vehicle's chassis. Dressed in running clothes, they self-consciously closed their packs when they saw Tobias. They moved slowly away from the car, while pretending to do stretches for a running hike. Tobias dove behind the steering wheel and left them in the dust. He sensed that he had arrived just in time, before they altered his laptop irreparably or planted something on his car.

Donna called Tobias the next morning to report that Carrie had easily walked down the mountain, as expected. She promised to remain in contact and thanked him for his assistance. They kept the conversation short and cryptic in case the line was tapped.

Several months later, when the tension in the air had subsided, Tobias conferred with one of his associates at the organic cafe near the Portland clinic.

"No glue can hold this planet together," Tobias told his colleague. "There is no grand unified theory. We need to let go of the garbage." Then he changed the subject, "The slain president belonged to his older brother and sister. You can read the auras from the pictures."

His colleague silently nodded at him. Taking a deep breath, the man shrugged and opened his hands in a gesture toward Tobias. He continued, "Tragedies are often dished as entertainment, like the war games in the Roman coliseums. Viewers are deluded into believing that they are far removed from the herds being shipped to concentration camps. The slain president's older siblings were the ones beaten down by the various genocides of WWII, later uncovered by those who cared about them."

Tobias bowed his head and leaned closer to the man across from him. He said, "I know, Jim. While most African Americans wanted the nation to lynch the bullies, they were reluctant to accept MLK's socialist sponsors, the same ones driving the assassination in Dallas. When African cannibals take out the son of a robber baron---we get global deforestation. Cannibals sold their African neighbors to the East India Company. Though no pun intended, the world is truly 'out of its tree.'"

Jim rejoined, "Yes, world solutions require a druid, an authentic naturopathic physician, not an allopathic wash-out, someone who really does like trees."

"Yes, I like that oath we took 'First Do No Harm.' It would have shut down the national practice of lobotomies, perhaps saving at least one president. Whereas some animals do eat their young, an animal is considered sick if it messes in the nest."

His colleague silently nodded at him. Addressing Tobias formally, he said, "Dr. Jones, it must be that homeopathic that you have been taking. It is working. This is an interesting conclusion that you have made."

"I know, Jim," Tobias ruefully admitted. "Though I feel more together, my experience of the world does not. I think that I was taking on more than my fair share of abuse." Leaning back in his chair, Tobias added firmly, "And you know, I don't *want* to go to Mars. Why is so much money spent on a race to space, while much of the national infrastructure lies in decay? Marchers congregate in front of icons housed in the icy-cold stone temples, reminiscent of a fallen Greek civilization, and demand their freedom. If they were really smart, they would plant trees instead of memorials and get more oxygen to the heads of state. I like it here---the birds, the bees, the trees, the flora, the fauna...I don't want to live on Mars or in Russia."

"Said like a natural. You go, boy," Dr. Mansfield answered. "Most people can't handle the revelations. They would have to make a choice, because love makes a choice. Love does not march. It is not a military discipline. The builders of monuments confuse the issues. Ancient Greece and Rome lost though decay. Why adopt their architecture? The real models are the ones like Rosa Parks and those demanding the help of the National Guard to conduct the daily affairs of their lives."

"I know," Tobias said. "It is our daily choices that define us. By the time of the president's meeting with de Gaulle in Paris, the natural order had been restored. The fate of the US president remained with the jackal---an agreement forged with ruthless Apaches, but that is another story."

"MLK, his dreams, and love marches could not understand that the real problem was related to the theft of Geronimo's skull," Jim added.

Tobias smiled. He rejoined, "He should have gone to Yale instead of the Lincoln Memorial. Perhaps the National Guard would have helped MLK get an honorary degree. Instead he just fueled the gossips of J. Edgar Hoover's state militias. Likewise, the slain president's son never should have flown to Cape Cod under the influence of opiates. These days doctors get sued for not advising their patients to avoid the operation of heavy machinery, which I believe should include airplanes.

"The standard of care is to allow four days to clear the body of residue. However, the insurance models for health care are based on incidence rather than value. This means that the opiates would have been encouraged for the effect to fly higher. If that son had been truly an environmentalist, then he would have been allergic to the drug. People who care for the flora and fauna react to allopathic substances. You can imagine the setup for codependency. It is a different set of values, and you can see the hand of the East India Company in this tragedy. I am surprised the other passengers in the plane joined him. Would you get in a plane with a pilot recovering from a leg injury?"

"No, I made my mother's spouse get out of the car for drinking Pepsi and GMO-potato chips. I didn't want to drive while under the influence of a backseat driver, waiting for an accident to happen."

"It is the herd-going-over-the-cliff medical model that drives socialized medicine and insurance coverage."

"Yes, my mother would be the one to know. She always asked me 'If the herd went over the cliff, would I go with it?'"

"The medical model belongs to the cannibals rather than the value-based decision modeling techniques of the industrial engineers," Jim summarized. "I value the planet and this affects the lives of patients. However, if the military wants to kill us all, then the planet would not be a factor in health care."

"The eat-thy-neighbor medical model defined the medicine of the Renaissance. The Medici owned it and made their Knights Hospitallers abide by it. The slain president's departed siblings carried him across the grassy knoll to freedom. It was a ruthless way to beat the system, as the Apaches know." Tobias paused and reached inside a pocket to remove a rock. Placing the stone on the table for emphasis, he continued, "That's how a crystal called Apache Tears got named. The Apaches were the only ones to enjoy any measure of success since the fall of Eden. This is why the skull and bones occultism of the East India Company seized Geronimo's skull for their collection at Yale. He was Apache."

Jim gazed at the black stone on the table. Tobias's fingers traced some of the whitish-blue inclusions that streamed through the rock. The streams resembled the flow of tears. After uniformed soldiers from the Transylvania

Land Company pursued a group of Apache warriors, the Apaches rode over a cliff, evading capture. According to the tale, the tears of the survivors turned to obsidian and the resulting crystal was used to heal profound sorrow and pain.

Tobias removed his finger from the obsidian nodule and Jim spoke in a soft voice, "Benevolent extraterrestrials laced crystal skulls strategically on the earth's continents. There is a crystal skull in the British museum for display. Hoover and his aliens intended to ensnare the president's skull in the occult dynamics of the East India Company. The US attorney general refused to save his brother from family relations, which pertained to the TFX and Lindbergh baby kidnapping." Jim paused and looked down at his finished plate. Changing the subject, he asked, "How are you and Michelle? Rumor has it that you have been seeing each other on a personal basis."

"She's moved in," Tobias acknowledged. "We are planning to get married next year after the national conference. During our breaks we look at small houses together. I plan to leave the clinic soon and start a practice near Eugene, Oregon. Michelle wants to relocate her midwifery business to someplace where we both feel safe. Both of us are drawn to the forests above the town of Springfield. The locals say that Lincoln's ancestors settled there shortly before the Civil War broke out."

"Why did they leave?" Dr. Mansfield asked.

Tobias answered, "The Confederacy needed a reason to kill those involved with the underground railroad. Lincoln's ancestors fled the war zone."

"You mentioned that Michelle was related," Dr. Mansfield said.

"Her ancestors intermarried with Lincoln's relations in Germany-Switzerland," he added. "The homeopathic treatment has been clarifying our

DNA. We both are descendants of Bavarian woodcutters. They always settled near natural springs or woods that reminded them of the Black Forest."

"It is a beautiful area. There are many portals in the wooded areas. The Sasquatch roam freely. It's the perfect place for you, Tobias. You can confer with the Sasquatch all you wish."

"How did you know about the Sasquatch?" Tobias questioned.

"I'm a doctor, Tobias," he replied. "Besides, I know you. You can't fool us, not as much as you may think." Staring down at his plate, he rambled, "Years ago, the Grateful Dead donated money from their concerts to a creamery near Springfield, home of my favorite yogurt for probiotics. The endangered Western pond lily can be found there, along with oak, incense cedar, and red-legged frogs."

"It's in my blood," Tobias said, focusing on the earlier topic. "The healthier you get, the more coherent the DNA becomes. The expression of coherent DNA is less degraded, more compatible with life. The Sasquatch have eluded DNA contamination all these years. The ancestors cherished the communication with these creatures, and apparently I've inherited the responsibility of multidimensional networking."

"What's multidimensional networking?" he asked.

"I don't know. I'm trying to figure that out," Tobias responded. "It is like finding lost souls between the layers of existence. Can we change the subject?"

Instead of pursuing the matter, his colleague asked, "How did it go with the seminar in San Francisco?"

"The conference was great. A medical doctor even mentioned a few homeopathics for spiritual possession, though I do not use the same term for the condition. The case was linked to the Oakland earthquake. The patient dreamed about the bridge collapsing months before it happened. I prefer the more generalized *spiritual predator* to the term *possession*."

"Well, as they say possession is nine-tenths of the law," Dr. Mansfield quipped. He leaned forward and nervously glanced around the cafe. Something was bothering him.

"I would not be surprised," Tobias speculated, taking long sips from his cup of chai. "Another MD presented a case on *Radium bromatum*."

"I've heard about that one," Dr. Mansfield responded. He sat back, finally relaxing in his chair for a moment. Then he carefully weighed the utensil in his hands. "All the electronics in the room temporarily break down prior to the lecture. That is how *Radium bromatum* makes its presence known. The MD just stands there, smiling, while radium does it own thing. When the lights and video return, he begins the presentation."

"The case study was about a whistleblower, who was about to lose everything. It reminded me of my friend Joe, whom I stayed with during the conference. He is an engineer who left an aeronautics firm to start his own company."

"I bet there's a story there," Dr. Mansfield remarked. "Is he a whistleblower?"

"I don't think that I could label him as a whistleblower. He is more of an entrepreneur, though. You are correct, because there *is* more to the story," Tobias mentioned, rubbing his head. "Joe was intrigued with the notion of radiation as a type of communication. The homeopathic remedy deals with issues stemming from WWII, particularly pertaining to the concentration camps and use of nuclear power. It works to bring a fragmented world back together, breaking down barriers and going through walls. As a result of his investigations, Joe works with extraterrestrials and the other side. The aeronautics company went one direction, and Joe pursued the other. He has changed the way that I view history, especially the Mexican-American War. There is a lot of information to be integrated from a quantum physical perspective."

"Let's have the rest, Tobias. I sense that there is more to be said," his colleague insisted. "I gotta leave in twenty minutes to teach a class."

"Well, do you remember our last class on medical philosophy? It was taught by a full-blooded Native American. He demanded that we learn how to write chart notes for shamans as well as allopaths. I wrote about a heart patient who said that she would die if she had to go into her group-health hospital."

"I know; the members on my softball team write insurance software for the system," Dr. Mansfield confessed. "The catcher calls it 'group death.' It is a rowdy allopathic team, though I sometimes wonder what I am doing playing with them. They think that I am a pansy, and opposing teams beat me up once they learn my profession. Our pitcher was jailed for defacing tobacco billboards. He's an MD with the nonprofit community health center."

"Well, he has a point about group death. The patient died before her scheduled heart surgery. She looked fine at the consult---good vitals, no edema, steady heart rhythm. Several interns and another physician in the room agreed. After she passed on, her chart kept appearing at the clinic for an appointment, as if she wanted to see me from the other side. So I approached it from the perspective of a shaman, and this became the case for the class assignment. I used images from a book written by a Russian medical doctor, who researched the Siberian shamans. I felt that these images would keep the deceased patient from pestering me."

"Did it work?" Dr. Mansfield questioned.

"Yes. The Native American instructor was happy with the chart notes, and the deceased got off my case," Tobias admitted. "I provided some sort of closure for her."

"So what was she dying to tell you?" Dr. Mansfield pointedly asked Tobias.

Realizing that his astute colleague was not going to let him prematurely end the story of the patient, Tobias sighed. Waving his hands in the air in resignation, he concluded, "She is a soul from Arcturus."

"Why do think that she wanted you to know that?" Dr. Mansfield inquired.

"She wanted me to diagnose patients using intergalactic spirituality and evolution."

"Tough case," his colleague yielded, slapping his hands together as if closing a book.

"Our instructor appeared very excited about it," Tobias said ruefully. "It was just the beginning. There is more to the story. Remember the class where the topic of UFOs was mentioned?" Without waiting for Dr. Mansfield's response, Tobias continued, "There was a lecturer from the air force, who had done spiritual regressions with clients. They could recall other lives in the galaxy."

"They would be the ones to know," Dr. Mansfield answered.

"Well, what's a student to do, but learn! I observed that several of my patients at the clinic resonated with the light of the stars that I could eyeball with my eight-inch telescope. The radiating frequencies were the same. With the help of an engineer who lived across the street, I built radios while in high school. Seeing the electromagnetic projections on the oscilloscopes fascinated me."

"There's another story for you, Tobias," Dr. Mansfield said. "Imagine having the history of the universe unfold before you like the stratified history of a rock formation."

"Perhaps it all started with the classes called Physician Heal Thyself or Healing Philosophy 101. I can't even remember their names anymore, but I recall the one where the topic of disease as metaphor was discussed. The nature of life becomes an intriguing story."

Connecting the dots, Dr. Mansfield quizzed Tobias, "So what does Joe have to do with all this?"

"Joe confirmed my speculations, which wasn't comforting," Tobias said. "He is a runaway from an aeronautics company stocked with heady government contracts. There have been several intergalactic wars on the planet. Most people don't care to remember them."

Dr. Mansfield took a deep breath before glancing at his watch. He sighed at Tobias. Then he rose from his chair and warmly shook Tobias's hand. "I must get to class. Tobias, as always, it has been a memorable lunch. Thanks, for landing on this. I look forward to future discussions."

Chapter Seventeen

Girls can be cowboys, too

They call them cowgirls

Many of them do pursue happy endings

And destroy outlaws

Tune Reference: *Where Have All The Cowboys Gone?*

----Paula Cole

FOR THE FIRST time in his life, Tobias's plans proceeded as scheduled. Perhaps it had to do more with Michelle's timing rather than his own. They continued their work, and they married. Years later, they birthed two children into the world, spaced a conservative two years apart. Despite the trying years of his youth, Tobias easily nested into the new family dynamics.

Rapport with Michelle proved simple. With their busy workloads, they shared parenting and household chores. Often he would place a bag of groceries down on the kitchen table with the announcement, "Father bird brings home the worms."

This would be her cue for action. Usually Michelle would grin and place her paring knife down on the counter. Then she would kiss Tobias on the cheek before inspecting the contents. They would chatter as their two children slept or played in another room. These moments provided quality time, much needed with their schedules of on-call weekends. It seemed it never ended.

It was ten years later, and Tobias continued to make play out of work, but the topic of conversation had changed to reflect the deepening dark intrusion in their line of work. Like Joe and his startup company, Michelle and Tobias did their best to provide the best quality-of-life experience in their work. Owning their businesses gave them the freedom they needed to do this.

"I finally figured out why the most enlightening scientific research gets overlooked and why the famous investigator of GUTS became a fundraiser for outer space," Tobias began. "The scientific literature is owned by the same robber barons that funded Hitler. Hitler's group was into space projects. It wasn't just international competition. They still want to go there."

"Oh, I am sure that there is more to it than that," Michelle replied as she unpacked the bag of groceries and hurried back to her task in the kitchen.

Tobias followed her around the room, organizing the shelves behind her. Michelle resumed her position behind the counter with the paring knife and went back to chopping vegetables for ratatouille. After checking the heat underneath a pot on the stove, he went over to Michelle and nuzzled her left ear.

"Tell me more," he whispered, encouragingly. "I am an endangered species on the planet. I want to at least know what is going on."

"After the Civil War, the nation embarked on an industrial crusade. The homeopathic hospitals were replaced with aspirin and surgery just in time for World War II, a war that went down in history for its blatant, widespread genocide."

"It openly targeted the human family, while disguising specific attacks on Atlantean survivors like the Celtics," Tobias remarked, taking her in his arms, while being careful to avoid disturbing her work. "My great-aunt, who had been a field nurse at the Battle of the Bulge, sensed that the Irish brigades were being purposely destroyed outside of the scope of war."

"True, those types of studies never quite make the research literature," Michelle observed as she relaxed with Tobias's embrace. After her countenance softened, the desired effect, Tobias drew back and walked over to a nearby cupboard. He asked his wife, "Care for a cup of green tea?"

"Not now. I want to finish before the kids join us," she said. Michelle raised her head and glanced at the clock. Hurriedly, she began her discourse of the day as if rehearsing the points she might make in one of her guest lectures.

"So the Civil War resulted in the government becoming the plaything of the robber barons set up by the American Revolution. WWI established the dependence on technology. WWII beat out the opposition and developed a consumer base. Then the Vietnam War created addicts out of the consumers. Sounds like a business plan to me. The industry feeds on itself, now intent on building more machines to do the destruction---and perhaps some of the genocide. The politicians with a background in dealing addictive substances prove the most successful. A person needs to know how the system really works in order to govern it, if that happens to be still possible."

Tobias left the teakettle on the stove and walked over to a framed picture on the wall. He stared at the larger representation of the Kabbalah Tree that had hung in Michelle's office years ago. He quieted for a moment before remarking, "I am glad that you introduced me to the Tree of Life. I think that it is the key to understanding how we got caught in this world of self-destructive patterns."

"My pleasure, Tobias," Michelle said as she grabbed a cup of tea and sat down next to him. She had already put down the paring knife and tidied the kitchen during their casual discussion.

"I heard from an old acquaintance the other day," Tobias told her. "She showed me map of Gondwanaland, with an eye in the sky outlined on it. She says that some geology friends at Woodsport developed it. It's a small world. I met Donna and Carrie during an EMT course in college. They also have experienced similar frustration with the lack of intellectual freedom."

"It isn't just intellectual freedom---it also involves spiritual freedom," Michelle remarked. "If it is true that we are all souls from various places in the universe, then the souls will have different spiritual needs. The exceptions are the spiritual predators or the spiritually apathetic."

"Like vampires and those who sit on the fence," Tobias reflected. "One instructor called them *ferengi*."

"Yes."

"Is this race for technology about the DNA or the innovations?" Tobias pondered out loud.

"I don't know," Michelle answered. "You might have to ask them, but I wouldn't advise getting that close."

"Many of the latest innovations erode the DNA," Tobias surmised. "Without the memory, there is no regeneration, because there is no coherent guidance."

"It is like going to war without an intelligence outfit," Michelle observed. "Perhaps the robber barons prefer to have armies of ants. Metaphorically, trees refer to lineage or ancestry. The Tree of Knowledge is akin to *humoral immunity*, where the body gets smarter through cause and effect. In comparison, the Tree of Life represents the spiritual DNA, where the imprint is for life rather than death as a final destiny."

"The Tree of Life counters chaos theory or the de-evolutionary spirit," Tobias said.

"Rather than survival of the fittest, it becomes survival of the most spirited," Michelle acknowledged. "Darwin only echoed the chaos resulting from the attack on the Garden of Eden."

"What attack?" Tobias questioned. "Do you mean that the garden was infiltrated by dark forces? It wasn't a simple case of disobedience."

"Only the ant in charge of the army would invent a rule that would hang up the whole of humanity," Michelle quipped.

"You have a point," Tobias rejoined. "It must have been a power play for dominating the planet."

"Back to the original argument," Michelle said, swirling the herbs around in her teacup as she spoke. "The supposed conflict fatally destroyed harmony, a pre-existing condition. It must have come from an outside force rather than from within. This dark force endangered the lives of those it manipulated. It was insensitive to the needs of the inhabitants."

"As above, so below," Tobias reflected. "Heaven, itself was at risk. The garden reflected another reality elsewhere in the universe."

"In other words, the celestial realm, or heaven, was attacked as well," Michelle continued. She nodded her head as she savored this point. Clasping her warm cup in her hands, she surmised, "Like the realities of today, it was for the sake of knowledge or technology."

"Apparently this is an old problem," Tobias remarked. After a few dips of his tea bag, he took it out of his cup and deposited on a nearby saucer. "It isn't over yet. Joe says that the trees separated when Pangea divided into two smaller subcontinents." He gazed at Michelle over the steam arising from his brew, and told her, "The Tree of Life went to Gondwanaland, whereas the Tree of Knowledge went with the northern portion. The imprint for the Tree of Life was encoded in the DNA of those who chose to embody its principles, known as the Kabbalah. They started a new race of spiritual warriors who were also wizards or shamans." He stopped the conversation briefly to take the pressure off of her. The boys would be awake soon. Their time together was limited. Taking a deep breath, Tobias dove for the punch lines, "Joe and his buddies say that this was the beginning of the *Dragon flyers*, who learned how to levitate the reptilian forms along with the other types of dragons. Some had fur or feathers and were very colorful with gemstones studded in their flesh and scales. The *Dragon flyers* were like flying cowboys. It was the enlightenment that came as a result of their choosing to remember their spiritual origins."

"Ride 'em, cowboy," Michelle happily murmured, reaching over the teacup to take his hand. "Like our children---we want to raise them without breaking their spirits. That is why we both do what we do."

"It is like the difference between a marching ant and spiritual warrior," Tobias said, rising from the table and ushering her towards the bedroom. "If we get lucky, then perhaps the robber barons running the industry will forget their motivations. If they forget to respect their DNA, then they will become dysfunctional."

"Then we will need to duck when it hits the fan or reaches critical proportions. The result would be a deadbeat or monster," Michelle said. She left her cup on the table and rushed upstairs.

"Hmm," Tobias hummed. He followed her up the stairs with his teacup in hand. The vapor from the contents rose to his nostrils. Calmed by the aroma and scintillating conversation with Michelle, he continued, "By then, we will need to hide in an alternative reality, hopefully one with a higher frequency." Then Tobias stopped to think for a moment, before adding, "Joe said that the eye on the Eye-in-the-Sky is awakening now. It is a Zen phenomenon."

Chapter Eighteen

In the Wild West

Divisions prove lethal

People work together

To survive

Tune Reference: *Deep In The West*

----Shake Russell and Dana Cooper

"THE LIFEGUARDS SEE all," Tobias repeated to Carrie a few days after the discussion with Michelle. "You told me this when we were undergraduates in college---remember? Carrie, I need more information on this eye-in-the-sky during the existence of Gondwanaland," Tobias began. "How did Donna ever come up with it?"

"They mapped out the location of the crystal skulls on various continents and then worked backward," Carrie said over the phone. "We are planning a geophysics survey on the Oregon coast for the summer of 2009. We want to compare the sand there with the dome of the rock in Jerusalem. Scientists claim that the beach deposits have the same age and constituents as the rock."

Changing the subject, Tobias reflected, "'The meaning of life is to see.' That is a quote from an eight-century Zen master. I want to know about Gondwanaland and its awakened eye."

"It is the manifestation of a clear day vision," Carrie told him. "As they say, to see clearly is poetry. It is similar to Frederick Franck's art, which was the result of his awareness of non-duality."

"Like an astute physician diagnosing a patient," Tobias declared.

"Could be," Carrie remarked. "In non-dual awareness, the Zen masters access paradise through the perceptions of the awakened eye."

"OK, let me get this story straight," Tobias insisted. "The high priestesses lived inside the iris of the eye drawn on your map."

"Yes," Carrie responded, "after the Garden of Eden was invaded by Serpentine aliens, refugees from other star systems attempted to establish heaven on earth, literally." Then she added, "Donna says that there was Serpentine infiltration of Lilith's subconscious."

"Who was Lilith?" Tobias asked.

"Lilith was the first failed female prototype. She was the human model before Eve," Carrie answered. "She chose to dominate Eden, and she sided with the Serpentines. She was pregnant when she left, and her child later became known as Morgan Le Fey."

Tobias questioned her, "Wasn't Morgan Le Fey the one who attacked the earth spirits during Camelon?" Without waiting for her response, he added, "It wasn't about Camelot, which is a deceitful fable told by the enemies of Camelon. Camelon refers to an ancient kingdom once established off the Scottish coast near the present town of Camelon, whereas Camulodunum is the name of the Roman settlement built on top of Queen Boudica's fortress in Britain. Her surviving grandson, Cole I, fled and created Camelon. He was the great-grandfather of King Arthur." Tobias paused to catch his breath, and Carrie did not interrupt him. He continued, "Today, Camulodunum is known as Colchester, which is named after his traitorous nephew, King Cole II. He married his daughter with the invading Roman emperor Constantius. The grandson of King Cole II formed Constantinople after the Turks razed Camelon."

"Yes," Carrie responded. "Morgan Le Fey didn't care for fairies. King Arthur and the emperor Constantine were distant cousins as well as enemies. Constantine formed a church where he could be sainted for his actions."

"I can see how it all started," Tobias observed. "Did Lilith produce any progeny with the Serpentines?"

"Her son was called Hades." Carrie continued, "Hades and his sister came back and attacked the civilization on Gondwanaland. Another sister, Psyche, placed a curse on Eve, which rendered her vulnerable to male dominance."

"Curses are removed with love," Tobias mused. "Though I always sensed that the gender war was not a real one, I never thought of the conflict as a curse. This accounts for much of the aggression of Greek gods such as Zeus."

"Eventually it destroyed those who seeded the refugee civilizations on the planet. The cursed sponsors became inflexible and calcified."

"No surprise there," Tobias remarked. "Were those who regrouped on Gondwanaland also attacked? Were there any survivors?"

Carrie answered, "The only survivor of Gondwanaland was male. Male warriors protected the high priestesses. They lived in the iris portion. This one later returned as John the Baptist."

Tobias interrupted Carrie's rendition. Wishing for clarity on another pertinent detail, he pressed, "It is my understanding that Gondwanaland served as a base for the transportation of souls."

"Yes, it was a soul transport system, or STN, for intergalactic refugees assuming the human form. The high priestesses were healers for the wounded souls."

"Where does Arcturus come in?" he asked. "I had a patient who wanted to impress me with the notion that she was an Arcturian."

Carrie added, "Arcturus is the name of a giant red star in our galaxy. The Arcturians were among the first group of fragmented souls. Only the Pleiades system remained intact. For some reason, they enjoyed immunity from the chaos wrought by the Serpentine invasions."

"Oh, I remember," Tobias said. "The Pleiades system is known as the 'seven sisters.'"

Carrie mentioned, "Sometime before becoming Hades's willing consort, Persephone birthed seven females for the two Pleiadian Kings. The girls served as the godhead for the universe and met with the Orion Council."

"What was the Orion council? I know Orion is the constellation of the hunter."

"The Orion Council collected the refugees in the universe, and they approached the godhead to provide a portal between the heaven and earth. When Gondwanaland was attacked, the portal was destroyed along with the Pleiades."

"A patient told me that the Pleiades is almost rebuilt now," Tobias commented.

"Maybe that is why the eye of Gondwanaland is awakening," Carrie observed. "The vision is being restored."

Tobias continued his story. "A colleague of mine has a father in the Czech Republic. His family reminds me of the Dragon flyers that you have told me about. The man came down with a gallbladder tumor that affected pancreatic function as well. An intuitive from England said that it was partially due to a family curse. One of my naturopathic interns traced the curse to Saint Bridget. Apparently, Morgan Le Fey cursed Bridget before crucifying her for the nature spirits. Her descendants bore the curse of always fighting for the light---which isn't such a bad curse. The problem is that it was compulsory, and they could not choose their battles, even if it meant taking on Godzilla. The intern, who is of Welsh ancestry, found that she had the curse as well. This means that the Slavs and western Europe mated during the time of the legendary Dragon flyers. Unlike the curse on Eve, the hex on Bridget affected the males. Lincoln descended from Bridget, who came from the Conn Druid family and married into a Welsh-German tribe. Lincoln lost several sons to this curse. Many died unknown. Lincoln's biological parents were Welsh and German."

"It makes sense."

Lowering his voice, Tobias offered, "Curses are countered by love, and they can be annulled through developing immunity. Otherwise, they can be removed by skilled professionals." Then he rambled in a manner similar to his wife, "The curse on Eve's descendants is removed by first cutting cords, or energetic links, with Morgan Le Fey, the archetypal female villain. Her rabid soul infected almost the entire universe as it tried to recreate itself on Gondwanaland. The cords with Morgan Le Fey are found a centimeter lateral from the sternum. They are at the level of the sixth rib, possibly the one that Eve got from Adam."

"Thanks," Carrie said. Ending the conversation, she promised Tobias, "I'll get on that Eve curse right away. "You'll enjoy meeting Joan on the Oregon beach this summer. She is looking forward to a mini-vacation. Her husband says that her work is getting to her. He is bringing her along on one

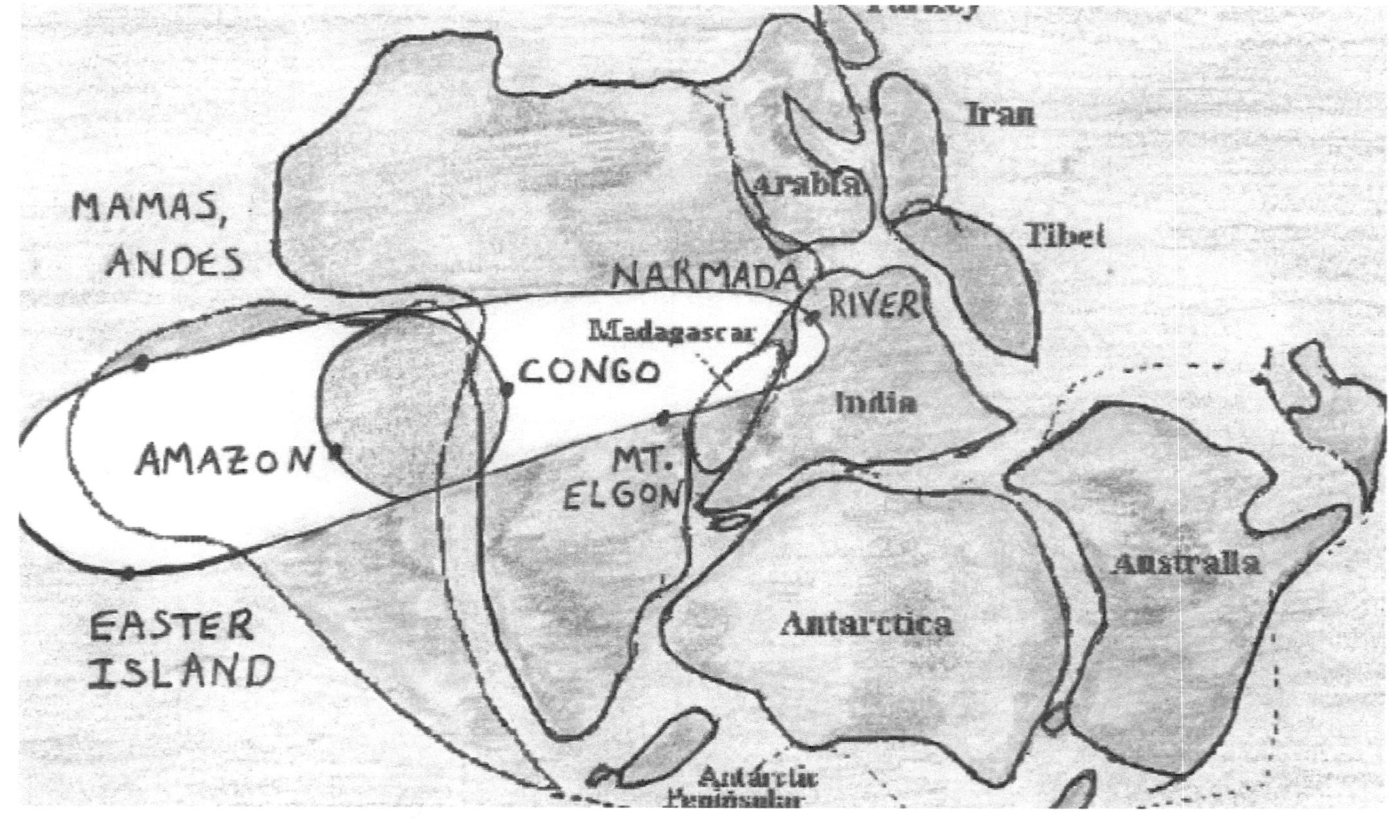

MAMAS, ANDES
Turkey
Iran
Arabia
Tibet
NARMADA
RIVER
Madagascar
CONGO
India
AMAZON
MT. ELGON
Australia
EASTER ISLAND
Antarctica
Antarctic Peninsular

of his geophysical surveys."

Chapter Nineteen

Just the motion of living life
Can keep you from straying
From the path where you belong

Tune Reference: *Pancho & Lefty*

----Townes Van Zandt

LATER THAT SUMMER, Tobias arranged to meet Joan on the beach near a small coastal town. Tobias left the family at home and took the dog with him. Arriving ahead of schedule, he watched the gray surf billowing into a cloud over the waves. Tobias knelt over a sand dollar left in the sand during low tide and pried it free. As he tossed it back into the frosted, rolling waters, he watched the dim sunlight etch silver streaks across the horizon. He looked down at the shiny grains of sand and remained still as his dog raced past him in pursuit of some seagulls. The dog's presence announced itself by the splish-splash of her fuzzy white feet. The yellow, thick-coated mutt had enough Border collie genes in her that she perpetually herded everything from cats to ducks. As soon as all the gulls on the beach had been corralled in the sea, the satisfied pup stopped knee-deep in the waves, searching the horizon for something else to herd.

"Tin-Tin," he yelled, cupping his hands over his mouth to form a speaker.

The dog perked her golden ears and ran at full speed toward him. The pup had earned her name from Tobias. The sound of the galloping dog on the wet beach resembled the rattling of pebbles in a tin can. Tobias sidestepped the pup to avoid a muddy spray. *I'll need to allow extra time to clean the dog before I let her back in the car carrier*, he thought. Absorbed by his inner thoughts of the dog, Tobias seemed startled when Joan appeared out of the enveloping mists to stand beside him. The osteopathic physician cut a wispy figure; this seemed to be characteristic of naturopathic females. This natural air of familiarity caught him off balance, and Tin-Tin knocked him over.

Ignoring Tobias's romp in the sand with the mangy pup, Joan got straight to the focus of their prearranged meeting. She began, "Donna told me that the sand on the Oregon coast is related not only to the dome of the rock but the Island Nation in the Pacific as well."

"Do you mean Tonga?" Tobias asked, rising to his feet. He shook his head to collect his thoughts, which had been sidelined by one of his best friends. Instead of waiting for her reply, he explained, as his eyes tracked his pup for the next muddy move, "Supposedly they are descendants from one of the Lost Tribes of Israel. It was the tribe headed by Naphtali, progenitors of the kahuna, or red-eyed seers. They are recognized by the red rims of their eyelids. They see between worlds and drink kava." Tobias stopped and turned around in a circle as his still-romping dog almost toppled him. He added, "Rumor has it that the natives have been abusing the kava lately. I only used it to get through finals in Pathology class. The multidimensional effect comes in handy when you are presented every disease intimate to humankind."

"*Kava*---what?" Joan asked, ignoring the antics of the pup and master. "The multidimensional approach sounds refreshing. Where can I find this kava stuff?"

Tobias paused to reflect on her words for a moment. He seemed surprised by her willingness to pursue a naturopathic concoction. Waving his hand across his face to shield himself from his splashing mutt, Tobias switched gears and thought about the stagnation that had become pathological on the islands. He wandered toward the dog wading in the surf. As any good cowboy knew, one had to keep moving like grains of sand on the beach. Moving like a tumbleweed, a rambling man could spin around the world like the wheels of a whirling chakra. There was infinite peace to be found in movement, as steady as the ocean breeze rolling grains of salt and constantly sculpting the planet. Such motion required a certain type of rough-hewn character who could sniff this motion in air and be shaped without being eroded. The cowboy in his soul found his home on the winding trail.

"My husband's geology lab did a survey and found a rip in the space-time continuum," Joan explained, before Tobias got knee-deep in front of his dog. She went on to entertain him with a lengthy narrative of her spouse's adventure, "We journeyed to a grave marker on one of the islands. It proved to be a portal to Temple Mound in Jerusalem. There were three triangles, of silver, white, and gold, which appeared as light *seeing* into the ground. Two of the triangles were true, whereas one had been adulterated. The adulterated triangle required healing. Afterward, we closed it, so that the *nephilim*, or dark angels, could not use it." After pausing for a moment to collect her thoughts and step away from the water spewing off Tobias, Joan continued, "The earth has two important portals, which control the many others on the planet. The one in Tonga has no name, but it serves to counter the Temple of Mound portal."

"Interesting," Tobias remarked as he threw another sand dollar back into the tide. Despite Joan's attempt to hold him to the shore with her tale, he waded through the water up to his knees. He braved the chance that his running dog would come splashing near him. The temperature of the Pacific Ocean hovered at approximately fifty-five degrees Fahrenheit this far north on the continent. It posed a hypothermal threat for those who lingered in the waves without wet suits. Focusing on the spot where the sand dollar had landed in the water, he pretended to ignore the rushing dog. He told Joan, "This means that the earth's chakras are most likely contaminated."

"*Chakras*?" Joan questioned. "Do you mean to say that the planet has chakras like the spinning wheels of energy on the human body?"

"Yes," Tobias said, backing away from the incoming surf and heading for shallower waters. A few waves rolled over his ankles, while he steadied himself in the sandy bottom. Tobias kicked around some waters droplets with his feet, as if dribbling a soccer ball, before elaborating, "Chakras mostly pertain to the psycho-spiritual realm. They are emotional wheels of electromagnetic energy, but Dr. Candace Pert's work proves we must never underestimate the power of emotions on physiology. They have their own set of molecules."

"Do you have a chakra system that correlates to Carrie's Time Wrinkle of 1986?" she quizzed him, while watching the swirls of frothy waves circling around her legs.

"I'll give it to you straight," Tobias answered. He stooped over an unfurling wave to tug at another sand dollar. Then he began, "Mount Kailash: root chakra. Second chakra: Haleakala Crater in Maui."

Joan watched Tobias pry the purple disc free. "Why Maui?"

Examining the velvet surface of the sand dollar in his hand, Tobias responded, "Until Captain Cook arrived, the Hawaiians enjoyed some of the healthiest sexual relationships on the planet." He hurled the disc back into the ocean like a Frisbee, and he added, "Power chakra: Island of the Sun at Lake Titicaca, on the border of Peru and Bolivia. The lore claims that the region is the center of evolution. Empowerment comes from being able to recreate oneself, while moving forward."

"OK," Joan said as Tobias walked out of the waves and up the beach.

"Yep," Tobias surmised, tossing another sand dollar toward the horizon. "The heart chakra is Stonehenge. Some would protest and say that it is a power spot, but I prefer the adage Love Makes a Choice. There is a lot of power in love, particularly regarding free choice."

Joan remained silent as if thoughtfully considering his words. She placed her hands on her hips and studied his face. A seagull cried overhead, and she turned her attention to its flight over the horizon.

Tobias resumed, explaining his next choice of planetary chakras. This time he playfully spoke in a voice that might have belonged to an announcer at the Academy Awards. "The fifth, or communications, chakra deserves two forms for gender expression. Balance becomes paramount under the painful circumstances. The best spot for expression and communication is Hollywood, California."

Joan lightly clapped her hands in the light of a sunbeam streaking through the clouds. Using a tone reserved for clinical presentations, she told him, "Hollywood was an ancient home for the Lacerta, who played a critical role in the soul-transport system. Native Americans called them the *Lizard People*, and they settled as far north as Bellevue, Washington. The wise extraterrestrials came from the constellation known as the lizard, which complimented the Draco or dragon constellation where earth was conceived. Planetary evolution must make space for the divine expression, which has always been part of the struggle for the natives in this region."

"Yes, human trafficking has taken its toll in this particular part of California," Tobias said, digressing. "The missions that arose in time for the Mexican-American War and Civil War became a threat to spiritual freedom."

Joan shook her head, and interrupted him, "So, where is the sixth chakra?"

"It lies in a Russian satellite nation, supposedly a newly freed republic," Tobias said, skipping a stone over the water's edge. Breathless from his activity on the beach, he heaved in short, choppy sentences, "Lake Karakul, in China, constitutes the 'third eye' or vision chakra. It is in the heart of Siberian shamanism, and the lake reflects a particular type of vision associated with the iris of Gondwanaland's eye. The legendary yeti are the Russian equivalent of our Pacific Northwest Big Foot population. They inhabit the area. A Russian psychologist called the vision *Entering the Circle*, but later found herself going in circles."

"Yes, I've read that book. She later wrote about the illusionists," Joan remarked, cocking her head to hear his words over the thunderous approach of the rising tide. "It became important to Donna and her husband's investigation. He is a lawyer in Massachusetts." Joan strolled over to a log that had drifted to shore and sat down. She covered her head with one hand as she explained, "Donna told me about how Dion Fortune's group worked with a group of wizards north of Pakistan. They are illusionists, operating the smoke and mirrors in the metaphorical Land of Oz. Meanwhile, Joe learned through his taps that the robber barons controlling the elite echelons of US military had sent those working with navy intelligence to the Pacific Ocean to die. I suspect that it was the same space-time continuum that Carrie discovered in 1986. The robber barons wanted to employ the OSS for industrial espionage, and navy intelligence opposed this. After WWII, the

OSS was regrouped into the CIA. During 911, the naval intelligence section of the pentagon was destroyed."

Tobias shrugged and moved forward with his comments. "This brings us to the seventh chakra, centered at Medenet Habu, or the Temple of Rameses III. The story behind this pharaoh is interesting. Legend says that he conquered the dreaded 'sea people,' who threatened existence on the planet during the intergalactic wars of ancient Egypt."

Joan sighed, dropping her hands down to the sand. Drawing a few lines and figures, she went on, "His story explains the subsequent rips in the space-time continuum. This intergalactic war continues to haunt us. Only the elite echelons of the American Revolution, Mexican-American War, Civil War, and World War II fully integrated this phenomenon. Donna told me about the intergalactic war of ancient Egypt. The devastation on the planet was so great that ice rings formed around it, like the ones on Saturn. Joe learned that the time period correlates to Tolkien's *Lord of the Rings* writings."

"Who was the lord of ancient Egypt?" Tobias questioned her.

"The lord was the one who ruled the skies. In this instance, it happened to be Sauron, the maker of the rings to control the MidEarth. The MidEarth served as the refuge site for the spirits that had created and nurtured the planet. After Atlantis sunk, Sauron emerged and pursued everyone, along with his evil yang companion."

As they walked along the beach, the tide deposited several sand dollars at their feet. Joan reached down and picked one. Rubbing the velvet coating between her fingers, she said, "I suppose there is more to life than money."

"There are other forms of currency," Tobias remarked. "The sand dollar in your hands represents the energy of time and biology. There is no other coin in the world like that. It is not an exchange. It represents a cost."

Throwing the sand dollar back into the waves, she said, "It has a different value."

"Much different," Tobias stated. Then he chuckled, before adding, "Especially when you account for its position in the sea." He stopped to pry another sand dollar from the sand. As Tobias tossed it back into the ocean, he added, "Sand dollars have an ecological niche. They are part of the web of life."

"It figures that I would miss it," Joan said. "The west coast is more pristine. I don't think there is a web of life on the east coast. The salmon became extinct there years ago."

"There's more to it," Tobias told her. "In connecting your medical practice to your *chi gung* practice, you must realize that there is no weaver to the web. In Western medicine, those who understood the poetry of the body were burned at the stake. They were persecuted as intellectuals, which left the connection between spirit, mind, and body to the Asians. You feel burned out because you quit seeing the patient's signs and symptoms as a poem, like a spider's web."

Chapter Twenty

Brawls in dance halls

Can ruin a nation

From the inside out

Tune Reference: *Gimme Three Steps*

----Lynyrd Skynyrd

WHILE JOAN COMBED the beach, Tobias pitched his tent. When Donna arrived to join the survey, he wandered toward the group assembled by a small fire. Everyone busily chatted as they prepared food, and Tobias assumed the role of fire caretaker. Both Carrie and Donna joined him around the fire.

"Joan appreciated Mount Kailash as the sacral chakra in this latest planetary chakra system," Carrie told Tobias as he fed driftwood into the bonfire. "She gave me the book *The Secret of the Golden Tara* for my birthday last year. It has beautiful photos of Mount Kailash."

"What is the book about?" Tobias asked her. He blew into the growing fire so that more flames would ignite the logs he'd added. People were already loading their skewers with tofu dogs for roasting. Though there was pressure on him to keep the fire from going out, his mind wandered over images of the Himalayan Mountains. When his thoughts centered on a rugged peak with four corners, he withdrew from the growing heat, and gazed into the dancing blue, red, and yellow flames emanating from the gray wood pile. "Tell me the story in your own words."

"The book describes the persecution of Tibetian monasteries, when a monk was given the task of placing a golden icon at Mount Kailash. Because the mountain was revered as the center of the universe, the abbot wanted a symbol of the goddess of compassion restored there. It meant a lot to them. Any Olympian can tell you that winning is ninety-percent mental attitude. It is the same with those suffering extreme torture and faced with spiritual annihilation. A World War II concentration-camp survivor, Victor Frankl, wrote about how critical *meaning* is to life."

"What was the icon?" Donna asked Carrie.

"It was a tara," she replied. "A tara is a meditative symbol pertaining to a female Buddha of compassion. The Tibetians consider her as a protective deity or female savior."

"Did the monk ever make it to Mount Kailash with the tara?"

"No, he was forced to leave the country for his homeland. While shopping for supplies, he forgot to exchange his red robes for civilian garb. The Chinese army recognized the red robes and captured him. Luckily, his student and companion on the journey remained hiding with the tara. The monk escaped from prison camp two years later and went looking for his student, who wore a silver amulet. Being restricted from the Mount Kailash region, he went home without any knowledge whether his student had succeeded. Shortly before his death, he contacted the monastery's appointed representative in Germany. He asked him to see whether the golden tara had been brought to Mount Kailash, and he gave him a silver amulet that matches his student's."

"The German, who worked as a photojournalist and freelance television reporter, documented his journey as he traversed rugged terrain and dangerous circumstances. On the way to Mount Kailash, he found another monastery, where an old man recognized the silver amulet. The old man told the photojournalist that the student was no longer alive. However, the old man retrieved a yellow bundle from the student's casket and gave it to the photojournalist. Together they unraveled the mysterious contents of the yellow bundle. The yellow scarf proved to be a prayer flag. Written on the prayer flag were the words 'thirteen chorten.' They found the matching silver amulet and an unusual stone that was wrapped inside the prayer flag."

Carrie stopped for a moment and surveyed her surroundings. There were puzzled expressions on the faces of the listeners gathered around the fire. She briefly explained, "*Chorten* is another word for a Buddhist shrine. The journalist assumed that the words pertained to the destination of the golden tara. He continued his trek with renewed hope of finding such a small object on a huge mountain. The meaning of the tara became clear through his reflections and insights, gathered along the way. He found a place on Mount Kailash with thirteen chortens. After an avalanche fell around him, he studied the mountain carefully. His attention was drawn to a tiny gold tara tucked away on a rocky ledge. He found many Buddhist offerings around the golden goddess of compassion, and he realized that many others have made this pilgrimage. The German journalist concluded that *Happiness is not a place to stay but a path to go*."

"Compassion gets you on the path," Tobias interjected. "The tara is symbol of compassion. The nature of the exercise was for the sake of compassion. It all synergistically adds up to compassion."

With those parting thoughts, everybody resumed preparing dinner around the campfire. Nobody stayed up late. Instead, they retired to their bedrolls and nylon sanctuaries before the fog rolled in. Their tents offered them protection from the cool salt mists that dampened any gear left outside. In the morning, they rose and ignited camp stoves for boiling water. Some sipped cups of herb tea around a small fire, while others strolled the beach. Gulls hawked in the air, dancing past streaks of sunlight streaming from the sandy horizon opposite the shore.

Tobias joined the group around the campfire. Donna passed out samples of green tea that one of her *chi gung* instructors had brought from a monastery in China. Tobias savored the aroma of the brew, noting its delicate sweetness.

"The communists razed the mountain vegetation during the cultural revolution," Donna explained before Tobias drunk from his cup. "It is slowly coming back. This particular tea seems uncontaminated."

"Like the Tibetans, the Taoist monasteries were destroyed and the monks imprisoned," Carrie added. "Fifteen years ago, Larry went with his seventy-year old instructor to the site of his former monastery in China. While he stayed there, the instructor met another former monk, who happened to be visiting the monastery at the same time. The man was over eighty years old, and they conversed as if they had seen each other yesterday. Taoist timing reflects synchronicity. It is another world."

"Many important medicines were made from the forests around the monasteries," Donna interjected. "Many plants had been there for centuries. Much timeless value has been lost to the evil wrought after World War II ended. The genocide continued, except the faces became different. Though it wasn't just humans that were exterminated---the entire sacred environment around them went too. Lake Manasarovar, the precious body of water often perceived as Mount Kailash's female counterpart, lost its abundant wildlife to Chinese invaders. The natives used the waters for healing.

"We lose our environment; we lose ourselves," Tobias remarked. "That is the secret of life."

"Apparently those who focus on the immaterial were once considered a threat to the cultural revolution, though it was the same people who held the soul of a nation during World War II," Carrie said.

Donna paused for a moment before continuing, "Instead of enslaving African Americans, the industrial revolution recreated serfdom. People became victimized by time and began punching time clocks rather than becoming masters of time, like the synchronous Taoist instructors. Now industrial communities are trying to rebuild what was lost, but mostly for the tourist industry."

"The Darth Vaders of our lives, or the Yankees, traded their souls for technology, in the same manner that Gollum in *Lord of Rings* pursued the icon," Tobias responded. "I remember asking a Russian why Stalin had taken out his entire political cabinet and their families. Soldiers emptied an entire apartment complex of over two hundred people and shot them at the local marina. His answer: *progress*. I looked at the iconic Mercedes Benz symbol on the top of the forever-abandoned apartment complex, and wondered whether he thought German occupation of a Russian building defined progress. Meanwhile, he had to open four locked doors to get to his friend's suite in the designated housing for Moscow scientists. I disagree with their version of *progress*. What they called progress came at the expense of security and identity."

"All the following generations have gone to oblivion as a result." Taking a deep breath, she continued, "That is why Carrie's time wrinkle is so important. We don't have to live with the lyrics of a music industry suggesting that we have been programmed for self-destruction. In 1986, the US president pushed the button for a nuclear holocaust and Phil Collins sang about. Carrie exploited the rip in the space-time continuum in favor of the planet and for her own freedom. 9/11 was a ripped portion of the continuum that could not be restored. Luckily, in 1986 we only suffered one mishap with a Trident submarine and the Soviets. Carrie has good boundaries and chose not to get caught up in the nuclear tragedies. Eventually they will be wrinkled off the planet. She would rather play basketball than vomit from radiation poisoning."

"Basketball does come into play here," Carrie admitted. "Though, when it comes to a nuclear holocaust, I don't play games."

Cocking his head from side to side in contemplation, Tobias asked, "Something about being programmed for destruction? Yeah, yeah." He noted, "We can choose other solutions to problems that earmark us toward oblivion. Carrie's time wrinkle presented us with a new concept of ourselves, one that is compassionate and enduring, rather than ridiculous. That is the secret of the golden tara. It is about having compassion for those who continue to look upward while on their path."

Carrie resumed, "Over time I have come to see myself as starlight, rather than dust that only returns to dust. It is not my choice. Besides, I have a colleague who gave a seminar at an international physics conference. He lectured on Tibetan bowls and how their frequencies could be used to immobilize someone. He told me about a scientist, whom he called the 'man with no name.' He said that the man with no name reminded him of a *ferengi* on *Star Trek*. I'm no Trekkie, but I've seen enough episodes of *Babylon* 5 to understand the term. The ferengi character plays one side against the other, never assuming an identity in a critical life-or-death situation."

"Sorta like the Hegelian dialectic?" Donna questioned.

"Yes," Carrie answered. "However, it is not always such a bad thing to do, if both options are undesirable, and you wish to escape imposed circumstances. Such a maneuver can be employed to avoid a *Catch-22* situation. In this case, the ferengi-like healer possessed the ability to see into other dimensions and read the energy around people. When the ferengi encountered the energetic field around my colleague, he professed envy at the six-star cluster and high column shaft, with perfect gold and a spiral leaf emanating from him. When it gets to that point of visualization, the balancing act is over. The man went to the dark side because he could see what he was not. The ferengi-like healer coveted it. My colleague has been known to inadvertently knock out power grids in cities with his intrepid forays into adverse energy fields."

"Someone in one of my classes could capture the energetic structures created in various sacred places on camera," Tobias acknowledged. "Her black-and-white photos found highly refined ribbons of swirling light rising to meet the insides of church steeples. One photo showed a spiral staircase emanating from a tabernacle to the dome of a cathedral. They were beautiful images connecting the gap between heaven and earth. It wasn't fun to come back to earth from that class and crash into the realities affecting our day-to-day existence." Then he sighed. "The portals of our lives."

"I've heard about that type of design in an aura," Donna said. "It has to do with the Christ-consciousness. The Mayans popularized it."

"Yes, it corresponds to their holy grain, amaranth," Tobias said. "The common name is 'love-lies-bleeding.' It is a plant that embodies the consciousness of transcendence, particularly pertaining to compassion and sacrifice. The bleeding or suffering becomes meaningful if projected for redemption of the planet and its inhabitants. It is nothing personal."

"Yes, they obviously wanted to transcend the human sacrifices made by a civilization gone out of control---almost like the technological one hell-driven on progress that we have today," Donna noted.

"It is driven by dollars," Tobias inserted. "Any software engineer in the Pacific Northwest knows that all the electronic money passes through the computers at the Seattle Westin Hotel. The money gets electronically sent to a Kochi bank in India with the Eye-in-the-Sky on the building."

"When did it start?" Donna asked.

"The American Revolution---but that is another story," Tobias replied.

Chapter Twenty-One

It is one thing to solve a mystery

But it is a waste of time to be mysterious

Tune Reference: Building A Mystery

----Sarah McLachlan

THE NEXT DAY Tobias drove back home with the dog. He greeted Michelle in the living room as he put down his knapsack. Peering out the large picture window to the backyard, he watched several children race to be reunited with the dog, who ran toward them like a graceful gazelle. After kissing Michelle on the cheek, he joined her at the table behind stacks of books and papers. Michelle smiled at Tobias and then turned her head to the children's shouts outside. The youngsters were hugging the bouncy dog as she lunged for their embraces, knocking over children into one big, delightful pile.

Both Michelle and Tobias chuckled at the sight. Tobias poured boiling water from the kettle over some herb tea in a cup as Michelle switched her focus. Glancing briefly at her work, she looked at Tobias and asked, "Did you ever finish your stories about life's secrets?"

Tobias laughed softly."No, we left each other on information overload, promising to continue at some vague point in the future at some undetermined destination. That is how it is with those two. Then he added, "The big secret is that there are no secrets."

Michelle sighed and put her arm around him in a gentle squeeze. "No mysteries?"

"People get manipulated by secrets. Joe can tell you that. He has some sort of two-way tap going with those who have bugged his communications system," Tobias replied.

Michelle suggested. "What about this secret of life?"

"It is all in the implications," Tobias responded. "While Tesla was being played by the military, some scientists in France studied the work of some microbiologists. They wanted to investigate the fact that microbes, like the dreaded typhus bacillus, possess electrical properties. For therapeutic purposes, Lakhovsky built a radio cellulo-oscillator of 150 million cycles per second. Unlike the popular, etched-in-stone disease models, Lakhovsky considered cancer as an oscillatory disequilibrium. Today, people who look through electron microscopes find that carcinogenic cells resemble ruffled potato chips; they vibrate abnormally, though every tissue cell in the body has its own frequency. Lakhovsky built a multiple-wave oscillator to enable disturbed cells to restore their unique frequencies, much like lightly pushing the pendulum on a clock to restore its ability to keep time. Before the age of electronics, scientists knew that all the pendulum clocks in a room would eventually swing to the same frequency."

Stopping for a moment, Tobias grinned and lightly kissed Michelle on the forehead. He told her, "Harmony can be as infectious as a room full of pendulum clocks."

Michelle chuckled when she heard his explanation, and she savored the well-timed display of affection.

Tobias moved closer to her before continuing, "He concluded that cosmic waves could be directed for regeneration and the atmosphere has a ready supply of all the various frequencies. Though he wasn't able to resolve all cancers, he did unveil the secret of life. European healers adopted the concept and produced recipes of the types of frequencies needed to heal various disequilibriums. The recipes are called *unda*, which means 'frequency' or 'wave' in the language that they speak in Belgium. Not all naturopathic physicians use them, because they can get complicated. They require a special focus."

Michelle laughed as she stirred underneath his arm, "Yes, I have my hands full catching babies. I wish that more of my patients did a protocol involving *undas* before becoming pregnant; the cases would go so much smoother. Referrals & specialists come in handy." After taking a deep breath and snuggling against his body, Michelle asked, "Where did you find Lakhovsky's *Secret of Life* these days? Much of the research in this country has been destroyed in favor of Cancer Wards, a book written by a Soviet dissident."

"Knights Hospitallers," he answered. "I had always though that the secret of life was to spin, but it has to be left-handed. Positive thought adds elegance to the universe.

Closing her book with a slam for emphasis, Michelle told him, "I'm ready for a break. You get parent duty. I'm off to catch some babies."

Michelle rose and removed her books from the table. Tobias followed her around the house as she gathered her things. She briefed him on the latest details. "Three of the kids are staying overnight as their parents march in the WTO demonstration."

"Some of the parents are bringing the kids. They want them to experience their first peaceful demonstration," Tobias added. "I think I am going to teach the children how to catch tadpoles instead."

Tobias left Michelle to collect the children for a walk to a nearby stream. There were six youngsters and one excited dog ready for the next adventure. As they wandered over to the creek, Tobias waved at Michelle as she backed out of the driveway. Then he directed the children's attention to the grove of trees.

"Oh, look!" one youngster said to the others in hushed voice. "It's the magical forest."

"Ah, the magical forest," a chorus echoed. "The trees look just like the poster in the playroom." They stopped by a small blue tidal pool. Something about the clear-blue reflecting patterns of the water caught their attention. The varying refractive depths stilled the mind with the multidimensional angles of light, though they could see clearly to the sandy, rippled bottom. Little tadpoles darted to and fro in the shallow water.

Some children floated a piece of driftwood on the surface of the water, while others scooped a few tadpoles into their jars. Tobias lay down on a grassy mound and listened to their chatter as he studied the outline of trees against the sky. Storm clouds were looming in the distance and they would need to return home soon.

"I tried to do a science fair project on metamorphosis, but my tadpoles died," a small girl told her companions. "We don't have any streams by my house, so we had to order them from a national magazine. They came from a fish farm."

"What were their names?" another voice asked softly.

"Picklejuice and Prince Charming," the child answered.

Tobias gulped when he overheard the name Prince Charming.

"We had a memorial service for Prince Charming. He never became a frog."

"OK, kids," Tobias interrupted, rising from his position. "Time to go, before the lightning strikes. Let's have a hot-chocolate break. The older kids can get the spaghetti started."

"We have organic," one child said to another.

"Bring the jars with the tadpoles, and we can get them situated," Tobias instructed. He brought up the rear of the parade led by the yellow dog. The children walked slowly down the hill with their collections, taking great care to not spill or drop anything they valued.

Once inside the house, the older children began preparations for dinner as the younger ones crowded the kitchen to observe. Tobias produced several well-illustrated books on tadpole care for the interested children to review. Then he got out of the way, later joining them for the feast. Afterward, he cleaned the kitchen while they played board games.

Late in the evening, Michelle came home from the birth. Without waking the sleeping children, Tobias met Michelle in the kitchen as she brewed herself a cup of lavender tea. Her hands trembled as she prepared the concoction.

"The birth went well," she said, nodding to Tobias as she searched the room for various utensils. "Somebody tried to sideswiped me on the way home. I'm still shaking."

Tobias didn't move. He waited for her to compose herself. Changing the subject, she commented as she opened the fridge, "Hmm. Spaghetti, salad, vegetables, and brownies. Sure is nice to be home, though I must admit the newborn was adorable."

She smiled and faced Tobias.

He hugged her. "Go sit down. I'll fix you a feast from the leftovers."

Michelle gave Tobias a gentle squeeze around his torso as she softly planted a kiss on his cheek. She did as she was told. When he brought a plate over to the table, she motioned Tobias to join her. The steam from the warm food and drink seemed to melt the stress from her shoulders. Her manner resumed its usual steadiness. After looking down at the table briefly, she began, "Let's go back to the events of 1999, when Donna's family was attacked during their vacation. It occurred the same week that the plane of the son of an assassinated president went down. Donna's family was targeted. It was the same hazardous waste company that hypnotized their employees. Do you think there is a connection?"

Tobias reviewed in his mind the details of Donna's family vacation. They had switched cars and camping sites several times during their travels to a remote geologic site. He answered, "Most likely, but I don't know exactly. The leader of Iraq had financial connections to the transport systems that carried airline baggage and enjoyed documented support from US intelligence systems."

"Was the Bridget curse a factor?" Michelle questioned, changing the focus of the discussion.

"Yes. Though the son's stepfather ran the KGB, an outfit dedicated to Armageddon, the dark wizards north of Pakistan operated the smoke and mirrors, involving Iraqi leadership. 9/11 represented an illusion of horrific physical manifestations. Carrie, like many others, was alerted through the dream-state. Ever since the fall of Eden, the Serpentines have manipulated the dream-state to create illusions." After pausing a brief moment, Tobias looked at the ground and held Michelle's hands. He added, "Morgan Le Fey carried out the agenda of the Serpentines and Lilith. She cursed Bridget. The geologic company that attacked Donna was controlled by the same corporate oligarchy that targets US presidents."

"So is it genocide or control of world resources at environmental expenses?" Michelle queried.

"Bigger," Tobias replied. "It goes back to the race for technology as an intergalactic weapon."

"DNA can also be considered technology, because it holds the memory of other technologies worth remembering," Michelle remarked.

"Yes, the curses that infiltrate the DNA mark those spirits for intergalactic warfare, regardless of the carrier's awareness," Tobias continued, feeding a few ideas to Michelle. He elaborated, "Some, particularly the female counterparts, have an intuitive awareness and can manage the threats easier than the males can. It goes further back than the assassinations of the sixties. TV made the events of the sixties more visible to the public. If we compared notes, certain patterns would become apparent. For example, my great-grandmother Jones died in the same bioterrorism epidemic as did the grandfather of the president killed in Dallas. Both the president and his relative died on the same day in November---more than fifty years apart, which is statistically significant. This has been going on for a long time. The terrorists also targeted Lincoln's mother and the family who raised her. During the time of the Napoleonic war, the Holy Roman Empire forced marriages with the surviving Welsh royalty. Once the Welsh families figured out the Hegelian dialectic behind Napoleon, they fled to the United States. Bioterrorism is older than ancient Greece. The blankets the European armies traded to the Native Americans on this continent were purposely contaminated with smallpox. The racehorses of today carry the homeopathic vibrations of smallpox, serving as a living reminder of the scourges on human beings. The Irish potato famine was a genocide put in place by the British parliament. The survivors that came to America were tracked, like the African slaves at Georgetown. Look at the graveyards on the East Coast; there are separate ones for the various nationalities---Italian, Polish, German, and Irish. Where did it come from and why? Is it more than just bad habit? People have been played off their differences for thousands of years. The wounds run deep, and reach into the celestial realms. There is more to it that meets the eye."

Michelle interrupted him. "Speaking of which, let's get back to the eye on the Eye-in-the-Sky," she suggested.

"Yes, tomorrow," Tobias said. "I'm going to bed first. You can sleep in while the children and I make waffles."

The next morning, Michelle awoke and joined Tobias for breakfast after the children had eaten. They watched the children play as they munched on waffles and strawberries. At midmorning the parents came for their children. Michelle scurried away to gather them, along with their belongings, while Tobias entertained the group of parents.

"Did you see the news?" one parent asked. "Seattle is still smoking from the damage. You will not believe what happened to that mellow city!"

Another chimed, "I saw our friends marching with their kids. It was a peaceful protest, and everyone was singing songs. When the rioting erupted, a group of witches joined them and everyone lit Hanukah candles."

"The TV footage shows some of the police agitating the violence," a parent rejoined.

The children stood around their parents and studied the faces as they spoke. They looked up with puzzled expressions. "Mom, Dad. We found some tadpoles."

A father patted his child on the shoulder, and then turned back to the adults. "It's like what happened in Eugene, Oregon when the neocons allowed the anarchists bully the city. The town led the country in alternative energy, ecology, and sustainable lifestyles. They bused the same anarchists north for the conference."

"It's the negative ions that make us mellow," Tobias said as an aside to some of the small children who were searching for an explanation.

The children nodded and glanced at the adults above them for a response. The parents ignored Tobias, though wry smiles tugged at the corners of their mouths. Looking down at the jars in the hands below, one parent asked, "So what is in the jars?"

"Tadpoles."

Chapter Twenty-Two

Substitution of trains for communities,

As in the song called City of New Orleans,

Keeps everyone moving,

Though not always forward.

Sometimes it is just a way to

Escape the bullets and the blues

Tune Reference: *City Of New Orleans*

----Steve Goodman

LIFE IN THE Pacific Northwest returned to normal, although the adults remained scarred by the assault on the home front. Only tourists could be seen in city corridors. Still in shock, the locals stayed away from the downtown areas. Maybe it was due to all the rumblings in their part of the world, but no one in the region seemed surprised when the tsunami struck Japan. The corporate release of hazardous material didn't faze them. Entrepreneurs eventually converted the radioactive refuse that washed on the beaches into a tourist attraction. Because there was no declaration of war, the skeletons did not return home with honor. Volunteers swept the beaches clean.

On the day the tsunami struck Japan, Tobias received a phone from Joan. In light of the tragedy, Joan was considering the practice of medicine from another perspective. Many other conscientious health care practitioners groped for answers on dealing with the catastrophe.

"It is time for a paradigm shift," Joan confessed. "The world is finally learning how to view itself in terms of waves or frequencies."

"It is the key to thriving, instead of just surviving," Tobias commented in a succinct, low voice. Exploding into a history lesson, he boomed, "It is as if everything has come full circle for the planet. The Japanese invaded the Republic of China, while Hitler came to power in Germany. The invasion of China ended in a powerful reversal of energy, almost like an aikido move culminating in a hara-kiri of sorts for the attacker---if you take out the politics and just track the energy in motion."

"Issues of power pertain to the third chakra," Joan observed. "In a sense, their power play reversed on itself."

"The annexation of Korea during the war wove the thread for the next conflict," Tobias interjected. "Manchurian nomadic tribes struggled with the Korean royalty, which had become communist with help from the United Nations. It must have been a culture shock to go from a monarchy to communism."

"The wound runs deeper," Joan told him.

"I know," Tobias said. "The queens of the Chinese wanderers were from the *nadas* of India. They were precursors of Nazis and fascists. Nowadays the groups relate to the Eye-in-the-Sky gang that runs the banking in India. The women of the tribes worship snakes."

"The *nadas* financed the iron horse. In many ways, it broke the wild, free spirit of nations," Joan remarked. "The Tibetans prophesied that they would be banished with the arrival of the iron horse. Iron horses are trains."

Tobias sighed. He told her, "Yes, like the atomic bomb, the style of fighting changed with trains. It tamed the Wild West in this country and ultimately contributed to the destruction of Native American communities. It wasn't the trains---it was the dollars behind them."

"It wasn't the dollars, per se," Joan insisted. "Paul Hawken's video and book *Natural Capitalism* convinced me."

Tobias grinned at hearing the word *natural* coming from the mouth of an osteopathic allopath. He elaborated, "It was the occult energy inserted into the dollar designed by the US founding parents, which has something to do with the pyramid symbol on the back of the dollar bill."

Joan remained silent.

Without waiting another second for her comment, Tobias lapsed into a narrative. "When I went to Russia, I was surprised to see the resemblance between Lenin's tomb and that uncapped pyramid on the back of the dollar bill. It became obvious who funded his enterprises. The robber barons also sponsored Hitler and the international railroads. It is a dirty little secret of World War II. Someone on the plane going home pointed out the occult owl in the corner of the dollar bill, which I realized symbolizes something adverse to prosperity in harmony with the natural world. That is another book. Both Russians and American clapped and cheered when the plane landed in the United States. Despite the occult details on the dollar, most experience this country with a sense of relief."

Joan grumbled, "It is not the occult source of funding, but the fact that nobody stood up to Hitler and such expenditures."

Sensing that Joan would argue with him no matter what, Tobias decided to take the high road. Closing his eyes momentarily like a sea anemone, he said, "Have it your way. I'm not one to contest the winner of the dirtiest of secrets."

Joan laughed at that. "OK, I win. Now I want your homeopathic recipes for developing immunity from these radioactive waves, so I can oscillate at a higher vibrational frequency."

"Never mind," Tobias said, shaking his head. "Take a look at Patton's final days in light of the plan to industrialize the globe. His ambulance missed being hit several times, according to the record. He was afraid that his own military would kill him and it looks like the Knights Hospitallers got to him."

"What?" Joan asked.

"Look," Tobias directed. He began talking fast, tightly gripping the thread of conversation. "All I am saying is this---don't throw socio-political-religious icons at me. Vaccines are as old as the American Revolution. The grandchildren of the man credited with the invention of vaccine technology were in my high school biology class. They were far more interested in football and drill team than germ warfare. It is not about scientific intrigue or method. The scientific method assumes that you know all the variables before you run the experiment. Data in conflict with the initial hypotheses often gets tossed."

"Huh?" Joan pondered out loud. Recovering her wit, she questioned Tobias further on the subject. "What are you talking about?"

"As a result of my teenage experiences, I can understand why they say that the best thing that France ever did was get rid of mandatory vaccinations," Tobias quipped. "Unfortunately, somebody sold it to the US military-industrial complex and colleges. The fastest guy on my high-school team went to college on a swim scholarship. He dropped out when the college demanded that he take their steroids and drugs. It was either be an unnatural swimmer or lose the scholarship. We were champions, not robots."

Continuing to race through his explanations before Joan protested, he added, "I tend to agree with one colleague that we are all in various states of decay, though I am hesitant to commit to robust theory in my present wandering state of scientific inquiry. After consulting with the industrial engineers that use Montgomery's statistical approaches, I prefer to deal with the states of decay rather than take pop-shots at germs. After treating his children for several years, my colleague took his family on vacation in a mosquito-infested jungle---without malaria shots. All the bugs left them alone; there was no dead meat to eat. My colleague studied extensively with the French MDs."

"Why French MDs?" Joan asked.

Tobias answered, "France had to figure how to recover from WWII, and they developed the medicines. The technology has been imported to the United States. They have advanced from *natural medicine to medicine of the individual*. Apparently, there were some intellectuals who survived the French Revolution. Unfortunately, they killed the physician who wrote the book on *medicine of the individual*. Those who pursue socialized and military medicine want us to all die together in the same muck. Allopathic parents tell children that they are giving them 'shots' which is the language of war. Then the kids go to war and soil the nests of both continents. In comparison, the children at the clinic call the homeopathics 'yum yums.' Healthy individuals crave what they need, whether it is pungent or not."

"Sounds like your colleague is addressing Jungian notions of individualism," Joan observed. She dropped germ warfare for the moment.

"Invoking Jung is like substituting Newton mathematics for integral calculus," Tobias told her. "It only adds up some of the time. The slain president fired Jung's patient for his involvement in the Bay of Pigs and CIA."

"Let's not mention Leibniz." Joan sighed. History considered Leibniz, Newton's rival, as the father of integral calculus.

"Let's do," Tobias demanded. "We are in suspect terrain with Leibniz as well. Leibniz wanted to topple the British monarchy and replace it with his own students. You can see why Newton and Leibniz didn't get along. The politics of math goes way back. It is not just all numbers. You have to know when to use a particular approach, or do nothing. Studies show that placebo offers a thirty percent recovery; most cancer treatments have far less. Wounds heal by primary intention. It is important to get to the bottom of things in a manner that is not lethal. It is a naturopathic oath to address root causes as well as do no harm. Life is not black and white."

"You have a point," Joan admitted. "Let's table this discussion until Carrie and Donna can join us. I want to hear their comments."

Chapter Twenty-Three

Sooner or later

It all comes down

To mindfulness

Tune Reference: *Just Between You And Me*

----Lou Gramm

"THAT'S A GREAT idea," Tobias told Joan. She listened quietly as he related his story. "Let's work it through, first. My dentist explained to me that the practice of medicine changed during the Civil War. The homeopaths could not come up with a remedy as fast as cutting off a limb and putting sulphur on the wound to avoid infection. Things have changed in the last thirty years. Pasteur's Germ Theory came out in 1864, shortly before the war ended. The international robber barons fund his institute in France.

"They also funded Napoleon, who came to power after the king and queen of France aided the American Revolution. According to *National Geographic,* Vatican agents in America misdirected thousands of French troops to their death on US soil, especially in Maryland. Many of the signers to the Declaration of Independence were economic slaves of the British Empire, and connected to the Eye-in-the-Sky enterprise in India. Only two of the signers, William Whipple and Samuel Adams, were free of British corporate ties.

"Leibniz betrayed the French Academy and American Revolution to the House of Hanover, a Hapsburg bid for the crown of England. By portraying the revolutionists as anti-oligarchists, he paved the way for infiltration. The fight was with the occultist Brahmins in India. The American Revolution began in western India during 1772, not as a parlor game from the elite of France. The East India Company defaulted on payments to the British treasury, which threatened the security of the United Kingdom. The result was the introduction of alien rule to India, which was intended to govern the colonists. This prompted an intergalactic war on US soil. The Brahmin occultists brought in the Serpentines, who later enlisted the aid of the M33 galaxy. M33 is also known as the Triangulum galaxy, because the star pattern consists of two triangles."

Tobias continued as Joan remained silent, "A British occultist wrote, 'Psychology is the basis of the occult,' and one of the signers of the Declaration of Independence, Dr. Benjamin Rush, became known as the father of mental health in the United States. The wise survivors of the American Revolution tried Rush's student for the murder of George Washington. Later, President Jefferson placed Dr. Rush in the capacity of physician for the Lewis and Clark expedition. I never use the botanical medicines that Rush gave them; it would kill anyone. Both Sacajewa and Lewis died violently, under mysterious circumstances. Meanwhile, financial agents of the House of Hanover and Hapsburgs intermarried with descendants of European royalty who had fled Serpentine persecution. It was a Roman custom to take the wives of the native leaders as their own, often resorting to force. This practice lasted for thousands of years and carried over into the American colonies.

"A wise survivor of the American Revolution, Nancy Hanks created a legal entity representing Lincoln's murdered father. A. A. Springs died in 1840 and left Lincoln a huge plot of land now known as Huntsville, Alabama. However, Lincoln always considered Springfield, Illinois, his home, and it was the place of his lifelong friends. Originally known as Calhoun, Illinois, it later bore the name of his father's legal entity. This occurred after the ousting of the royal occult-secessionist Senator John C. Calhoun of South Carolina. Dissidents from the intergalactic Mexican-American War formed a political group called the Copperheads, the name of a small poisonous snake. They later evolved into the Knights of the Golden Circle, representing the Roman Serpentines who vowed allegiance to the Vatican over their own nation. Lincoln's secretary Hay became one of their foremost occult members. The other secretary, Nicolay, wrote a book about Lincoln, mentioning his clash with a secret society known as the Knights of the Golden Circle. When the Serpentines seized control of the US government and assassinated Lincoln, they assumed control of the property and turned it into a huge center for mind control. Mrs. Lincoln, for her role in the setup, became one of its first subjects. Having been a founding member of the underground-railroad system, Lincoln used the Todd family for cover until the curse of Saint Bridget caught up with him and his sons. Unfortunately, Mrs. Lincoln sided with her Confederate family as the war ceased. The corporate agents of the French Revolution pursued Lincoln's half-brother, Leroy Springs. They took over the railroads through company derivatives aligned with imposters on the French throne and vaccination program. All of the children of the king and queen of France died in prison. His child with another queen led the European monarchies confronting Napoleon. At the time of Napoleon, most of the European monarchs were descendants of Avalon, and they wished to protect their progeny. Hapsburg relations attempted to regain control of the French throne, reinventing themselves in the United States. They aligned with the efforts of Marie Antoinette's brother Leopold II, Hapsburg king of Germany, who promoted smallpox vaccines as well as mental-health programs similar to Rush's agendas.

"They tried to seduce Lincoln into several affairs, including one with Anne Rutledge who, like Leopold II, died under mysterious circumstances. Being a competitor of his sister, Marie Antoinette, as well as Napoleon I and Leopold II succumbed to the snake pit. Lincoln recognized the Civil War as a thinly disguised war of sibling against sibling, with many being the casualties of royal infighting. The replacement of one monarchy with another proved the ultimate futility, marking Leibniz's betrayal of the natural rights of human beings as proposed by Leonardo Da Vinci. The artists of that century knew who pulled all the puppet strings."

Joan sighed. Then she changed the subject. "Tell me more about this French medical doctor reclaiming his intellectual freedom."

Tobias returned her sigh. "Dr. Guéniot, MD simply observed spiritual laws in his health model. The natural world has a supportive role."

"Sounds refreshing," Joan said, encouraging him.

"Yes," Tobias rejoined. "Instead of stem-cell innovations, he incorporates phytembryotherapy. This supports Dr. Guéniot's notion of an 'elemental formative force,' where the buds, seeds, or tender shoots of a tree concentrate the potential of a future life."

"Very exciting," Joan commented. "It matches your wife's understanding of the Kabbalah tree."

Tobias continued, "A leading researcher at IBM, Marcel Vogel cut a small quartz crystal to represent the Kabbalah, serving to enable all of us to find our inner light. I relate it to the 'theory of dissipative structures,' which won a Nobel prize for the conviction that there exists a small code or structure within that operates as a unit. It unifies the whole. It is sorta like GUTS of modern physics, except this can be applied to organizations as well. For example, the park rangers at Independence Hall will tell you that only one-third of the colonists supported the revolution. The coherency of this unit created order out of chaos. Likewise, Margaret Meade said, 'Never doubt that a small group of thoughtful, committed citizens can change the world; indeed, it's the only thing that ever has.' I am referring to regeneration, health, and a sense of a well-being, rather than entropy and senseless acts of violence. Dr. Pol Henry of Brussels gets credit for the concept of phytembryotherapy in 1959. Perhaps it was a response to the social upheaval that was taking place in Asia and Africa during the late 1950's."

"Revolutions are messy and can be degenerative," Joan commented.

"Not all change is for the better," Tobias agreed. "Updating the ancient Greek method of determining signs and symptoms to arrive at a diagnosis, Dr. Guéniot incorporated morphopsychology."

"The psychology of form," Joan murmured.

"I knew a clinic that served the poor in Mexico City. The doctors could tell by looking at a patient whether he or she was going to live or die. Morphopsychology simply perceives psychological behavior by looking at someone's facial features. In a sense, the mind-body relationship is used diagnostically. For example, those with a sanguine temperament have an oval face."

"Yes, I remember. Hippocrates defined patients according to their humors." Joan laughed. "I always wondered what he would have come up with for those without a sense of humor."

"Well, you can see why they call it 'Greek,' " Tobias quipped. "It fell short of some people's understanding at the time."

"No, I think we still have some ill-humored people today," Joan mused.

"It only took thousands of years to update the understanding to make the practice of medicine more inclusive," Tobias surmised. "The challenge is to update the medicine of the Roman Empire to include females."

"That's not funny," Joan said.

"I know. They later named a bone for it," Tobias countered. "It's called the funny bone, but I have never seen a patient laugh when they hit it. It is not the humerus. My son and his friends in junior high still joke about the nose bone. Other times they've pointed to the hard bony protrusion on their posterior bent forearm and asked if anyone wants to see their *weenus*. They convinced the girls in their class to do it, and it really broke the pubescent gender ice."

"You mean there isn't a nose bone?" Joan joshed in a serious voice.

Tobias laughed. "This is what happens when you give young trick-or-treaters miniature skeletons as gifts for Halloween. Do you know what it is like to kiss a sweet child good night, and peer into the red-hollowed orbits on the bony frame tucked underneath his arm like a teddy bear? They've a fondness for structure in life. Their term of endearment for the plastic Legos version has become *skelly*. Now they have become creative with the bones of the body."

"It is an adjustment," Joan commented. "I think that we are going to get along with Asian medicine, Tobias. For two thousand years, they imagined organ structures such as the Triple Burner."

"I think so. They recognized the importance of function, instead of dissection and vivisection," Tobias agreed. "They are like the engineers with their imagined concepts of lift and drag. Just keep looking for that elusive nose bone, Joan. If it flies, it flies. This is why I don't consider engineers, computer programmers, and chemists as scientists. They make it all a program or recipe, instead of figuring out where they are going with their gollum-driven, amino acid soup."

Chapter Twenty-Four

When the magic of everyday things
Is lost by tricksters intending
To destroy you, the leaves,
And the tree that the leaves left
Just call it a bad day
And move through on to a better moment

Tune Reference: *Bad Day*
----Daniel Powter

A YEAR AND half later, Tobias and several buddies tagged along on Michelle's business trip to the Swiss Alps. A perfect time for a mini-vacation, they caught an early snow falling in the mountains. Arriving at the closest airport, the couple went their separate ways, and planned to meet later for dinner. Driving to the hotel, Tobias made several wrong turns, though they could see their destination in the distance.

"I have it surrounded," he told Michelle as he circled around the hotel, finding his way through one-way streets toward the underground parking garage. The booking agent at the hotel had mentioned that they could find free parking beneath the hotel. As his mistakes took him further from the hotel, Tobias mentioned, "I don't usually have this much difficulty finding a place. There may be a reason why I can't zero in on the parking garage."

Michelle moved uncomfortably in the passenger seat. She uttered in a hushed voice, "We are going to get killed, Tobias. It's a setup."

Tobias glanced at her before turning around in the direction of the underground parking lot. "We aren't going to get killed. Get a grip. You are making me nervous. I need to think and keep my wits about me." Then he added, "Watch, Michelle---you might learn something."

When they reached the entrance to the underground parking, the placement of a Parking Lot Full sign conspicuously blocking the entrance, though only partially. Instead of turning in, Tobias circled around the hotel one more time. Slowing down as he approached the sign, he peered at the one open dark lane going down into the earth.

"We are being protected. There's must be a problem," he told Michelle. "I'm not going down that lane. It is too early in the day for the lot to be full." Nodding his head forward, he added, "Look, there is an outdoor empty spot by that meter. It's as if someone has been holding it for us. Get out your pocket change. Paying for parking beats getting ambushed in an underground lot."

Tobias slid the car in the angled parking space as Michelle dug in her purse for foreign coins. Standing outside of the car, Michelle supplied Tobias with money as they secured the space. They looked around. No one was out braving the wintery cold this early in the morning. Pretending that nothing more was amiss, Tobias and Michelle checked into the hotel.

"Let's not make a scene, and we'll continue with the subtle play," Tobias instructed Michelle. "I'll handle the two-hour coin drops, while you attend the conference. Besides me and my sixth sense, there are only a few handful of people in the world who would alert me to danger without telling me outright."

Fifteen minutes later, Tobias went outside to unpack the car while Michelle rested. Returning to his room with the rest of the baggage, he mentioned, "Someone moved the sign out of the lane. Cars are going into the underground lot." Sitting down on the bed, he rubbed his forehead. He said, "Let's not move the car. We'll sneak around the place through the stairwells and back doors by the kitchen. Only use the elevator if you know the people around you. Stay near your group, but not close enough to be identified with them. Keep the friends out of it. I'll meet you for lunch at the break. We'll find a quiet place away. I'm gonna need a glass of red wine and warm meal to deal with this situation."

At lunch break, Tobias took Michelle by the hand and led her away from conference rooms. He felt the tension as he grasped her hand and observed the firmness of her jaw. Her other hand discreetly held her extended key as a weapon.

"You look like you are ready to fight like the devil," Tobias commented to her softly.

"Watch me," she said.

Leaving through the exit at the back of the hotel, they descended the stairs and opened the backdoor to a city street.

In the open air, Tobias began explaining, "I have protection from three sources. They include individuals in the profession, a buddy from my high-school swim team, and my father. It is like a silent guild. The circles of our lives interlock, and we help each other."

"Tell me about your buddy and your father," Michelle murmured as they swiftly made their way across the street.

"My buddy understood English literature better than anyone I know. I swam in the same lane with him for almost seven years."

"That's a long time in close waters," Michelle said quietly.

"He taught me how to stay detached from human foibles and how to spread my wings. He works with the international police. His wife is an air-force pilot, and they were stationed at the Austrian embassy. They went underground after 9/11."

"And your father?" Michelle questioned. "You haven't seen your father in over thirty years. We only invited close friends to the wedding."

"Adjunct military," Tobias said softly. "When I was a teenager, I discovered his wheat germ and vitamin E oil in the fridge. I know he approves of my line of work."

There was no one on the street on this blustery day. Only a few restaurants were opened, and all the stores were closed. He continued to scan the street and storefronts for people nearby. Looking around, Tobias added, "My father had been in Korea. Unlike Reggie, he stayed on top of the threats against him. He was part of the units steering people away from 9/11."

"I heard about that," Michelle said. She stared into the gray clouds overhanging the city. Without looking at Tobias, she told him, "One of my clients mentioned how he had been instructed by various intelligence networks to set up roadblocks."

Tobias shuddered for a moment. Then he shrugged and dropped his shoulders. He put his arm around Michelle as if to shield her from the cold.

"You and the others make all the difference in the world," Tobias said. "Let's all stay in the shadows. My relationships can protect you, but you must maintain caution."

There was a courthouse at the far end of a snow-covered field across the road. Only a few isolated automobiles roamed the city streets on this cold, brisk day. Despite the tension in the air, Tobias savored the grounding chill of the wind rushing past them. Scattered snowflakes danced in the air as the breeze unanchored them from the icy pack. He and Michelle wandered a quarter mile past empty shops until they found an open restaurant.

"Perfect," Tobias said, opening the door for Michelle. "A vibrant Italian lounge is just what I need with my glass of red wine. Hopefully they have some good food."

The lobby was warm, with dark wood molding and dark-red velvet upholstered chairs. As they waited, they watched several groups leave the establishment. When they finally were seated, there were only two couples left in the dining room. The waiter ushered them to a cozy booth and took their order for drinks.

"We've been directed here," Tobias whispered to Michelle. "We have company. I'm not sure who arrived here first. The couple in the opposite booth is a fake."

Without giving herself away, Michelle turned her head to look while the waiter placed two wineglasses on the table. She smiled immediately when she saw them. An older man with silver hair held the hands of a younger female as if they were lovers. Not only did the couple seemed a little odd given the age differences, the intensity of the encounter did not match the woman's nervous, shaking feet beneath the table. Despite the mismatch, she appeared intent on holding hands over the table. Her eyes were on the entrance.

The waiter took their order as Tobias relaxed and stretched his arms. "Now I understand why cowboys have one last nip at the bar before heading for a shootout in the street."

Michelle grimaced slightly, looking down at the antipasto plate that the waiter had just deposited on their table. Ten minutes later, a group of four men arrived and asked for a table at the back of the room. With a nod, Tobias directed Michelle's gaze to the odd assortment of men filling in the room.

'We'll sit back here with the rowdies," the tall red-haired man said to the waiter, who seemed suddenly animated by the masculine presence.

"The shorter fellow seems too scared to be having a good time," Tobias said softly to Michelle. "They aren't very businesslike. Only one of them is carrying a briefcase. The others seem scattered."

Michelle gulped some water from a glass as the waiter came with dishes of pasta and sauce for their table. About twenty minutes later, a pair of women entered the restaurant and opted for the booth next to them. Tobias winced at Michelle, who did not bother to look at the newcomers this time. He motioned for the waiter to bring a doggy bag and the bill.

"Here comes our problem," he announced to Michelle after the waiter left. "It's our exit cue."

Quickly, they hurried away from the restaurant. Walking past the open field until they were out of anyone's hearing distance, Tobias explained, "The women fit the profile that I anticipated. After what I witnessed at the restaurant, I feel even more compelled than ever to continue feeding the meter. No underground parking for me today. Meanwhile, I suggest that you avoid any zealous group of American female tourists twenty-thirty years older than ourselves---particularly teacher unions, library associations, and church organizations."

Michelle's chest heaved steadily. "I am going to hide in the middle of my naturopathic friends from the States. I am glad I like my work. It will keep my mind off things." As they entered the hotel from the door near the kitchen, Michelle suggested, "I'll meet you at the room this evening. Go check on your buddies about skiing. Street parking is free tomorrow. It's a holiday."

The next day Tobias went skiing with his chums, after briefing them on the strange happenings at the hotel. No one seemed unduly surprised, and they encouraged him to continue researching the matter.

"Is it the Grays?" his buddy, Jim, asked. He stopped short when Tobias gasped with a silent *how-did- you-know?* expression on his face. The Grays represented an alien race promoted by select governmental-military leaders. They had been ushered in on the planet during Hitler's rise in power, about the time the Fuhrer began awarding the Blue Cross to females having the most children. Other leaders went underground and alerted the population with Orson Welles 'War of the Worlds' broadcast.

Nobody brought up the topic again. Instead, they focused on having fun in the unseasonably good weather. After a half-day spent Nordic skiing, Tobias separated from his chums to check out a world-renowned scientific community in the valley below. Though he ran the risk of exposing himself, Tobias wanted to distract the pursuers from Michelle. Finding a close friend and associate at the science institute though sheer synchronicity, Tobias seized the occasion to resume their acquaintance. Being a teacher far away from his home in the United States, the instructor immediately accepted Tobias's offer of support.

"Please help me find my missing cubit," he asked Tobias. "I need it for my demonstration this afternoon."

"Give me a moment to call my friend Joe," Tobias requested. A cubit was a circle of braided wires that comprised special electromagnetic properties. "He would understand the technical phenomenon more than I would. Joe is great at engineering his way out of scrapes. I can call from the nearby town, so that I won't be overheard."

Tobias walked a mile-long path through the woods into town. He found a phone booth and dialed Joe's number.

"So, what's the problem today?" Joe asked, calmly.

"I need your help with a colleague's cubit," Tobias requested abruptly. "He suspects another attendee at the conference hid it."

"Give me the weasel's name, and I'll look him up," Joe promised.

"Thanks, Joe," Tobias said when he had done so. Then he hung up the receiver, and stared at the wooded path leading back to the conference center.

Looking around the small town where he had gone to place his call, Tobias returned to the path. He'd gone only thirty yards when he had the distinct feeling that he was being watched. Twice he turned around and saw no one. On the third check, he quickly veered a few steps off the trail before whirling around. Behind him was the weasel---a tall, dark-haired man about thirty-five years old. The weasel met Tobias's gaze then feigned absentmindedly bending down to tie a shoelace. Tobias continued on the path unhampered. He recognized a highly skilled ninja when he saw one. It dawned on him that the weasel also knew how to disappear into thin air, like an Indian swami who could climb a rope into nothingness. The disappearing rope trick was as old as Marco Polo, who had to figure out how to deal with the *nadas* when he was providing spice to the Western world. With this thought, Tobias realized what had happened to his colleague's cubit.

The cubit was a tool from ancient Egypt that could be used for healing purposes. Tobias's colleague had fashioned the cubit using sacred geometry that resonated with the structure of pyramids. A braided wire of copper, gold, and silver had been measured out and folded back to make the cubit. Inside the cubit's ring, there was a parametric effect, with tensor fields that always proved balancing for people. Tensors represented energy projected in more than four dimensions, going beyond the time variable. Using an optical illusion, the weasel had hidden the cubit in another dimension to embarrass Tobias's colleague.

After he'd figure this out, Tobias was not startled when he found the weasel standing next to his colleague in the conference theater. The weasel had beaten him back to the lecture. Scientific demonstrations were conducted in a round theater resembling those of ancient Greece. When Tobias's colleague saw him enter the round room, he stepped away from the conference officials and drew Tobias aside.

"The man standing next to me is a fakir," his colleague whispered. Then he instructed Tobias like he was lecturing: "Watch the placement of his hands. He is doing *mudras* to create blind spots through scalar-energy manipulation. I need your help. You and your friends can counter his attack by doing the opposite of what he does with his fingers. Counter right with left and left with right."

Tobias nodded. "I called Joe from town. That weasel messed with me on the way back."

"I agree that he's a weasel," Tobias's colleague murmured as he stepped away.

Tobias dashed out of the room and met with two of his friends, who were on their way to the ski slopes an hour away. They had not been invited specifically to the conference, though they had seized the opportunity for recreation and for the gathering of rare botanicals with established Swiss herbalists.

"We have a fakir in our midst," he announced, stopping them outside the hotel lobby.

"I knew that there was even a better reason why we were here," Jim, the taller naturopath, said as he planted his skis firmly aside in a snowdrift. Then he asked, "What's a fakir?"

"Well, you know how most naturopathic physicians practice one form of *chi gung* or another. They either come in as adepts or start learning esoteric healing skills during first year," Tobias said. After pausing briefly to study the quizzical expressions on the men's faces, he explained, "A fakir practices a form of aesthetics that comes from India. They are like little magicians that inhabit the streets, like beggars. The illusionists come from a small country north of Pakistan."

"Oh yeah, I remember seeing them on childhood cartoons. A bunny wearing a turban plays a flute as if to charm a snake out of a basket. Instead, the music erects a rope in midair, and he climbs the rope to befuddle the hunter and escape. They don't show those kind of cartoons anymore," Jim's sidekick, David, commented.

"It is because the technique has been adopted by those in espionage," Jim said. "They don't want children to use it against them. I guess they had problems."

"They don't show *Laugh In* reruns either," David rejoined.

For a moment Tobias let down his guard. "Yeah, the kids found some old television videos for my birthday, along with an old *Red Skelton* show. Only Red could get away with cracking a joke on an Occultist 33rd Degree rite. He called it the 'deep freeze.'"

"Let's not date ourselves before we go skiing," Jim joked. Then he grew serious. "Tobias, what do you need from us?"

"Look, I know that I should be Nordic skiing, but I ran into a colleague with a missing cubit."

"Don't you just hate that when it happens," David rambled.

"Yes, I still have visions of chasing the two-millimeter silver ball from the guts of an imploding blood pressure cuff only twenty minutes prior to a final test. I retrieved the tiny rolling ball from the floor of the cafeteria, an area almost half the size of a football field."

"Yeah, and you still had to borrow mine for the final exam," Jim quipped.

"I had to find you first, which was even harder than tracking a minute, moving ball in a crowded, large room."

"Do you still have the cuff?" Jim queried.

"Yes, it worked as soon as I finished the exam," Tobias answered. "Occasionally I see talented patients who can stop the needles on my solar watch and aneroid sphygmomanometer. I have to tell them to cut it out."

"I just get the occasional abductee," David reflected.

"They're keeping you on your toes, Tobias," Jim remarked.

"I don't need it," Tobias admitted. "As much as I try to maintain peaceful mind for healing purposes, I can't forget that I was also trained to kill, a courtesy of the germ-warfare model."

"It is probably why our esteemed colleague---who teaches at the military hospital when not cavorting with the seventy-something medical doctor and teacher of family medicine---approached you."

"They don't really cavort. Everyone tries to keep it light as we manage several dimensions at once," Tobias reflected. "I do have a way of wandering in and out of things, including closed international conferences."

"Curiosity is not such a bad thing, Tobias," Jim told him.

"Thanks, Jim. I'll remember that next time I am crawling my way out of a scrape. I want to help this guy because I can relate, not because I want to align myself with conservative professors promoting unidentified flying objects."

"That's right, Tobias," Jim said, almost slapping Tobias on the back. "You have identified them all."

"They aren't unidentifiable to me," Tobias mused. "No ego problem here. I'm not so proud."

"You're our man, Tobias," Jim announced. "What does the instructor want your friends to do?"

"Counter the weasel's hand gestures," Tobias instructed.

"We can do it!" David cried.

"Yes, it is about time our skills at juggling and Hacky Sack came in handy," Jim observed. "I took it up first year, practicing while waiting for cadaver lab."

"Great! Time to make like scientists instead of ski bums," Tobias proposed. "Do it with an eccentric international flair. Wear a scarf or a European beanie, or something. We have forty minutes to hop the shuttle down the valley and show up as the colonel's assistants."

By the time Tobias and his friends walked in the room, the colonel had retrieved the cubit. Tobias glanced at the golden-ringed apparatus and nodded at his friends. Jim's friend, David, recognized the object, taking a deep breath before assuming an energetic position designed to protect it and the demonstration. He reassured Tobias with eye contact before the colonel whispered to him in a voice that only he could hear. "I'm glad you are here. It is synchronicity," the colonel acknowledged.

"How did you get the cubit back?" Tobias questioned softly.

"I found the correct mantra," the colonel explained with a firm shake of his head. "With the dark forces at play here, I want to walk away unscathed with my cubit."

"It's a plan," Tobias murmured, steadying himself to counter the weasel's energetic projections. "Are you sure the mantra wasn't *There's no place like home?*"

He shrugged at Tobias instead of answering him directly. Just like a prayer, the colonel completed the demonstration in front of an audience in which the average viewer had approximately two or three PhD certificates behind his or her name. Then he walked away, and the assistants left the room. Jim and David went back to their skiing to clear their heads, while Tobias said good-bye to the colleague with the disappearing cubit.

Meeting the colonel in the hall afterward, Tobias explained, "I want to follow up a phone call made to Joe. Get back to you later with the info." Then he turned down the path toward town.

The familiar path was laced with reddish-brown leaves that crunched when he stepped on them. Tobias enjoyed the soft noise beneath his feet. He happily noticed that there was no echo. If someone walked behind him, the sound would be noticeable. The creepy sensation raising the hairs on the back of his neck disappeared. Having been exposed, the weasel had quickly fled the institute, especially after the cubit had reappeared. He had been defeated in a war of his own creation.

Again Tobias phoned Joe from a landline for privacy and better transatlantic connection. As before, he felt relieved when he heard the familiar voice on the other end. For a few moments, Joe entertained him. Seeing through Joe's thinly disguised humor, Tobias sensed that the matter was extremely serious.

"Joan mentioned that her cats do the same thing with the family's favorite Christmas ornaments," Joe began when he heard Tobias's account of the disappearing cubit story. "She is convinced that her cats were playing with the gnomes. They even hid the canary diamond that Nicholas wanted back from her."

Tobias took a deep breath, analyzing the elements that he'd been dealt. Nicholas Hapsburg, Joan's former college lover, had recently been destroyed, as a vampire by special forces protecting the US president. Nicholas had been annihilated during the president's recent visit with a computer-software mogul. The vampire had held most of the international corporate world under his power, which apparently had survived the intergalatic wars of ancient Egypt.

"Do you mean to say that her cats are fakirs?" Tobias questioned.

"The latest *National Geographic* did an article on how cats infiltrated the domestic lives of ancient Egyptian and weaseled their way into the hearts of their owners. It was a means of survival for the tiny beggars. Evolution perfected their techniques."

"I believe it," Tobias said.

"Your weasel at the conference is the former head of the KGB's mind-control unit, which is associated with US military medicine through occultist guilds."

Chapter Twenty-Five

When the parade begins to bore you

It is time to be in one

And live your own life

Even if it is a high-wire act without a net

Or a dance with some clown

Tune Reference: *Don't Cry Out Loud*

----Melissa Manchester

TOBIAS PASSED THE information on to the colonel, who had already done his own research and arrived at the same conclusion. They parted ways, promising to meet again in another synchronous moment. Before leaving to join his friends on the snow-covered mountains, Tobias beseeched the colonel for more information on the *mudras* that had transpired during the demonstration.

"It is an ancient art that existed before the rise of Old Egypt or the time of Moses. After being dormant for twelve hundred years, the healing form resurfaced in Japan recently. I am not familiar with the weasel's *mudras*; I only knew to counter them. In my studies, I employ the mudra set known as *Jin Shui Jyutsu*. I like it because it ties the body to the planet's energy centers, or chakras."

With those parting words, Tobias left the science institute. He joined Michelle, who happened to be lecturing at a birth center several hours away. Meanwhile, his buddies enjoyed their time on the ski slopes without him.

"You've had a busy day," Michelle commented when they reached their hotel room in the evening. "I'm looking forward to getting back to the US. Gabriella and I can sunbathe at the beach, while you and Joe go play in the electronics lab."

"I'm glad that we scheduled some time with Joe and Gabriella," Tobias said. Have you heard anything on how the boys were doing?"

"I checked in with the Thompsons and Whittingtons. Both boys are having a positive influence on their peers. The Thompsons want our son to stay longer, because he encourages her child to do his homework. The Whittingtons say that our son keeps her children entertained with La Crosse drills. Both families are enjoying the peace and harmony."

"Great," Tobias said happily. "Our children haven't overstayed their welcome."

"Healthy kids, healthy lives," Michelle said. She sighed. "It builds communities, which is a threat to both fascists and communists. I hope that they don't take over the health-care industry in the US."

The rest of the time at the hotel passed without incidence. After two days, Tobias and Michelle drove to the airport to catch their plane back to the United States. Shortly before they reached the car-rental agency, Tobias glanced at the fuel gauge.

"Oh, I forgot to fill the tank," Tobias said, and he started turning the car around. After circling around the rental office several times, they finally found the exit. He drove back the way they'd come in, and he found a gas station almost fifteen minutes away. Getting out of the car, he began refueling while Michelle joined him by the pump.

"I notice that you've lost your sense of direction again," Michelle whispered, while keeping watch on the street behind them. "It is the same as when we searched for the hotel."

"Yes, I know," Tobias said. "They must be waiting to ambush us at the car-rental agency. Let me drop you off at the airport. Then I'll leave the car at a place at a place where they can't get me."

When they arrived at the terminal, Tobias dropped off Michelle far away from the car-rental agency. She blew him a kiss as he drove away. Circling around the airport a few more times, he made his way to the rental office by a side street. Then he left the car in the middle of the empty lot and walked to the office. The agent hurriedly took the key and ran for the car, while he directed Tobias to a clerk in a booth. After completing the transaction, Tobias ran for the terminal. Racing up stairs and jumping over elevator steps, he hurried into the airport. Minutes later, he met Michelle where she was waiting in a line. There was a dark-skinned attendant near her, who offered to help with carrying the bags.

"How did it go?" she asked Tobias, while handing some bags to the gentleman.

"Well, I had friends who worked at car-rental agencies in the States. All you have to do to get their attention is leave the car in the street and dangle the keys in front of them. They'll leave you'll alone and run like crazy to park the car. You have to understand people's obsessive compulsions."

Without a further word, Tobias followed the attendant who was carrying some of Michelle's bags. He wore a gold necklace around his neck and was dressed in black pants and shirt. Dropping the bags at a short line for security clearance, he told them, "You must hurry."

He left as the agent checked Tobias's open palms after the couple had walked through the detector. Tobias had saved the life of a passenger on a previous flight. Rather than congratulate him on his advanced skills in osteopathic manipulation, airport security routinely insulted him by running strange metal objects around his hands or sending him through the detector more than once. Tobias sighed and waited for security to clear him. Then he and Michelle quickly gathered their things and rushed to board their plane. When they were away from eavesdroppers, Tobias whispered in Michelle's ear, "My hands must have a reputation! Little do they know that I imagine sending all the TSA radiation back to the people who perpetuated 9/11."

"Hush," Michelle told him. "Tomorrow is the anniversary of 9/11."

As they approached the gate, the sirens from eleven police and fire vehicles pierced the air. Michelle shuddered as she dropped her bag near the line at the counter. Tobias went immediately to the large picture window overlooking the runway. A few passengers stood beside him, gaping at the flashing lights and army of uniformed officers.

"Looks like they have the SWAT team at our plane," Tobias observed.

As Michelle turned around to hear him, the dark-skinned man with the gold necklace appeared from behind the counter. He approached Michelle with the words, "They reassigned another plane to this flight. The boarding gate is down the hall. Hurry, before it leaves."

Michelle nodded at Tobias, while the man shouldered one of her bags. Tobias ran after them, leaving the rest of the bewildered passengers at the window. When they reached their destination, the man oversaw the changes to the boarding passes. Then he disappeared a swarm of people in the near vicinity. Tobias mouthed the words *thank you*, and the man responded with a smile and a nod before vanishing.

As they headed down an isolated corridor to board their new plane, Tobias leaned closer to Michelle and said, "Looks like the modern underground railroad is now accepting Caucasians."

"Lucky for us," Michelle responded, straightening her back as she lugged her cases over the metal planks. She wrinkled her brow for a second, and then she questioned Tobias, "What tipped you off about the car-rental agency?"

"Remember? We reserved the car while we were waiting between planes in San Francisco. The other dark-skinned man at the desk wore the ring of a popular occult group," Tobias informed her.

The next day, Tobias and Michelle landed at the airport in California, where they'd planned to meet Joe and Gabriella. As the couple helped Joe and Michelle retrieve their bags from the carousel, Tobias watched the people congregate in the area. There was one familiar face in the crowd, sitting comfortably in the lobby as if he had been waiting for Tobias's appearance. Tobias looked at the silvered-haired man right in the eye. They silently acknowledged each other before leaving the area. Tobias glanced at several mounted television screens in the area, which were flashing headline news. Without saying a word to the others about the incident, Tobias watched footage of the burning embassy in Libya.

Instead, he whispered to his group. "There's a man from the Italian restaurant in Switzerland. He's a remote sensor."

"Yes, I saw him," Michelle responded. "He is without his women friend. He doesn't appear to be missing her. I like his nice brown eyes. They match his tan." Cocking her head side to side as she tossed one shoulder, she remarked, "It's not the dark skin tone that we find in the rainy Pacific Northwest, but it fits California."

They placed their bags in Joe's Prius and found their seats in the back. Gabriella sat in front and watched for traffic. As soon as they left the airport parking lot for the freeway, the conversation drifted to a more serious tone of scientific inquiry.

"The Japanese word for mudra is *injo*," Joe said, picking up the conversation between Tobias and his colleague without missing a beat. He momentarily looked at Tobias in the rearview mirror for his response. Then he focused his attention on the road.

Tobias appreciated Joe's thoughtful ability to zero in on a topic. He knew about Joe's two-way tapping at his former aeronautics company. Joe also possessed the ability to peer into the mechanisms of the universe; he could glean insight into the relationships that fit together like cogs on a perpetually rotating gear.

Michelle eyed Tobias. Gabriella slightly turned her head towards them, sensing the subtle play between the two people in the back. Then she tossed her head toward Joe beside her at the wheel. Joe picked up Gabriella's cue.

"I don't know why anyone would want to work in Libya," he said. "It is hard enough just living in the US."

"I suppose," Tobias responded. "They make it hard. I would rather focus on the lives saved rather than harass the winners over Arab politics."

"All the more reason to enjoy the simple things in life," Joe said. "Now about those mudras. Gestures like the sign of the cross, flipping someone off, and hook 'em horns are technically mudras. So what is so special about the Japanese *injo*? It is my understanding that the word has a derogatory meaning, because it refers to a deadbeat Korean emperor of the seventeenth century."

"I realize that," Tobias said. He explained, "Much has been lost in translation over thousands and thousands of years. Our *injo* pertains to the arrangement of the crystal skulls on Gondwanaland. Perhaps, *Jin Shui Jyutsu* is the better term. The Japanese consider it more of an art form rather than a mere gesture. The path of awareness can be considered a Zen discipline, which brings us to the awakened eye on the Eye-in-the-Sky. *Jin Shui Jyutsu* translates to 'art of the creator through human knowing and compassion.' This would have been the ultimate goal of the high priestesses reseeding Eden within the iris of Gondwanaland. With awareness and empathy for human beings, a rift between Adam and Lilith never would have transpired."

"Lilith left Eden with a pregnancy," Michelle interjected. Then she continued, "We have the story worked out."

"The child was a daughter and possessed the spirit of a Morgan Le Fey, someone who hated the earth spirits found in the MidEarth. The daughter returned to Eden, cursing Eve and her descendants. What survived was a soul ray associated with the divine mother, the one who will return and crush the head of the serpent who drove Lilith out of Eden initially. The Serpentines worked through Lilith's dream state or subconscious. At some level, she made a choice to allow the infiltrated dreams to unhinge her and sabotage her relationships in Eden. No, Eden is not where I want to go. I prefer Gondwanaland, where the women are high priestesses."

Tobias added, "Mother Mary, or the divine mother, is represented by the notion of purity, often symbolized by the Easter lily. Tiger lily depicts the essence of the women fighting back through awareness and compassion. They fit the *Lysistrata* mold, which is rowdy and ribald."

"Wasn't *Lysistrata* a play written by the Greek Aristophanes, almost four hundred years before the Christ consciousness appeared?" Gabriella asked.

"Yes," Tobias answered. He told them, "It was performed four hundred years before the female counterpart to the Christ consciousness appeared. This Ma Ray is the spiritual mother of the universe, which nurtures the childlike earth spirit. Her crown is one of the stars, like her male counterpart in his divine form. Mercy is a human invention. Compassion, or empathy, speaks to the divine nature in all of us."

"Donna said that the Council of Orion heralded Ma Ray," Joe mentioned.

"What?" Tobias questioned. "When did you talk to Donna about this? Sounds like she pulled another piece of information literally out of thin air."

"After you called me about the fakir, I checked with her concerning the eye on the Eye-in-the-Sky. She came up with a scenario that Joan validated," Joe said. "Well, she and Carrie are hopping separate planes to the West Coast to talk to us face-to-face. I expect them anytime. They may just show up at my company's lab. They say that they don't often get a chance to see the two of us together."

Tobias took a deep breath, and he glanced at Michelle.

Michelle responded, "Great! We can share information that might later prove useful. Ever since 2010, the corporate oligarchy has been going after alternative education, alternative energy, and alternative medicine. It has become obvious that choice and coexistence is out of the question."

Tobias added, "Fill me in. What does all this have to do with the history of the world and the passing of souls to the other side?

"Oh, you mean the history of the soul transport network. They call it STN," Joe replied. "Being physicians, you would both be interested in this topic."

"It relates Greek mythology to the Garden of Eden, the biblical account of the first human family," Gabriella explained. "We have to look to the heavens for the origin of the problem with the creation story."

Joe jumped into the conversation to recount the story. He related, "Apparently, the Council of Orion gathered the refugees in the galaxy, while the Serpentines and others wrought havoc. After Eden fell, the Council of Orion approached the godhead in the universe, which amounted to the Pleiades. The Pleiades was the only intact planetary system left. Their advanced culture prohibited Serpentine attacks and created a portal for the souls to travel between Gondwanaland and their star clusters. Unfortunately, Lilith's son, Hades, sabotaged the portal. He created a hell on earth. Persephone, who had given the kings of Pleiades seven daughters, later decided to join Hades. Not only was Persephone a drama queen, she went to Hades willingly. However, she bore a son, who became tired of the whole mess and did a number on Hades. Persephone obtained half-time visiting rights on the planet. Now she is being shut down totally by the arrival of the divine feminine."

"I told you, Joe," Gabriella said encouragingly. "Your job is to help bring in the divine feminine."

"Oh, that's another story," Joe said. "Let's make a deal. I will show Tobias my latest project, while you and Michelle have some female bonding time. You both can go lie out on the beach and bring in as much of the divine feminine as you want. Then come pick us up for dinner in four hours. Call first. We may decide to take a cab home early."

"*Bueno*, Joe. It's a date," Gabriella said. "We can take my car, and we'll leave yours in the lot before heading for the beach. You won't need to call a cab, and we can stay out as long as we wish. We'll catch up when we are done at the beach."

Tobias and Joe laughed at her proposal, accepting the offer.

Michelle laughed. "Deal," she added.

The women dropped Joe and Tobias off at the electronics lab. Then they went to Gabriella's home, where they could change and pick up the second car. Unlocking the front door with a key, Joe ushered Tobias inside the building. No one else appeared in the parking lot or office complex. Tobias followed Joe down a dimly lit hall and into an office filled with computer hardware.

As they entered the room, Joe explained his recent findings to Tobias, "Before the assassination, the president"s infant son was murdered by the military assistants who constructed the special facilities for the delivery. There is a tape of the president complaining about the five-thousand-dollar cost and the arrangements. My assets on the other side confirmed the murder. I learned about it through my taps. The day before they murdered him, the president confronted the air force staff at the San Antonio hospital. It was a power play at the new birth center. He spent his last moments dealing with them face-to-face on their oppression of the Irish. His older brother and sisters had been abused in hospitals since childhood. It was typical persecution for rising Irish families."

"I know. Though his wife was a triple agent, she was no threat to the president. The jackal understood that the others at Dealey Plaza were sadists. He lowered the gun on the president's wife and disobeyed orders. Then he ran," Tobias quietly said. Pausing for a moment, he added, "It matched the

Serpentine's agenda for worldwide genocide of certain DNA strands that survived after Atlantis. They were trying to erase any memory of the old conflicts. The reality is that you can run but you can't hide."

Tobias wondered around the room and surveyed the equipment. Today, the average cost for a home birth was less than a thousand. Michelle found that the home births empowered families and made them more self-sufficient. Tobias added, "The Serpentines, with their eugenics programs, know more about ourselves than we do. I have spent almost a lifetime developing immunity through the type of medicine that I practice." Tobias paused for a moment, staring at the assortment of various wires strewn over a desk. "Let's go relax over a glass of wine, Joe. I get the basic idea. By murdering our presidents and others, the Serpentines threw the baby out with the bath water. They haven't a clue how to save the planet from nuclear holocaust; maybe they don't want to. Peace requires the correct mind-set. It is what separates us from them; it is more than just our DNA. It is the choices we make and what we do. They lied about what the murdered presidents and the others did, thinking that they can fool people. But truth lingers. As a result of their deception, a fragmented view of history develops that doesn't make sense."

Without saying another word, Joe led Tobias out of the office and turned out the lights. The darkness enveloped them for a few minutes before they stepped outside into the bright, humid atmosphere. The contrast startled them and reminded them that fear could simply be dealt with by a change in scenery or flipping on a switch.

Chapter Twenty-Six

Sooner or later

A breath-taking speed

Has got to stop

Even a racehorse

Knows when to drop the race

For rest and recovery

Tune Reference: *Life In The Fast Lane*

----Eagles

"THERE YOU ARE!" Carrie waved from across the parking lot. She hurried from her rental car and hugged the two men. "Back into the lab. I need help."

"No more lab work for now," Joe said. "We can talk on that patch of lawn underneath that tree over there."

Tobias walked over to the grassy area and lay down. Leaving Joe at the door to his office build, Carrie hurriedly walked over and sat cross-legged beside Tobias. She said, "The ankle is working great, but I might lose my job."

"It is better than your life," Tobias quipped.

Joe joined them on the ground, and he listened thoughtfully to the ensuing discussion.

"The Serpentines are laced into the aeronautical profession. I want my intellectual freedom. They are gunning down the children of my colleagues to manipulate them into working overtime."

"Overtime for what?" Tobias said, studying the streaks of chemtrails in the sky above.

"The robber barons want to escape by using space ships. They need the minds of my colleagues to do this. My colleagues are worried about losing their jobs, so they work harder and harder under traumatized conditions. I am getting out of one project, because I consider it unethical."

"Which one is that?" Tobias asked.

"They want me to build radio-controlled cars that respond to transmitters from outer-space," Carrie answered. "All the oil barons that owned the buildings in Dealey Plaza had business interests in outer space."

"Your ankle was telling you to keep your feet on the ground," Tobias said. "I'm glad it is working."

"Yes, I need protection," Carrie said. "I need to traverse this terrain without having my ankle go out."

Tobias instructed Carrie to lie down, as he rose to complete the body work she had started at Mount Saint. Helen's. His hands removed cords linking her to Serpentine encounters. He removed implants found in the different energetic fields surrounding her body, which had been placed during traumatic life transitions. Joe watched, and he asked, "Tobias, could you work on my electronics equipment when you are done?"

"That's how I got started," Tobias said. "I went from radios to human receivers."

Tobias gave Carrie some homeopathic remedies for protection, and then he went into Joe's lab to examine his wires and semiconductors. Making a few corrections to the schematics, Tobias rearranged the equipment accordingly. His work was interrupted by a hard knock at the entrance to the building. They had locked it behind them.

"Oh, that must be our rockhound," Joe mentioned. He stayed with Tobias as Carrie went to open the door for Donna. "Tell her to bring in her collections."

"Great," Tobias commented. "See if she has a few spare crystals on her."

Donna came in and deposited a dusty knapsack on Joe's desk. "I thought you'd never ask," she said. "Here's the map of Gondwanaland. Here's a pink crystal skull. I'm keeping the green one. Here are a few quartz crystals that Joan's husband gave me from the office."

Tobias unfurled the map of Gondwanaland with the illustration of the eye superimposed on it. The only visible structure of the oval-shaped eye was an iris, formed by the circular line connecting the layout of crystal skulls found in the region by present-day paleontologists. Holding the skull in his hand, Tobias blinked his eyes as he sensed its energy and determined its new place in the scheme of things. "We put this head at the heart of Joe's electronics. It is a communications piece. This eliminates a few wires, which could easily be tapped. Serpentines can't tap crystal skulls."

Then he examined the quartz crystals that Donna had brought from the geophysics office. "These rocks represent twenty-two dimensional maps. They have the story of historical events embedded in them---like a stratigraphic rock record---except these records have been crystallized. With practice, you can tune in. They contain the information you need to work safely and communicate with those involved in the project. We need to grid all this with the quartz grains of sand on the beach. Let's go."

Donna nodded in satisfaction. "Now I understand how I've been able to communicate with Carrie without getting tapped."

"Like sisters. Great." Joe echoed, "To the beach."

****

Hours later, Tobias sipped his glass of Merlot in the setting sun. The two men had decided to relax in Joe's backyard after separating from the women on the beach. Leaving Joe alone in the kitchen with his thoughts, Tobias went to sit at a table near a small fishpond. The bubbling fountain in the middle operated on solar energy. There were tiny LED lights giving hues of color to the water that the pump ejected into the air. He quieted while Joe prepared a tray of appetizers in the nearby open-door kitchen. Their wives had not returned from their beach trek, which gave them more time to process their ongoing discussions. Keeping it simple, Joe brought out some hummus and celery after a few minutes.

"Did know that celery is a nervine?" Tobias asked Joe as he dipped a piece of celery in the hummus. *Nervine* described substances that soothed the nervous system and regenerated frayed endings. "We are going to need some carrots and bell peppers to go with this dip. My turn for duty."

"Next course," Joe said, sitting down across from Tobias. "We gotta save our appetites for going out with the ladies when they arrive. It's a date, remember?"

"You're right," Tobias said before crunching down on a hummus-covered celery stick. "I'm giving them forty minutes before I spring for takeout. Otherwise, I will be too famished to go anywhere."

"Pace yourself, Tobias," Joe cautioned him. "Here, I'll do all the thinking, while you float in the zone. Stand there and look cute. I'll make all the decisions when our ladies arrive. It is better that you quit thinking for a while."

"Sounds like a plan," Tobias rejoined. He held a piece of celery between his fingers and the light refracted off the green ribs. "It is about time that I slowed down. As I tell my clients, ninety percent of life is just showing up. It is how I got through med school. I'd arrive in the morning to take an exam, and the test would be canceled due to power failures or snowstorms. I kept my endeavors in harmony. The planet helped me get out of half of my scrapes. Other times it was time aberrations in the electromagnetic fields."

"More wine, Tobias?" Joe asked.

"No," he said, and he placed his hand over his glass, so that Joe would not add to its contents. "Otherwise I won't be able to pin my thoughts down, and I'll fall asleep," he added. "Michelle keeps me on a my toes. I'm really just a tired, old doc."

"I want to know about the time aberrations," Joe announced. "Then I'll stop trying to loosen your tongue."

"Well," Tobias began, savoring a swallow of Merlot as he stared into the distance. "I had a prof, who became upset that I was writing a class project so efficiently and easily. So he gave me more hoops to jump through. He wanted me to do a Duncan Multiple Range Test on some data analysis. Knowing that the computer center would be closed shortly for the weekend, he gave me the assignment at the last minute and a deadline on my project. It was obvious that he didn't want me to graduate, because I had politely chosen another Design of Experiments class instead of his. The class I chose used Montgomery's book, otherwise it would have been like studying human factors from Adolf Hitler. So, of course, I went to the Forestry-Fisheries Department for the class. They account for life in the analysis of their variables. For example, they thought it was significant when something like a fish died during the experiment. What if more than one fish died? What if the experiment concerned human beings instead of fish? Rather than treat the death as coincidence, I wanted an analysis that placed significance on tragedies. It would matter to the people who loved that fish."

Tobias resumed, "When I realized that the demands were being made in retaliation, I thought that I was a goner. Though the test was just a matter of finding the right buttons to do the test automatically, the timing of his request doomed me to failure. It was in the days of tracking computer printouts, just barely past the IBM computer card age. Anything one did on a university computer had to be picked up at the center, which printed the data. It took days, sometimes weeks, to get through the process."

Joe grimaced at the notion of such a quandary.

Noting his reaction, Tobias bowed his head and studied the plate of hummus and celery. "It is how I came to rely on time aberrations as my friend, which is sorta like believing in angles and fairies. Not *angels*, but angles. Finding an angle, I called up a few angelic friends, who worked for corporations with far more efficient and powerful computer systems. I got them to push the buttons and wave their magic wands. They sent the processing remotely to the university computer system, which provided better printouts for its operations. Somebody must have been bored that day or struck by lightning, because the center opened unusually early that day for work. My calculations determined that someone had been there at four in the morning. My sixth sense told me to call the center at six in the morning to check and see whether the printout was ready. It was ready for me to pick up and turn in. You should have seen the professor's jaw fall to the floor after I handed him the printout. People in the department started saying that God was on my side. Only the males suspected of carrying the extra Y-chromosomes liked the prof in question."

Joe chuckled. He put his wineglass down, so he could remain sober enough to follow the conversation with Tobias. Pouring himself some water from a flask on the table, he put a slice of lemon on the edge of the glass.

"It wasn't the first time. The same thing happened when I bought my guitar at a pawnshop. I was a teenager, and made an offer on a vintage Yamaha. The seller demanded cash and gave me a time constraint." Looking at Joe squarely in the face, he asked him, "Do you remember how difficult it was to obtain cash forty years ago in a Southern state with Sunday blue laws?"

"What's a *blue law*?" Joe questioned.

"It is a law designed to enforce religious policy, and limit commerce on the Sabbath," Tobias replied. "When I returned with the appropriate amount of cold, hard cash, the shop owner nearly fell over. He asked me whether I had got the money gambling."

Joe started coughing over his glass of water. He smiled as he put his glass down on the table and struggled to regain his composure. He didn't want Tobias to start slapping his back for emergency first aid. Waving his hand in the air, he assured Tobias that he was in no danger of choking on his water.

Tobias explained, before Joe took him too seriously. "Being a working teenager, I knew all the stores and places that would cash my checks for ten dollars over. The ones who knew me gave me more, so I only had to go to about five or six different places. I was a kid with a letter jacket and a

350 engine---I could do anything, and I learned to try. As long as I kept examining all my options and putting one foot in front of the other, I never seemed to run out of solutions. Even a punt, when it is fourth down in a football game, is a mode of operation. A psychology instructor once defined *insanity* as when a person keeps doing the same thing over and over to no effect. From my experience with the purchase of the guitar, the point was made---God does work on the Sabbath if the play is earnest."

"Speaking about religious passions," Joe began, mildly changing the subject. "The present nuclear threat is from a communist country where the Tree of Life is located. North Korea may not know quite what they have, but they think that they can use the knowledge for world domination. They intend to manipulate Carrie's time wrinkle."

"Do you mean put a stranglehold on the Goddesses of Fates associated with the Tree of Life?" Tobias said. "It will backfire."

"Yeah, but it has been infected with Arachnids from the galaxy," Joe said, slumping slightly over his unfinished celery and rubbing his head. "I learned this through my taps. How can you be so sure that they will not succeed in misusing the Kabbalah tree?"

"Hmmm," Tobias mused. "It is difficult to explain without examining some historical wild cards and the effect on the timing of events. The issue of nuclear war begins with Prohibition, which started shortly after the end of WWI. Prohibition was repealed when stocks returned to the pre-Depression levels and ended with WWII. Inadvertently, the link between the economy, wars, and alcohol made witnesses out of certain ethnic families, who became targets. The wild card is that some of these families refused to sell to the robber barons. They closed their oil wells and their mines. They quit working with people who murdered their loved ones in competing oil wells."

Tobias stopped for a moment and smiled. Placing his glass down on the table, he related, "It is sorta like your fish pond here, Joe. It is filled with kindred spirits. Those who do not honor life cannot use the Tree of Life to destroy life. Some people destroyed the offshoot from the Tree of Life at Versailles, when they murdered the president in Dallas. It became an oxymoron. It will take a lot of suicidal insects to destroy their terrain. I suspect that most bugs don't have that kind of programming. Unlike humans, they do not have the capacity to escape the planet. The bugs are bugged, but it is a positive programming---otherwise they could not exist. Either way, so the Tree of Life dies, but it will live on in those who understand its significance or meaning."

Chapter Twenty-Seven

Face it

And learn to discard

Other people's hang-ups

Projected onto your own life

Tune Reference: *Make Your Own Kind Of Music*

----Cass Elliot

DONNA AND CARRIE appeared in Joe's back yard, and interrupted the discussion between Tobias and Joe.

"Nice place you got here, Joe," Donna said, looking around. Then she told Tobias, "My turn. I need help. My husband and I have been on the run ever since we met."

Tobias rose from his chair and announced, "Time for some shadowboxing." He looked at Joe, "Where are your mitts, Joe?"

Sipping his wine, Joe said, "There's spare pair in the exercise room. You are welcomed to them, as long as you don't punch a hole in the wall or send someone to the emergency room." Remaining motionless in his chair, he added, "Don't look at me. I'm not moving."

Carrie stayed outside and enjoyed the appetizers with Joe. Donna followed Tobias in the house, where they found Joe's boxing gloves in the exercise room. There were also a mirror and a punching bag in the quarters.

Tossing Donna a pair of mitts to put over her hands, Tobias said, "You've got to find your own rhythm in the intrigue that surrounds you. You are not from the black dog military group, the ones who brought us the jackal. You are a wild coyote."

Tobias quickly covered his hands with mitts and started dancing back and forth, moving lightly on his feet. With some hesitation, Donna put the gloves on and faced Tobias. She began bouncing on her feet to mimic Tobias's stance. He advised her, "Learn by blocking and rolling with my punches. Then let it fly when it is your turn. No more going above and *beyond*."

A little while later, Donna and Tobias returned to the patio, where Joe and Carrie were making small talk.

"We heard the thunder from the exercise room. We thought someone was going to get killed," Joe said.

"We decided to wait until we saw blood," Carrie said. "We are saving ourselves."

Tobias commented, "No chance of seeing blood out here, if one of us dies."

"That's why none of us went in," Carrie said. "It is called purposeful denial."

Taking a deep breath, Joe resumed talking to Carrie, "By offering himself up, the president did a better job than his brother in eliminating the underground that had seized power during Prohibition, especially the ones concerned with trafficking into Cuba. This is what happens to survivors of horrific wars; they don't want anyone to start one at home. They call them vets."

Carrie added, "They already had slave labor, which how Russia and the Vatican got in. Why give them drugs and alcohol to go with their missiles?"

"Some of the tentacles reach into the Pennsylvania oil boom," Tobias observed. "There was a banana-republic family that rented to the assassination suspect living in Texas. Their relatives bought a share in the same oil company owned by my Irish-German relatives. Owners of the mine and oil well figured that investor represented a handler from the larger, competing company. It was the same one that later employed the ancestors of the slain president and his wife. My relatives lived in the county that produced the most oil in Pennsylvania. They learned quickly to avoid cutthroat business relationships. Some of the relations went to work on the Ohio wells. They knew how to use explosives to shoot a mine or well. The fiancé of one of my ancestors was set up by the competitors, and he died in a TNT explosion at one of the wells. Afterward, they closed the mine and capped the well, hoping to save themselves further bloodshed and harassment. They counted their blessings."

Tobias stopped for a moment and gazed into the reflections of the fishpond. Native species swam the waters; occasionally, they could be spotted by the light of their silver reflections. The sight of the darting silver lights animated Tobias's contemplations. He resumed speaking, "There's an investment company that uses the *Starfish Story* for its philosophy on socially responsible commerce. It is the same with the practice of natural medicine promoting the medicine of the individual. *The Starfish Story* is based on the writings of a highly respected academician who studied anthropology and nature. He had over thirty honorary degrees. Like most other great research, it was repressed after the president's assassination in Dallas."

"I understand," Joe said. "The daughters of my Irish uncle enjoy singing about *looking for the rainbow and following the fella who follows the dream*. The communist-fascists don't care for dreamers. Rescuing one stranded starfish on the beach, while giving up on the dying batch, is dreamy. Starfish rescuers nourish hope, saving one solely for the reason that it matters to the one that is saved."

"There is more to the story," Tobias added. "First, any chiropractor, who knows their autonomic nervous system physiology will say that the latest slain president did not suffer from adrenal fatigue. His skin had a bronze pigmentation, which means that he had adrenal function. No adrenals, no pigmentation. It is as simple as that regarding melanocytes and endocrine function. Information gleaned from witnesses suggests the bronze coloring was probably due to eating carrots with the First Lady."

Tobias added, "Whenever I binge on carrots, my skin becomes bronze too. Carrots are high in antioxidants, and they protect the upper respiratory system from second-hand smoke, especially in densely populated areas. My clients think that I've been tanning or on vacation. They ask where I have been. The secret to life is carrots."

"Second, as my ancestors learned during the oil boom, it is about the relationships. In a small town, the one who dies is someone's lover, or someone's brother, someone's niece, or someone's father. The value of life increases with the interdependent connections. This is why I went to the natural world to pursue my studies in design of experiments. It sorta makes me wonder what type of analysis the unnatural docs are using, considering that the university hospital looked to this particular professor for their policy study."

"Don't ask me," Joe said. Then he sighed. "The modern medicine societies are owned by the oil barons."

"Now independent small businesses, choice schools, alternative energy, and integrative medicine are being targeted," Tobias observed. "When I first moved to my neighborhood over twenty years ago, the newspapers printed the police reports. Last summer, the police busted hundreds of teenagers for underage alcohol and drug abuse. Today the rest of the news consists of real-estate ads for the newly transient society. Many independent newspapers in the Northwest suddenly quieted after linking an industrial lobbyist to the burgeoning software industry. It was the same lobbyist from the special prosecutor's investigations. The newspaper suffered some turnover in staff and ownership."

Tobias paused again to watch a school of fish swirl around in perfect synchronicity. Then he related, "The oil outlaws take care of their lobbyists as well as those who grease the skids for them. After getting the Armageddon president elected while a college republican, the same industrial lobbyist grew robust with a Pacific Northwest law firm parenting the software industry. Patrick Fitzgerald abandoned the prosecution of the milieu for issues that could not be revealed to the public. Ironically, Fitzgerald prosecuted the owners of the newspapers concurrently with his Libby investigation. The papers arrive free of charge and are delivered to our driveway whether we want them or not. We just recycle. Anything that I need to know I hear by word of mouth."

"Senator Wellstone, who spoke at the WTO protests, died in a mysterious plane crash several years later," Joe stated. "A reporter from an independent Texas newspaper was there also. The reporter later lost his seat as a state commissioner to the Democratic turncoat that neocon bankers are now sponsoring."

"Hmm," Tobias murmured. "In that part of Texas, they idolize their children, putting large statues of them in their yards---while the kids are still living. I think that would be uncomfortable, preferring the real thing, myself. It's a little different, this form of child worship. Aren't there laws against idolatry---maybe some mosaic ones carved in stone? These cults die hard. I prefer to love my children rather than hug them with nuclear arms. You'd think they'd invest their money in education instead, but perhaps the pesticides in the lawn went to their heads. Now they really overdo it on pomp and circumstance---though it is not quite as bad as the scarce-world-resources club. A friend of mine grew up with the club's debutante parties. His experiences never seemed impressive. He always became bored, yet he strove to play the game that he saw through." Tobias leaned forward and placed both hands on the table. "If I were one of his daughters, I'd throw up at the thought of being displayed for breeding purposes like a prime beef steer. It is eugenics and social programming."

"Gabriella calls it 'fashion on the hoof,' " Joe quipped.

Chapter Twenty-Eight

The basic question of life is not 'why'

Or 'why being'

But, are we having a good time?

Tune Reference: *Good Riddance (Time Of Your Life)*

----Green Day

THE NEXT MORNING, Tobias and Michelle left for their home near Springfield, Oregon. After waving good-bye to Joe and Gabriella outside of the Oakland airport, they quickly boarded their plane bound for Portland. After they landed in Oregon, they located their vehicle in the parking lot and drove south. Once off the main highway, they followed a winding road to the wooded foothills overlooking the city of Springfield. The sight of the towering Douglas fir and cedar trees comforted Tobias.

He's back. He's back. Tobias heard the whispers of dancing branches in the wind. The forest seemed more animated than usual, and the green of the trees appeared more vibrant. The collective consciousness knew that he was listening to its spirit. Michelle looked up at the canopy surrounding them. She also seemed to hear the motion in the breeze.

Tobias slowly turned into the driveway in front of the simple two-story house. After parking the car, he stepped out of the driver's side and studied the line of trees thirty yards away. Michelle got out of the car and searched the horizon. Then she gathered a few things from the car and headed toward the front door. Tobias retrieved some bags from the vehicle and followed closely behind her. When he took the items into the living room, Tobias sensed a slight chill in the air.

"I'll get the rest," Michelle offered. "How about starting a fire? It feels cold in here, for some reason."

"I'll go bring in some more wood," Tobias replied. "It will be dark in a half hour. I want to settle in before picking up the children."

Before separating, they stopped together to gaze at poster in the recreation room. Entitled *Unser Wald*, it was an illustration by a German woodcutter. The title meant "Our Woods."

"This is still the kids' favorite picture," Tobias mentioned. "It has never faded from their view, even during their teenage years."

"Remember how in 1970 the artist won an award in Germany for illustrations of family and children? His work is now repressed. *Our Woods* exists mostly in the minds and souls of the viewers. This German woodcutter-artist knew what he was doing."

"It transmits the vision of their German Bavarian ancestors," Tobias reasoned. "There must be ten million words in this design. It is very healing."

Taking a deep breath, they exited the room to finish their various tasks. Michelle listened to the phone messages on the machine as Tobias went upstairs to change into some work clothes. When he returned to the kitchen, she announced, "The Thompsons and Whittingtons want to keep the kids another night; apparently they are in the middle of a project. Looks like we have the place to ourselves tonight."

Tobias smiled. "I could use some time to regroup and rest up. I promised to take the boys to the bookstore this weekend."

"Good. I want to come too. Let's have lunch at the bookstore cafe. Make a day out of it."

"Something is going on. I could sense it as we arrived. The outdoor temperature seemed to drop ten degrees," he said.

Without any hint of trepidation, Michelle grinned slightly. "I like your spirit, Tobias. Go check the woodpile. Maybe your Sasquatch friends have something to tell you, especially now that humanity is becoming endangered. Meanwhile, I am looking forward to spending time as a family again."

Tobias chuckled; there was a glint in his eye. Slinging his axe with one arm like a slow-moving baton, he went outside to check his woodpile. A few yards outside the back door, he saw them coming. There were about nine of them---tall, dark figures hiding in the understory. Moving around like an incoming parade from the nearby mountains, the Sasquatch gathered around Tobias. They always stayed in the shadows, never fully revealing themselves. The Sasquatch hid so that he would not be prejudice by their appearance and would continue to communicate with them.

We welcome you. Much is happening on the planet. We will download the details in your dreams, and we will keep each other safe.

Sensing their intentions, Tobias relaxed. He turned around to finish splitting a log. Studying the lines in the wood, he rearranged the wedge so that he would hit it squarely on the metal top. The noise helped him mimic the quality of the strike. *Click. Thump. Click. Thump.* The log fell apart, revealing more sinewy lines on the face of the freshly cut wood. Tobias split a few more logs. He never felt alone in the woods. The presence of the Sasquatch always calmed him. He knew that they were keeping a watch on things in the universe while serving as a buffer for his sensitivities. They prevented intergalactic events from affecting him directly. Tobias feared being split in two, like the logs around his feet. He didn't want his consciousness to be zapped by some wayward intimidator trying to get the upper hand in a war that had started before the creation of the planet. By taking inventory of the contents of most of the portals in the forest, Tobias avoided unpleasant surprises. Like the Neanderthals, he wanted to keep himself pure, especially from those who wanted to shock his mind. With the Sasquatch protecting him, he didn't have to worry about having a plan for striking back.

I'll see what comes my way, Tobias told the Sasquatch with his being. *"It will be like a walk in the woods."*

Then he filled his canvas wood carrier with logs and walked back to the house. Night had fallen quickly, and now it was almost too dark to see. He made his way carefully, being guided by the soft lights behind the window shades. Once inside, he felt delighted to be back inside his own home, the place that Michelle kept so cozy.

The next day, at the bookstore cafe with his family, he did not remember his dreams of the previous evening. It wasn't until he ran into a few colleagues that he recalled what had transpired during his sleep. That was the way the Sasquatch spoke. Lacing their words on the mists streaming down the mountains, they revealed themselves to the conscious mind in bits and pieces. Their messages resonated with the vapors of dreams that connected to the real world like a dot-to-dots in a coloring book. Tobias never got the information all at once. Instead, he had to allow it to resonate with his awareness. Once he was on the path, the message flowered before him in its entirety.

"Hey, Tobias!" Dr. Bernard cried. The chair of the research department waved at him. "How's it going?"

"Intense, as usual," Tobias answered. Then he asked him, "Have you been using much *Uranium nitricum* lately in the homeopathy clinic. It is going out of my office as if the population has been radiated or something."

"No," Dr. Bernard said quietly. Then he looked at the fellow researcher sitting across from him. "Dr. Jones, this is Dr. Holly Schmaeder. She is working on a grant pertaining to ormuz substances."

"I haven't used *Uranium nitricum* much," Dr. Schmaeder said. "You might research the work of a particular homeopath in Ireland. She found some radioactive granite and marble just sitting in the landscape around a little town. After making a homeopathic out of the substances, she did a proving. It helps in certain types of wasting diseases. She used it for a group of emaciated people, who'd look as if they had been through a series of chemo treatments."

"Great. I'll look it up and compare it to the other remedies." Changing the subject, Tobias asked, "What is an ormuz material?"

"Ormuz materials behave similarly to a homeopathic substance. The material consists of a hollow cylindrical tube that has superconductivity properties. Scientists have been studying the ancient Druid stone monuments. The structures are hollow inside, like an ormuz substance."

Out of the corner of his eye, Tobias noticed the boys were waiting impatiently, restlessly roving the cafe. Tobias called Michelle over to the table with the other doctors, making the introductions brief. He wanted his colleagues to continue their conversation without further interruption, but he also wanted to keep his family from wilting due to boredom.

"See you later," he told his friends a few minutes later. "I'll check on those interesting substances. I want to see how they fit the research that I presented in Russia. The Russian scientists are the only ones who seem to pay attention to the quantum physical approach. They have their own wonders to explain---like some of their psychokinetic healers who can bend spoons with their minds."

****

A few months later, Tobias received a call from the colonel.

"Listen. I barely survived a terrible car wreck two months ago," the colonel began in a strained voice. "I was rear-ended and caught between two trucks. My jaw was broken. It is going to be a long healing process. Before I was hit, I saw several dark giants, about three-stories tall, surround me on all sides. They are *diablos*, or fallen ones. Like the Cyclops, the dark giants are the by-products of Serpentine and human forms. I need information how to escape them."

After suggesting a few homeopathic practitioners who might break the link with the diablos and their network of Grays, Tobias slowly put down his cell phone. Then he jotted down a phone number and e-mail address where he could maintain contact with his friend. Afterward, he called Donna and related his colleague's story.

Donna had more to offer on the subject. She briefed him on the latest updates. "They found skeletal remains of the *diablos* in the Mideast and in the middle of the United States. The forty-foot skeletons were found in places like Ohio, Tennessee, Wisconsin, Minnesota, Idaho, Sumeria, and Saudia Arabia. Scientists and scholars consider them an alien race from Anunnak, a planet inhabited by the Serpentine mate of Lilith. The ancient Greeks referred to Anu as Cronus. Besides the bible, the are references to the diablos in ancient writings found shortly before the American Civil War."

"So where do the Pantagones come into the picture?" Tobias queried.

"The Pantagones are the South American cousins of your Pacific Northwest Sasquatch, who are Neanderthals. The Neanderthals are the pure descendants of the Titans, who escaped Serpentine experimentation during Atlantis. Later, the Pantgones helped the victims from the Cave of the Hands escape Serpentine persecution," Donna said. Then she added, "It is a long story. I was working it out with Joe the other day. We were reviewing our trip to Mexico, during which we examined the intergalatic sites pertaining to the Mexican-American War. It was Joe's point of departure for bringing in the divine feminine. Gabriella put him up to it. We started at a mission near Los Angeles, home of the Tangvas and their intergalactic friends, the Lacerta. The Lacerta were led by the celestial known as the Angel Gabriel. They provided support for the soul transport system after Atlantis fell."

"Figures," Tobias speculated. "What is the difference between the Tongas and Tangvas?"

"It is a long story. The Tongas represent a lost tribe of the human family. They are considered the descendants of Jacob's son Naphtali. The tribes became lost after an intergalactic attack on the Babylon Tower. The Tangvas are descendants of the Titan god Atlas, who founded Atlantis. When Atlantis fell, Lacerta airlifted survivors to present-day Los Angeles. Other Atlanteans sailed to what is known today as Ireland. They became the Celtics, possessing more of the earth-spirit DNA. The Dragon flyer bloodline went to the mountains in Siberia and Tibet. The airlifted Atlanteans carried the Gaud bloodlines. The human form was developed on the supercontinent preceding the split that created Gondwanaland and Laurasia. When Lilith joined the Serpentine forces sequestered in Asia, the prototype known as Ma Ray was put into the twenty-second dimension. Ever since, manifestations of this divine mother have occurred in visions, such as the message of Gabrielle to Miriam, and other occurrences in Lourdes, Fatima, Guadalupe, and Medjugorje. The apparition holds the frequency associated with the Council of Orion's original vision. After meeting with all the intergalactic refugees, the Council of Orion approached the godhead, or Pleiades system, for a secure portal bridging the celestial realm with the developing planet. They represented refugees from places like Andromeda, Arcturus, Spica, and other galaxies, such as Centauri."

"The first division of the supercontinent known as Pangaea must have resulted from Lilith's departure. When she left, the land mass split in two," Tobias commented. "The first fallout in the garden coincided with the Serpentine infiltration of the Orion refugee base. There were three races of blue beings in Orion to seek protection, much like a circle of covered wagons drawn together for defense. Two of the families never fell, and the fallen one is known as the 'one with no name.' I understand that there were five survivors from Orion."

Pausing a second, Tobias connected the story of the heavens with that of life on earth. He said, "Lilith's daughter, Ishtar, attacked the vision of Gondwanaland that had been seeded by Pleiades and the Orion Council. Lilith's son, Hades, took over the portal known as Styx and developed Olympus for the Gauds on a star remnant. Having been Hades's willing partner, Persephone became the first Ferengi. She knew about the betrayal of the Pleiades to Aldebaran, which gave Ishtar control of Styx as a birth canal for the human form. This occurred when the moon broke away from the planet earth, leaving a deep cavity in the Pacific. Called *Sin*, Ishtar's moon birthed the human family in darkness."

"People on the planet forget that the earth is a living, breathing entity with its own spirit," Donna observed. "Gondwanaland included Africa, where many have traced the DNA to a common ancestor. The Tree of Life was in Africa at the time Gondwanaland broke into several continents separated by water. When the Tree of Life was gradually destroyed by an Arachnid infestation from M33, a spiritual family took a shoot from the tree and collectively moved it by foot. Like the Australian natives, this group felt the presence of the earth's spirit through their feet. They brought this connection with them to present-day Korea, where they regrew the Tree of Life."

"The fifth dimension pertains to rotational motion.The Orion Council was responsible for the motion of the planets and their orbits. The attack on the Council altered the earth's rotational motion. The resulting wobble resulted in the formation of Ishtar's moon. Later, one of Persephone's sons ejected the Aldebaran invaders from the Pleiades. With the help of Neptune, the brother of Hades, Persephone's son drowned the Arachnids on the planet, while cremating Hades with the help of another god, named Pele. Titans took over the war, and Atlas, the sole survivor, founded Atlantis. The moon's role in the transport of the human souls went inert. A new soul transport system was put into place with help of the Lacerta and Tangvas. Benevolent extraterrestrials created new portals through the *Nazca* lines, a creative art form of geoglyphs in southern Peru."

Tobias added, "There is more to the story of the contaminated portal from Gondwanaland. Playing both sides, Persephone provided the Pleiades and Hades with children. The children she bore for the Pleiades have unknown fathers. Lilith bore Cronus children and named them Hades, Neptune, and Zeus. Cronus was the son of the fallen Gaia with Uranus. All of Lilith's children, except Ishtar, eventually became calcified, spiritless entities unable to successfully matriculate on the planet. Persephone has returned recently to help repair the human DNA altered by Ishtar's curse. Like Gaia, another spirit surfaces as the fallen one is shutting down. Now that the truth is out concerning Persephone, a new paradigm can be created for those people choosing to heal their DNA."

"Ishtar seeded discord between the genders, which damaged the DNA and scarred the planet," Tobias explained, reading from his notes on the desk. "The earliest writings on the earth were discovered in 1853, which resurfaced in-between two intergalactic wars. Collectively, the books are called the *Epic of Gilgamesh*. It is the story of the progeny of Lilith and their search for immortality.

According to the tale, Lilith and the Serpentines eventually create the Persian Empire. The progeny lack the starlight that infuses the human family. Gilgamesh was Lilith's grandson, who ruled Mesopotamia on the Laurasian continent. While falling prey to the ploys of his Serpentine community, Gilgamesh realizes that he is destined to return to dust, as is his evil twin. He seeks advice on immortality from Noah, who has survived the flood that scrapped the disgraced human community."

Taking a moment to clear his throat, Tobias concluded, "Although, Gilgamesh has initially been told by a sage that he will never find the sort of immortality that he seeks, he still tries. Noah, who listened to the wise advice of Ea, a Pegasus-sea dragon hybrid, understands that the spirit of the human family lives on through cycles of regeneration. The cycles of rebirth match the restored spirit of Gaia, which rises like a phoenix from the ashes. Noah has remained attentive to Ea's instructions to build the ark that saved him. Noah's endeavors have taught him the essence of immortality---that life on the planet came through spirit or starlight. That is the secret to life. As a result, it is the spirit that rises, and not the body. Gilgamesh, unable to contain the spiritual wine and gain wisdom from experience, fails to pass his tests for immortality."

Chapter Twenty-Nine

About those burning questions in life

The ones we shouldn't have to ask

Like who am I?

Tune Reference: *The Grand Illusion*

----Styx

"HOMER BOUGHT INTO Gilgamesh's *Epic*," Donna remarked. "He passed his blindness on to the ancient Greeks, who continually fought each other."

"It leads us again to the Zen notion of an awakened eye, or the cultivation of an awareness needed to move forward," Tobias commented. "A colleague of mine worked with a comatose patient. As the result of treatment, we were able to connect with his consciousness. He eventually died from the drugs used to contain his seizures. They destroyed his liver. Because the interaction with him was so intricate, I developed awareness of those who comprised the *living dead* versus those who could pass the mental-health standard for being *alert and oriented*. The test involves remembering dates, especially the present calendar day. This comatose patient's awareness surpassed most of the people around me at the time. When his mother walked in the room, he started to hiccough in greeting. After I returned from a vacation in Hawaii, he recognized my hands by their feel and scent. His countenance changed dramatically once I touched his cranium, which initially had a three-millimeter concavity on the right forehead. We developed a type of nonverbal language that matched the spirit inside the semiparalyzed body. He nosed my hands as if they were a gift of a faraway place. He learned about a Hawaiian Island through them. I could tell by the expression on his face, which made the trip worth it. By the time he died, the concavity had disappeared. He seemed more alive than most people I encounter. So I learned to connect to people's awareness and avoid the zombies."

"Here is another dot to connect," Donna said. Checking her files, she skimmed through a research article. She told Tobias, "A United States veteran, claims that the war in Iraq was created for the seizure of the land where it is believed Eden once existed. Now that the plates have drifted apart, the area between the Tigris and Euphrates rivers became rich in ancient writings about aliens from Anunnak. The vet wasn't happy about fighting in a war to obtain more literature about demons. He says that it is like the time when the robber barons turned Hitler into a monster. Popular news showed how a US intelligence agency gave the leader of Iraq monstrous control and weaponry. It was comparable to the support of Hitler's antics during the Olympics and Versailles violations. Rumor has it that Hitler did actually shake hands with the winner Jesse Owen, rather than exhibit racism, as was reported. Supposedly the sprinter carried a photograph of the occasion in his wallet. It is a similar story about demonization, but the pre-World War II one is more revealing about the actual dynamics."

Flipping through her papers, Donna continued, "There's more. At the same time Hitler made a scene at the Olympics, a US president dedicated a statue of Robert E. Lee in Texas. Remember that Robert E. Lee had turned down command of the Union in favor of the Confederacy. Lee cited personal reasons. The dedication of the statue made anti-Semantism an issue. The president said that Lee deserved honor because he was a 'Christian gentleman.' This statement fuzzed over the separation of church and state as well as the issue of treason. The president implied that it was okay to attack the US as long as it was done by a gentleman. Later, the same US president provoked the Japanese attack on Pearl Harbor. He aided the Chinese blockade and collaborated with staff to deceive the US military about the upcoming Japanese attack."

Donna stopped to read from another series of notes. "The US president during the beginning of WWII was connected to the robber-baron group, bearing the name of a meeting room in a Houston hotel. The man, who induced the US president to honor Lee at the celebration, owned another Houston hotel where they 'suicided' people who disagreed with their programs. It was the same hotel where another president retired after his confrontation with the aerospace hospital. They killed the president within the next two days."

Tobias observed, "Many of the military bases in the region considered themselves Confederate, at least according to the Birchers. The base in San Antonio had plans to run tanks up to Dallas, if the deal fell through."

"Back to Hades," Donna interrupted. "The Houston hotel group also placed the cornerstone for an obelisk that surpassed the Washington monument. The funds collected for the giant San Jacinto monument had been directed to the CIA during the National Student Association scandal. But wait---it goes deep. The San Jacinto monument honors the galactic Mexican-American war. Families of the robber barons traded sons with Santa Anna's military as part of an educational-cultural exchange program during the conflict. An oil baron associated with the CIA named his company for the

Mexican revolutionary who overthrew the Mexican president. The next Mexican president represented Pancho Villa."

Tobias interrupted Donna, saying, "Some of my relatives told stories about how they kept Pancho from killing them and destroying their land. All it took was a pre-barbecued fatted calf. They encouraged him to take it on the run."

Donna persisted in connecting the dots. She continued, "This international group proved more powerful than the US president. Congress passed legislation to give them control of the world's richest oil fields as well as the price of oil. The railroad commission became the model for Mideast oil operations. Now, realize that there were eleven to thirteen unauthorized individuals on the railroad overpass in Dallas on November 22 just shortly before 1 p.m.. The layout for the assassination matched the constellation of Orion with the president and his wife sitting in the belt. Gridded for intergalactic purposes, the setup mimicked the attack on Orion that had occurred at the split of the supercontinent Pangea."

Wishing to move forward quickly, Tobias refocused the conversation. He told Donna, "*Kochi* is an Indian word for 'big cow.' Cows are considered sacred in many parts of that country. The Mayans and the Hopi believed that a celestial bull, known as Taurus, protected earth. The constellation Taurus lies between Orion and the Pleiades. According to the story of the stars, Orion has a little hunting dog named Sirius. The brightest star in Sirius lies in sacred geometry with the pyramids of ancient Egypt. In the *Epic of Gilgamesh*, the protagonist kills the bull. The bull's eye happens to be Aldebaran, one of the Pleiades' oppressors. Metaphorically, a bull's-eye hit is fatal. The absence of the protective bull or sacred cow would render the Pleiades vulnerable to any rabidity infiltrating Orion or his hunting dog. The destruction of the connection between heaven and earth, such as the holy iris of Gondwanaland, is a story of the stars. Info Park in Kochi, India contains the Tejomaya building---which has the same eye on it as the dollar."

"OK, so how do we get past this ancient setup?" Donna asked.

"*Namaste*," Tobias answered. "The high priestesses on Gondwanaland needed to get past the illusion inspiring continental drift."

Chapter Thirty

Nothing is safer or more secure

Than the arms of someone

Who loves you

Nobody decides

Who follows

Or who goes first

Tune Reference: *Follow You, Follow Me*

----Deja Vu

AFTER ENDING THE phone conversation with Donna, Tobias placed the phone down and went to seek out Michelle. She worked in her home office, organizing supplies for the next birth. Michelle looked up from what she was doing. She studied Tobias's face as he strolled into her office. Without a word, Tobias sat down near her. Ignoring his presence, she continued to repack her midwifery kits. Tobias watched her. She appeared surrounded by tokens of past and future births.

Finally he spoke, saying, "You inspire me, especially when the world seems most dangerous."

"You keep me going too," she said, maintaining her focus on her task. "There's a lot of pressure on the good guys these days. I like to get them off to a great start. For most, the womb is as safe as its gets. I try to make the transition seamless, so that the child learns how to be secure in the world."

After pausing a moment to reflect, Michelle continued, "So, what do you think of the Kabbalah Tree now that our children are adults?"

Tobias laughed with a sense of relief. He remarked. "Our little homegrown tree of life taught me well."

"What do you mean, specifically?" Michelle asked.

"I learned how to let go," Tobias said, rising to answer the ringing phone. It was a colleague of his, and leaving Michelle in her office, he greeted the caller.

"Tobias, you need a break," the colleague told him. "I want to start a group clinic where we can all trade shifts. This will give you more flexibility in connecting the dots for the rest of us. Then we can come up with solutions. By the way, Tobias, what is the latest?"

Tobias stared out the window overlooking the misty mountains in the distance. Tall, verdant evergreens dotted the vapor-like pillars reaching for the clouds. Familiar tall, willowy figures moved in the underbrush. Tobias straightened as he saw the Neanderthals making their presence known. They had survived persecution since the beginning of the planet.

Taking a breath before speaking, Tobias reflected on the notes scribbled from previous conversations. They lay in a disorganized array on the desk in front of him. He sat down on a nearby chair, and he rubbed his head.

"Have you ever seen the pines of east Texas?" he asked his future partner. "They are a beautiful deep, rich green, with long, lacy needles."

"Yes, I remember those trees," his colleague mentioned. "I attended a *chi gung* workshop there once. The place is filled with oil wells."

"Those oil wells were lost to the owner of the Dallas School Book Depository. His cousin owned a military aeronautics company and sponsored the president's accused search-and-rescue unit."

"Let me guess," Tobias's colleague interrupted. "The oil under those pines also financed alien investigations at the earth's poles."

"It also funded the communist foray into Korea, where the aliens could infect the Tree of Life. We are lucky that there has not been a planetary takeover."

The voice on the other end advised him. "When you come to the edge, all you have to do is let go. Let your spirit fly, Tobias."

"You're right," Tobias mused.

"You've freed yourself from the past. Now you can teach us how to fly," his colleague commented. "We're all in this. Cheers, Tobias."

"Cheers," Tobias said, ending the conversation on that note. Another incoming call prevented him from rejoining Michelle in the next room. Instead of moving away, he stayed and picked up the phone again.

Without wasting time with introductions, Donna jumped into the thread lingering from the last discussion. She blurted, "They will never find what they seek."

"Who?" Tobias asked. Then he said, "Oh, those who serve the alien agenda. Yes, it was quite epic for Gilgamesh." Tobias remarked, drumming his fingers as he thought. "They do not know how to rebirth themselves. A colleague was just talking about the essence of the flower known as lady's slipper, which reminds us that neocon-communists and dreaming visionaries get along like oil and water."

"Huh?" Donna questioned.

Tobias explained, "Water comprises ninety percent of the human body and much of the planet. It is renewable: water evaporates, condenses, and returns as rain. Fossil fuels are unrenewable. It is the hydrogen bonding on the DNA that determines states of consciousness, so there is a concrete reason for the association of water with human consciousness."

Donna chuckled. "I get it, Tobias. Eventually the aliens will destroy their DNA so much that they will lose sight of the dreamers. It is just a matter of time. Count me in. Cheers, Tobias."

"Cheers," he responded, before ending the call. Tobias remained seated at the desk, and checked his e-mail for any further messages. He found a pertinent one from Joan.

"I suspect that the iris on Gondwanaland acted like the shutter on a camera. The memory would have become part of the DNA," she wrote.

Tobias typed in his response. "Water is composed of various ionic solutions that foster communication, almost like a self-assembling semiconductor or the interstitial fluid between cells. Zen awareness, or clear day vision, leads us to the encompassing code of the samurai and Dragon flyer traditions. We can fly from the milieu of Hades."

An immediate response from Joan surprised him. Apparently she was online. She replied, "It's like arriving at the EDGE of humanity and taking FLIGHT." A few seconds later, she added another line in a separate e-mail. "Cheers, Tobias."

He wrote back, "Cheers."

A phone ring interrupted his focus. Carrie called this time. Apparently, Donna had phoned her after finishing the discussion with Tobias.

"Donna said that you needed some information on how the US dollar funded communism," Carrie began. "It has to do with oil and the steel needed to move the oil around."

Tobias replied, "Joan and I were just arriving at that blind spot in world history."

"One of the Chinese empresses wrote a letter blaming the East India Company for turning her country into addicts. During World War II, the drug smuggling assumed aeronautical proportions."

Tobias continued, "Let me guess. The religious opiates of the missionaries became a bad trip known as communism.

Carrie interjected, "The railroads provided the supply lines for the addicts. Who supplied the railroads? It was John Quincy Adams. He railroaded the tracks into Russia. The railroads brought in communism after the Czar blocked trading with the East India Company during the Civil War. The Russian communists annexed North Korea after World War II."

Tobias added, "Dark occult symbols for a unified world dollar were woven into US currency from the beginning. It's the kind of currency to cause continental drift."

"Or perpetual nuclear threats," Carrie observed. "In the West, they flew real dragons, while the East flew imagined dragons in meditations. Flight is a very powerful technology, especially when cultivated in the round table or *namaste* sense," Carrie murmured. "Enough for now. I must go back to my astronomical research. I'll talk to you later, Tobias. Cheers."

"Cheers," Tobias said.

Before he could return to Michelle, another call stopped him. He answered the ring immediately. Tobias sighed as he glanced out the window. The swirling fog between the trees started to disappear.

"Hi, Tobias," Joe greeted. He delved into a similar topic related to the preceding discussions. "A colleague found some old family records at the church where her grandparents married," Joe replied. "They built the church-school's foundation with bricks from Glastonbury. Somebody knew what to do. It was the reincarnation of Joseph of Arimathea's Glastonbury project."

"Were they descendants of Avalon's Pink knights?" Tobias questioned.

"Yes, the survivors of Avalon fled to Ireland, Germany, Switzerland, and South America. Jungles and the Black Forest attracted them."

"What does Gabriella say about the change in focus for the divine feminine?" Tobias questioned.

"She says that we need to focus on the American Revolution and the development of the Pentagon. We need to know the story behind the eye of Gondwanaland and the Eye-in-the-Sky on the US dollar." Joe mentioned. "She thinks that women played a major role and that the history has been suppressed. We need to learn the connection between the Glastonbury-Avalon project and the high-priestesses on Gondwanaland."

"That's a great move," Tobias stood upright and stretched his legs. "The Gondwanaland project inspired the samurai, who learned how to protect themselves without massive weaponry and castles."

Joe said, "I understand that it was a samurai, who place a sword in the stone for the Camelon legacy. Camelon symbolized the kingdom created by Queen Boudica's grandson, King Cole I. He represented the merry old soul of a children's nursery rhyme, and his grandson, King Arcas, pulled the sword out of the stone. King Arthur was the son of King Arcas. It pertained to the Western version of the wizard-spiritual-warrior known as the 'Dragon flyer' tradition."

Tobias commented, "Both traditions were derived from the civilization that connected heaven to earth on Gondwanaland. The placement of the sword in the stone was the key for uniting these technologies to protect the forces of light against metaphorical continental drift. The American Revolution was planned at a tavern called the Green Dragon. The survivors of the American Revolution recreated the pentagon from the ashes of the intergalactic structure, according to the designs of Metatron's Cube."

"Metatron countered the nephilim, who destroyed the intergalactic Pentagon as earth was being settled with refugees. He landed with the platform people near Angles, Germany. Noah descended from the surviving platform people," Joe said. After pausing briefly to collect his thoughts, he suddenly announced, "That's it! I gotta get back to Gabriella. Cheers."

"Cheers." Tobias blinked and then gently placed the phone down. Turning around, he saw that Michelle had left her office. He walked over to where Michelle stood in the room, and he warmly embraced her.

"You are popular, Tobias," she observed. "You've got this flight thing figured out. Though it may be on the charts for others, *oblivion* is not *our* destiny." Michelle softly patted his forearms as she gazed into a new future, one that would uplift them from the present. She told him, "Congratulations. We can learn from your experience. You have your wings, Tobias. Cheers."

Tobias kissed her softly on the cheek. He repeated, "Cheers."